KU-235-647

YOUNG MAY MOON

On the silvery sands of West Wick, in Suffolk, just before her sixteenth birthday, Young May Moon, as she is known to family and friends, fulfils the promise made to her late father and becomes the Punch and Judy lady. Assisted by her younger sister, Pomona, Young May Moon discovers that performing is in her blood, as four years earlier, from this same place, their fiery mother Carmen, a flamenco dancer, absconded with the preacher from the rival entertainment. The girls are befriended by the O'Flaherty family, also lodging at The Swan, and May experiences first love and the pain of parting...

YOUNG MAY MOON

by

Sheila Newberry

Magna Large Print Books
Long Preston, North Yorkshire,
BD23 4ND, England.

British Library Cataloguing in Publication Data.

Newberry, Sheila
    Young May Moon.

    A catalogue record of this book is
    available from the British Library

    ISBN   978-0-7505-3810-7

First published in Great Britain in 2012 by Robert Hale Limited

Copyright © Sheila Newberry 2012

Cover illustration by arrangement with Robert Hale Ltd.

The right of Sheila Newberry to be identified as the author of the work
has been asserted by her in accordance with the Copyright, Designs
and Patents Act, 1988

Published in Large Print 2013 by arrangement with
Robert Hale Limited

All Rights reserved. No part of this publication may be reproduced,
stored in a retrieval system, or transmitted in any form or by any
means, electronic, mechanical, photocopying, recording or otherwise
without the prior permission of the Copyright owner.

STAFFORDSHIRE
LIBRARIES, ARTS
AND ARCHIVES

38014044966163	
MAGNA	30-9-13
F	£20-99

Magna Large Print is an imprint of Library Magna Books Ltd.

Printed and bound in Great Britain by
T.J. (International) Ltd., Cornwall, PL28 8RW

DEDICATION

Fond memories of my father, who had a Spanish grandmother and lived and worked in Barcelona for a time as a young man.

To Betty, who wrote lyrics for my version of *Cinderella,* and encouraged me in all my writing. She is much missed.

Also, to our delightful grandchildren, all twenty-two of them, several of whom show signs of following in Young May Moon's footsteps!

Thank you, John, as always, for your encouragement and especially for all your stories of along the Worple Road to Wimbledon in the 1930s.

Sheila Newberry

YOUNG MAY MOON. A jig for country dancing, with fiddle accompaniment. Sometimes known as **NEW MAY MOON.**

PART ONE

West Wick to Kettle Row

1925–26

One

It was a dew-damp morning, the sky still hazily grey, in late May, already warm, despite the early hour, when Young May Moon trundled into town. The nickname had been given her by her grandfather who'd played the tune on his fiddle at many a jig.

The high red wheels of the trap scraped against the walls of the narrow hump-backed stone bridge, over which she led the reluctant donkey, Smokey. She glanced over the parapet. The water below was hidden under a shifting mass of evil slime. On the opposite bank of the river were ramshackle wooden shacks, tarred black, with rank weeds growing round the foundations. These old smoking-huts appeared deserted, probably because of the decline in herring fishing.

May shivered involuntarily; fortunately, she thought, they would shortly leave this gloomy place behind, for now the smell of the sea was tantalizingly close.

May was almost sixteen, olive-skinned, dark-eyed, with a great knot of shining blue-black hair crammed under her father's best straw boater. She was feeling somewhat apprehensive, for this afternoon, on the familiar West Wick sands, she'd be setting up her very first show.

PROFESSOR JAS JOLLEY'S PUNCH & JUDY.

May would keep the legend, in memory of her late father, Jim, the popular Punch and Judy man. 'Professor' was of course an honorary title, but traditional. Smokey plodded on, sensing journey's end, after May climbed back into the driving seat. May and her younger sister Pomona had travelled almost twenty miles from their Aunt Min's home, on the outskirts of Kettle Row, a market town on the borders of Suffolk and Norfolk. Their grand-father had settled with his daughter when he gave up travelling with the show. To Min, who'd been widowed in the Boer War, the Jolleys were her family. Min was responsible for naming her younger niece after Pomona, the Roman goddess of orchards. This was fitting because Min made her living from the apple, pear and plum trees in the smallholding she'd inherited from her in-laws.

Jim and the children stayed on the farm during the winter, when Pomona attended the village school. May's education had ended at fourteen, so she and Jim spent this time refurbishing the puppets, sewing new costumes, painting fresh backcloths, inventing new props.

Sadly, soon after their return from the last sum-mer season, Jim succumbed to chronic conges-tion of the lungs. The condition had plagued him since he was gassed in the trenches during the Great War, the one it was said would end all wars. He had been invalided out of the Army in 1916. During his absence, Carmen, his wife, had left May with Min, while she toured with other dancers to entertain the troops. She'd not been best pleased when she was expected to return home to look after her sick husband, and then a new baby in 1917.

Jim's last words to May were: 'Will you girls carry on with the show?' She'd promised him that they would.

May and Pomona were about to fulfill this pledge. Their mother, Carmen, a volatile Spanish flamenco dancer, who'd left most of the girls' upbringing to their father, had flounced off four summers ago with an itinerant evangelist, after a huge row with Jim right in the middle of the rival entertainments, leaving both audiences gawping on the beach. *'That's* the way to do it!' Punch had cried, as the hymn singing faltered and faded. '*He* never liked her,' Jim muttered to May.

Now, Pomona, a sturdy child, sandy-haired and freckled, eight years old, swayed perilously atop the wooden trunk which housed the precious puppets, hand-carved over a hundred years ago by the first Jas Jolley, their great-grandfather. Quivering, alert, on Pomona's lap was Dog Toby – an elderly, but still agile female Toby, for they'd had enough in the past of male Tobys following some irresistible scent, and neglecting their duties. This little dog had been abandoned by its original owner, and taken in by the Jolleys. In return, she had learned new tricks and was a great asset to the Punch and Judy.

'Hold tight, Pom,' May reminded her sister. 'Why you have to sit up top I don't know.'

'Don't want old Mr Punch bursting out and

showing off for nothing,' Pomona replied, perfectly reasonably. May smiled to herself, for at Pomona's age, she too had imagined the puppets to have mysterious powers.

They passed the milestone, then the Saxon church. The donkey turned in to the forecourt of the Swan Inn, with its flint-napped walls, red pantiled roof, and small windows.

The proprietor's wife, Jane Wren, known as Jenny, who at the turn of the century had been a popular artiste in the end-of-the pier shows, was also a theatrical landlady.

Smokey clopped straight toward the old stables, and poked his nose over the open half-door.

'Smokey never forgets,' May remarked to Pomona. 'Hold on tight to Toby.'

Before May could jump down a hand was extended to fondle the donkey's plushy nose. Smokey's soft, expressive ears revealed his pleasure. Toby barked, to draw attention to herself.

'A visitor!' exclaimed an amused voice. 'I'm afraid your stable is occupied.'

May looked in at a young fellow, tousle-haired as if roused from sleep. She spotted a makeshift bed of straw behind him and a haversack. Was he a vagrant? Then in the shadows she discerned a black motor car, where their trap was usually kept under cover. You didn't see many motor vehicles in this part of Suffolk, she thought, or even electric trams or trolley buses. The horse or ox still drew wagons and ploughs; donkeys drew smaller conveyances. Not a tramp, then!

She was both cross and curious. 'We always stay here, every Whit week, didn't Jenny Wren tell

14

you?' she demanded of the youth, who leaned towards her, smiling. He was around her age, as dark as herself, with curling hair. But his eyes were blue.

'Patrick O'Flaherty, they call me Paddy,' he introduced himself. 'Our family are appearing in a show on the pier. Mrs Wren did tell us that the Punch and Judy man and his family had first claim to the rooms. However, when she heard that he had...' he hesitated, glancing at Pomona, who, with Toby under her arm, was descending by way of the wheel, 'passed away, she thought the show wouldn't come this summer.'

Toby launched herself from Pomona's arms, and Paddy caught the little fox terrier in mid-air. The next thing the girls knew was that the warning growl had ceased, and Toby was ecstatically licking the boy's face. Toby was usually wary of strangers, except when she was performing.

'I have no objection, you know, to sharing my quarters, with the donkey and the dog,' he said.

Hot tears pricked May's eyes. She blinked them fiercely away. She had coped bravely with the loss of her beloved father a few months ago, for Pomona's sake. He had done the same for them, after Carmen deserted the family. 'We're a team,' he'd said. 'Life goes on – better to be happy than sad.'

She thought now, I wish he hadn't used that expression: *passed away*. While we were travelling here, somehow I felt as if Dad was around still, encouraging us to carry on. That was comforting.

'We must see what Jenny thinks about that,' she said primly. She called to Pomona, 'Run up to

15

the house. I'll follow in the trap.'

Jenny Wren was comfortably plump in her brightly patterned overall, with her fuzzy grey hair carelessly arranged in a top-knot, from which she shed the occasional crinkled hair pin. She saw them through the open kitchen window and let out a delighted shriek. *'Here* you are, after all! Young May Moon, you take Smokey out of the shafts and let him in to the little meadow. Percy's in the milking parlour, he'll feed and water him. Smokey can keep the cow and our old horse company in the barn at night. Monty's retired, now Percy's the proud owner of an Austin motor. I made him buy it, I told him: "It's 1925 not 1905, we ought to move with the times..."' She drew a breath. 'Leave your bags by the door, for now. You're in time for breakfast, we'll catch up with the news then – do come in, Pom!'

Dodging the great ham dangling from the ceiling hook, Jenny welcomed Pomona with a hug, her face flushed with heat from the stove. Pomona was soon sitting at the kitchen table, drinking a glass of milk, while Jenny scrambled a panful of eggs.

As she opened the back door May became aware that someone had come up behind her. She turned to see Paddy, still with bits of straw clinging to his hair, grinning at her.

'Room at the inn, I reckon?' he remarked.

'I don't know yet,' she returned sharply. 'Why are you following me?'

The blue eyes flashed at her. 'I'm not! I'm here for my breakfast. I chose to sleep in the stable partly because I fancied it would be an adven-

16

ture, rather like camping out, as we've done in the past when times were hard, but mainly because I didn't want to share a room with Danny, my kid brother. He's very annoying at times. Ten years old, and thinks he knows it all.'

May almost admitted, 'I feel that way about my sister sometimes.' However, she didn't want to prolong the conversation.

She went into the kitchen and closed the door, while he continued along the passage to the dining room, from which emanated the cheerful voices of his family.

Jenny gave May a cuddle. 'I thought we wouldn't see you this summer. Your poor father, not unexpected, I suppose, with that weak chest... No, I thought, our Young May Moon will be looking for a steady job. When the O'Flahertys enquired – you can guess their roots of course, with a name like that, their grandparents came over here in the last century, during the potato famine in Ireland – I explained matters to them.' Jenny added: 'There's what used to be the snug, the room over the stairs – folks seem to prefer the bar now – would you mind sharing a bed? I would only charge five shillings a week for the two of you – though it's not the quietest room in the house; you'll hear me playing the piano below in the bar most nights.'

'Oh, we don't mind that!' May assured her. Jenny was a virtuoso on the piano, she thought, accompanying many a temperamental songstress during her summer seasons on the pier. Jenny possessed a powerful singing voice herself. She didn't need a microphone. She understood the

17

idiosyncrasies of performers, being one herself.

'Well, let's join the troubadours. Will you help carry the trays? They're nice people, they've been here a week already. I'm not sure how long they're staying. What about you?'

'Oh, Whit week, of course,' May told her. 'Then Pom must return to school. But, if it goes well this week, we'll be back for all of August, as usual.'

'You can't manage the rest of the summer, I gather, without dear Jim?'

May shook her head. 'I'm not too sure how we'll cope this week by ourselves ... this afternoon will be a real test.'

'Paddy's at a loose end during the day, as they are in the evening show. He might like to help you out.'

Mmm ... May thought, we've clashed already, so I imagine he *wouldn't!*

Paddy's father, Brendan, sprang to his feet and welcomed the girls with a firm handshake. 'It's good you decided to come!' He had the same striking looks as his elder son.

'I'm glad Jenny could find room for all of us,' said Brigid O'Flaherty. 'It will be nice for Danny to have a friend.'

'Where's your dog?' Danny, a skinny boy with bright red hair, like his mother, asked Pomona, who was seated next to him. He spoke with his mouth full, spraying crumbs, but Brigid didn't reprimand him.

Pomona eyed him with distaste. Aunt Min was insistent on good table manners. 'In the kitchen,' she said shortly.

Percy, a short, stocky man with a shining bald

18

head, joined the company. Jenny poured the tea and passed the cups.

After the meal May asked Jenny: 'May we go to our room? We must get on, we have the bills to hand out before the first performance this afternoon.'

'You'll want an early light lunch,' Jenny said, familiar with their ways; knowing May couldn't perform on a full stomach.

May sensed, with satisfaction, that Paddy had gone quietly away.

'Oh look,' Pomona said, when they opened the snug door,

'Paddy's fetched our bags up for us!'

He'd placed a copper jug of steaming water on the washstand, too. There was no bathroom in the inn. Water still came from the pump in the yard and was heated on the stove. The chamber pot was discreetly stowed away in the washstand cupboard.

May felt a guilty pang. He'd been kind without making a song and dance about it. Maybe, she thought, with a wry smile, this is a hint we need a good wash!

Two

May took a deep breath, glancing down at the smart, striped blazer which, she hoped, concealed her curves, at the narrow trousers which she'd had to turn up twice, and at the elastic-sided boots, their toes stuffed with newspaper to fit her. Was she a credible Jas Jolley IV?

Down the hill, towards the sparkling sea they went, at a walking pace, because Smokey knew the routine, past the busy shops, with their wares flowing on to the cobbled pavement. Pomona, in her eagerness, let the handwritten bills flutter down to all and sundry; to the whistling errand boys, wobbling on sturdy bicycles with goods piled in baskets attached to handlebars; to young mothers in low-waisted frocks, with shingled hair under neat cloche hats, clutching firmly at sticky, small hands. 'See you at three!' May called. 'Usual spot beside the pier!'

Along the promenade above the silver sand Smokey plodded, past the new wooden beach huts, which had superseded the old bathing huts, now that women were more liberated. These were painted in contrasting colours, with names like *Mon Repos*, and towels hanging out to dry on porch rails. Fisherfolk were emptying crab and lobster pots; they saw a couple of beached boats, and children in sagging, hand-knitted wool bathers frolicking in the foam as the tide obligingly receded. In the hired striped deckchairs fathers slumbered peacefully, still clad in suits, starched collars, ties, and laced black shoes, with knotted handkerchiefs round their perspiring heads. Mothers knitted busily, guarding their children's clothes and a large, ribbed bottle of calamine lotion for sunburn, watching them in the water.

May struggled to assemble the portable booth, with its red-and white striped canvas, while Pomona unpacked the puppets and hung them in position on the wire that stretched round the sides of the little theatre. May fixed the canvas sling into place below the stage. Here the puppets were dropped, when they had played their parts. She pinned into place the cloth backdrop, depicting an old English street scene.

A curious, expectant crowd was gathering. Heart thumping, and feeling rather sick, May checked, as her father had done, that all was ready: the props on their shelf, the puppets, Punch, his wife Judy, the baby Marmaduke, the doctor, the clergyman, the Beadle, the policeman and crocodile, in order, and most important, the swazzle which produced Punch's shrill, excitable voice. She poured water from a bottle into a dish, and dampened the swazzle before placing it between her lips. She had been practising ever since she'd made up her mind to carry on with the show, but this would be her debut as Punch.

'Roll up, roll up, for Jas Jolley's Punch and Judy!' Pomona was in her element. She would drum up the crowd, playing a tune or two on the penny whistle, and later act as bottler, taking round the battered ancient leather bottle with the coin slot, as Mr Punchinello and Company took their final bows. Toby danced about beside her, as deckchairs were dragged into position. In the front row, they spotted two now familiar faces.

'Hello, Paddy, Danny,' Pomona exclaimed cheerfully. 'Nice of you to come.'

'Oh, we wouldn't have missed seeing the Punch and Judy lady in action,' Paddy replied.

'You mustn't let on she's a *lady*,' Pomona hissed in his ear. He winked at her. 'Mum's – oh, sorry,

Pomona's – the word.'

The magic of the play began. The curtains swished apart and bold Mr Punch, splendid in scarlet, green and gold, great curved nose almost resting on his chin, duly appeared and, with aplomb, bowed three times to the audience, right, left and centre stage.

Praying fervently that she wouldn't swallow the swazzle, May was glad that her father had adapted the familiar story over the years, that he had toned down the more violent aspects. But Punch, of course, began in benevolent mood.

Boys and girls, pray how do you do?
If you are all happy, then I'm happy too.
Let's have some hush, now, for my little play,
If I make you laugh, mind, I expect you to pay...

As Punch ducked from view on May's right hand, up popped the policeman on her left. He strutted up and down the stage, waving his truncheon.

I am the village bobby.
and I have quite a hunch,
that there will soon be trouble,
with that scoundrel, Mr Punch.
He has a spouse named Judy,
and a little baby, too–
A saucy dog called Toby–
who now come into view...

'Don't panic,' May said to herself, as she divested herself of the bobby, dropped him in to

22

the bag, and fitted Judy in his place.

Meanwhile, Toby, resplendent in her ruff, leapt on to the stage and pirouetted round and round, to warm applause. May continued, gathering confidence from scene to scene, and when the audience cheered or booed in all the right places, she knew Jim would have been proud of her.

They were a generous crowd, and Pomona did her bit with the bottle. Then the front curtain opened slightly and Paddy peeped in at May, smiling broadly. 'Well done, Punch and Judy lady!' he congratulated her. 'Need any help with all this?'

'No thank you,' she said crossly, biting back: *Mind your own business!*

'We've two more shows to do before we pack up,' Pomona said.

As the curtains fell back into place, May realized that she had been ungracious. She came out to apologize, but Paddy and Danny had gone. Smokey, tethered in a shady spot, was being petted by a family of children. Pomona too had disappeared. May felt panic rising inside; Pomona – and the bottle full of coins! Then her sister emerged from the ice cream tent, licking a cornet, Toby at her heels.

'Pomona! You bad girl, spending our money on ice cream.'

'Sorry,' Pomona said, breaking off the end of the cone for the dog. 'But I didn't buy it. Paddy gave me sixpence. Said I'd earned a prize for my good work. So I bought two cornets and gave one to Danny. He collected some of the money for us, in a bucket.'

'Well...' May began. She took off her boater to stuff her hair under it more securely. Off-handedness had ruled out an ice for her.

'Look, Mum, the Punch and Judy man's a *girl!*' came an excited voice. May ducked hastily back into the booth.

Jenny had to hear all about it. 'Reckon you've done well,' she congratulated them both. There was cold rabbit pie for supper. They were joined by the boys. May ignored Paddy's smile.

'Their parents prefer to eat after the show,' Jenny explained.

'Eating doesn't affect *my* singing,' Paddy said complacently. 'I can't hit the right notes since my voice broke, so I whistle instead.'

'Doesn't make any difference to me,' his brother put in. 'I'm *always* hungry!'

May observed that Jenny looked tired. 'I'll help dish up,' she offered.

'I'll wash up the plates,' Pomona said eagerly, hoping to postpone bedtime.

'That leaves me to open up the bar, to draw a pint or two to keep 'em quiet 'til Percy appears. He's down the cellar, rolling out the barrel,' Jenny said, adding gratefully, 'You're a lovely lot you are, like family.'

A whistling noise down the speaking tube in the wall made them all jump. 'Boys,' it was Brendan's voice. 'Time to go. We're the opening act tonight, at 7.30...'

'Don't forget to ask your parents if they can get tickets for May and Pomona for the show next week,' Jenny reminded the boys.

24

It was a squeeze, sharing a single bed, the girls discovered. Pomona insisted on being next to the wall. 'I might roll out on to the floor if I'm on the outside,' she insisted. May took more after their mother in looks, but Pomona could be autocratic, like Carmen Jolley.

'So might I.' May sighed, but she gave in, thinking, *don't I always?* She placed a couple of cushions next to the bed as a precaution to soften any landing. As tomorrow is a special day, she yawned to herself, even if no-one else is aware of it, I'll make sure we change places tomorrow night!

Despite their apprehension they were both soon asleep. It had been a long day, after all.

May suddenly jerked awake when she heard singing. Jenny was rendering an old favourite from her music hall days.

Just a Song at Twilight,
When the lights are low
And the twinkling shadows
Softly come and go
Tho' the heart be weary
And the days be long—
Just a song at twilight,
Comes love's old sweet song
Comes loves' old sweet song

May recalled her friend telling them that it had been sung: 'not by me, dearie, but I was tickling the ivories, the night Percy and me met. It's been *our* song ever since.'

That's so romantic, May thought dreamily,

before she succumbed once more to sleep, despite the discomfort of their sleeping arrangements.

Three

They awoke to a tintinnabulation – they'd overslept and the church bells were ringing to proclaim the sabbath and herald the morning service. Most of the bedclothes appeared to be wound round Pomona, and her muffled voice said apologetically: 'Happy birthday, May!' It was Whit Sunday, 31 May, and now May was not 'almost' but actually sixteen.

There was a scraping noise. Something was being pushed under the door. An envelope. May waited for a few seconds, listening for descending footsteps on the stairs before she jumped out of bed and retrieved it.

Inside the envelope was a handmade card, with a pencil sketch of a Punch and Judy booth. Punch was front stage, and a bubble from his mouth proclaimed, HAPPY BIRTHDAY YOUNG MAY MOON! Inside was written, *Best wishes from Paddy and Danny.*

Her face flushed as she said, 'Cheek! I didn't say *they* could call me that...'

A tap on the door. 'May I come in?' asked Jenny. 'I heard you talking. Awake at last, eh? You must have been tired out.'

She was wearing her Sunday hat with a yellow

26

silk rose fastened to a wide band, matching her shiny satin blouse.

'Here's your hot-water jug and two mugs of fresh tea! I'll pop the tray on the washstand. The bells have just stopped ringing, I must dash, or I'll be late for church. Oh,' she turned at the door, 'many happy returns, May! I didn't forget! There's a bowl of fresh eggs in the pantry, if you fancy 'em boiled for breakfast. We had ours hours ago! The roast is already in the oven... 'Bye, my dears!'

Brigid was in the kitchen, peeling potatoes and dropping them with a splash into a large pan of water on the stove. 'I must wish you a happy birthday, May! I thought our busy landlady might be glad of a hand with the spuds... Paddy and his dad are helping Percy. Danny took Toby for a run in the meadow, I hope you don't mind?'

'Thank you, of course not,' May replied. What else could she say? 'It's very kind of you all,' she added.

'Can I go outside until breakfast is ready?' Pomona wheedled.

'Put your shoes on, then. The grass will be damp, even though it's looking to be a fine day,' her sister said.

'We're all enjoying a day off – even Smokey! I'll make sure he's been fed and watered,' Pomona said, as she wriggled her feet into her sandals without undoing the buckles.

Danny was kicking a ball in the air and Toby leapt up to catch it.

'She's an old dog, you know,' Pomona re-minded Danny when she joined them in the meadow.

'She can still do a back flip in the air,' he said cheerfully.

'So can I!' Pomona promptly demonstrated, ending up with her skirt around her ears. Fortunately May was not there to remonstrate with her; she could be quite prim at times, Pomona thought, Mum was the one who was outrageous in our family. She'd only been four when Carmen went off, but she still missed her mother, quick temper and all.

'You and Toby ought to be in the circus, I reckon.' Danny pulled up a long blade of grass and demonstrated how to make an earsplitting noise by blowing over it. 'You can both do tricks. Your talents are wasted in the Punch and Judy.'

'I play an important part, May says,' she flared.

'Paddy says May is jolly good, but she's watered the story down! Punch is a real villain. He whacks his wife and baby and chucks them out of a window. He gets hanged for his sins. But at least you had the crocodile in it!'

'Don't be so critical! My dad didn't like violence. He said enough shouting went on with my mother!'

'So that's where you get it from,' Danny said unwisely, before he scooted off to the house with Pomona in hot pursuit.

May was already dipping into her egg. 'I called you, Pom, but you didn't hear me, and I was hungry, so...' She was sitting at the kitchen table. Paddy was there, too, drinking a cup of tea.

There were cards on the mantelshelf. The china dogs that Jenny had won at a fair long ago propped them up. There was one with roses on it

28

from Jenny and Percy, a shiny card with deckled edges with a picture of a box of chocolates from Grandpa and Aunt Min, which May had brought with her, and another home-made card with a moonface with a wide grin, rather hastily made by Pomona, alongside the better-executed card by the boys.

'I thought we'd go for a stroll down to the sea before lunch,' May said to her sister. 'You could ride Smokey, eh?'

Pomona nodded, as Danny put in: 'I fancy doing that, too!'

'Who asked you?' Pomona retorted.

May looked from one to the other. She realized Pomona follows my example, she's too quick to snap back.

'You can take it in turns,' she said equably. 'Bareback riding, Danny – we don't have a saddle. I guess I'm left minding the dog!'

'Get up a nice appetite for your Sunday dinner.' Brigid smiled. 'What about you, Paddy – are you going, too?'

Paddy rose from the table, took his cup to the sink. 'I've something I want to finish making, in the barn. See you later.'

'Well, at least he's in the right place for his woodcarving,' Brigid observed. 'Percy cleaned off an old work bench for his use.' Seeing the look of interest on May's face, she added: 'My father makes walking-sticks, May. It was a family trade back in Ireland. He carves the most amazing handles, to suit gentlemen about town. I can always spot his sticks in society pictures in the newspapers.

'They were more in demand before the war, but he still has a steady flow of orders. He's passed his enthusiasm down to his grandson, it seems. I'm not sure that it would be a good livelihood nowadays. Not that our profession is secure either, particularly since all the strikes and unemployment over the country mean many folk won't be able to afford holidays, or entertainment.'

'How do you manage Danny's schooling?' May asked.

'If we get a long unbroken run somewhere he enrolls at the local school. Otherwise, Brendan tutors him. He was a teacher before we took to the road with our family act. He is a trained musician. I learned the harp at my mother's knee, so I'm told.'

'Maybe, if this week goes well, and Aunt Min agrees, Pom could go to school here, too, until August.'

'Oh, yes, please!' Pomona obviously liked the idea.

'It would depend on what Jenny thinks, of course.'

As if on cue, Jenny appeared, back from church. 'Well, how is the roast doing? Who would like to lay the table?'

'I will,' Brigid offered. 'They're going down to the beach.'

'One o'clock lunch,' Jenny said, 'Try to be back on time!'

The entertainments were not permitted on a Sunday, the slot machines on the pier were idle, no *What the Butler Saw*, nor the crane which let prizes slip from its jaws but sometimes yielded up

30

bright green sweets which tasted as if they had been in the machine since the year dot; no messages from Madame Zora the clairvoyant, with her chipped plaster nose and bright-red finger nails, but the young people watched the midday paddle steamer arrive and passengers disembarking on the pier. This was a favourite destination for Londoners. The little café on the promenade did a roaring trade in cups of tea with slabs of yellow fruitcake, and sold picture postcards and sticks of bright-pink mint rock. In the afternoon there would be a brass band in the bandstand on the green, beside the cannon, which still pointed out to sea to deter any invaders.

Sometimes there were guided tours round the historic little town, where the colourful painted ships' figureheads in the gardens were a focus of interest. Pomona always giggled at the carved wooden bosoms on display. May found them embarrassing and averted her eyes.

May, Pomona and Danny walked a fair distance along the beach. The sand was damp and rippled from the receding tide. Toby carried a long frond of seaweed in her mouth, and Smokey plodded along, pausing only to be petted by the holidaymakers. There was a pleasant breeze and puffy white clouds scudded along in a blue sky.

Danny presented May with a giant stick of rock. 'Happy birthday!'

May was suitably impressed. 'Thanks, Danny! We'll share it after lunch. We'll have to ask Percy to break it up with a hammer!'

This was not her only surprise gift. When they arrived back at the Swan, Paddy emerged from his den. 'Thought you might be glad of this,' he said gruffly. He held out a slapstick – one of Mr Punch's special props. This always made the shocked audience jump, when Punch wielded it, due to the explosive *crack!* 'Pomona told me you'd mislaid yours. It's made to her specifications,' he added disarmingly.

'Thank you, that's thoughtful of you.' May was embarrassed, but also impressed. She'd not been exactly friendly to him, she thought. Dad would have told her off. 'I'm sorry, you know – I haven't been very nice to you.'

'I can guess why,' he said quietly. 'Your first birthday without your father.'

She nodded. 'Come on, or we'll be late for lunch!'

Jenny was a superb cook, unlike Aunt Min, who had a heavy hand with suet dumplings and lumpy gravy. They ate thinly sliced succulent roast beef, perfectly browned crisp potatoes, buttered parsnips, mashed potatoes and lightly cooked shredded cabbage – the vegetables all grown by Percy in the garden.

To follow, there was apple pie in the softest of light pastry, dusted with sugar, with custard which poured from the jug and didn't need cutting with a knife, like Min's. Cream, too, from the house cow.

They could hardly move after leaving plates so clean. Pomona declared, 'They don't need washing up!' Her plate certainly didn't, after she'd chased every morsel with a hunk of homemade bread.

'Oh dear,' Jenny sighed, glancing at the clock,

'Time to pull the first pint. Needs must when the devil drives, as they say.'

'I hope you're not referring to *me*,' Percy said, with a grin. 'On a Sunday, too!'

Brendan settled down in the parlour with the newspaper. Pomona and Danny went outside again with Toby, Paddy retired to the stable, while May and Brigid cleared the table and made a pot of tea.

Brigid was easy to talk to, and later the two of them joined a dozing Brendan and sat beside him on the sofa, sipping their tea.

'Do you ever hear from your mother?' Brigid asked tentatively.

'No. It upset me a lot at first, but I knew it was worse for Dad. Aunt Min is very kind, but she has Grandpa to care for, too – his memory is not what it was, and sometimes he goes wandering, and then we have to go looking for him ... poor old chap hasn't really taken it in, that Dad is gone.'

'Have *you?*' Brigid said softly.

'Not quite,' May admitted.

Then they were silent, apart from a gentle snore from Brendan.

'Your mother doesn't know how lucky she is, to have two lovely girls like you,' Brigid said at last. 'You are bringing up your little sister – doing her job for her. Surely she must think of you?'

'She's not like you – you're a *real* mum!' May told her. 'And Brendan is a good dad, I can tell. My dad was like that...' She wiped a tear from her eye. 'I'm doing what I can for Pom. I know that's what he wished.'

Brigid gave her shoulder a comforting squeeze. 'Is the life of a Punch and Judy lady what you really want, I wonder? You know, I ran away from home at your age to be with Brendan. He persuaded me to go back to my parents until I had finished at school. I'm so glad I did. He waited for me to grow up, and then we married, as you see! Wouldn't you like to further your own education?'

'I promised Dad I'd carry on the business.'

'You could maybe do the summer season and study the rest of the year. Think about it,' Brigid advised.

She knew it was an illusion, but May seemed to hear an echo: 'Better to be happy than sad.'

Four

Whit Monday, 1 June, which May and Pomona had been anticipating as the highlight of their performing week, dawned wet and dismal. Unless it cleared up by lunchtime, it would not be worth their while to set up the Punch and Judy outfit.

'Don't look so despondent,' Jenny said at breakfast time. 'There's always folk worse off. A friend telephoned me from Beccles, that's not so far away from here, to tell me a *hurricane* whipped tiles off her roof, last night. D'you want to ring your aunt to let her know we were all right here? Apart from Percy, that is, complaining of wind in the early hours, but then he shouldn't have eaten those pickled onions with that lump

34

of cheese at midnight, as I told him.'

'You always manage to see the funny side of things, even the weather,' May said, smiling in spite of herself. 'It might worry Aunt Min more if I mention the hurricane, but I would like to phone home, please, to let her know we arrived safely. Also, Brigid mentioned that it might be possible for Pomona to attend school here, then we could stay on all summer – that's if you'll have us, of course!' Then she admitted: 'Although I wonder how I can carry on the putting up and taking down of the booth on my own. I know Dad did, after Mum left, but...'

Paddy had just come into the kitchen and had obviously overheard the conversation. He waited for Jenny's reply: 'Of course you can stay on, dearie. If the schoolmaster agrees your aunt will need to give her permission, as your guardian.' She gave a nod to Paddy, who took the hint.

'It looks as if we're booked here until September, so my offer still stands, to help with setting up and dismantling the Punch and Judy, if you'll let me,' he said.

'You will, eh, May?' Jenny could see that May was hesitating.

May gave in gracefully. 'I'd be silly to turn down a good offer – so I accept! Thanks, Paddy. We might have to postpone the show today – just look at the rain teeming down!'

'Fortunately, *our* show can go on, being under cover. We've tickets for you and Pomona for this evening.'

Pomona was busy towelling Toby by the stove. 'Good-oh!'

'What time does the show end?' May asked.

'Half past ten. We can squeeze you in to the car, as it's not far.'

'Don't say it's too late for *me* to be out!' pleaded Pomona.

May smiled. 'You'll sulk for days if I say no! So, all right!'

'Where's Danny?' Pomona put the damp towel down.

'In the dining room, with Mum and Dad,' Paddy told her. 'I wondered why I felt empty inside; no breakfast yet!'

'Hold you hard,' Jenny used a familiar expression, 'I'm doing my best! And you're hungry because you went out at the crack of dawn, your dad told me, to hunt for amber which I heard Percy tell you can sometimes be found on the beach after a rough night, and a high tide.'

'It was worth it today, because I found something that *might* be amber, but might not,' Paddy returned. 'Even though I got wet while I was beachcombing!'

'If it's still raining later this morning, but not too much, because it's an open air pool,' Pomona informed Danny, as they ate from soup bowls piled high with Force cornflakes, full-cream milk and sugar, 'I fancy a swim. Can you swim, Danny?'

He shook his head. 'Not very keen on the water,' he admitted. 'But I'll go with you. Something to do!'

'I'd like to swim the English Channel! There's a girl in America called Gertrude Ederle, a champion swimmer; she started young, like me, and she's going to attempt a Channel-swim this

36

August. But she's eighteen, I will have to beat that, won't I?'

'I shan't be surprised if you do,' Brendan looked up from his newspaper, smiling. 'You've got ten years to practise!'

The clouds parted, there was a brief respite from the rain and Punch and Judy managed one afternoon showing. Pomona, of course, had tittle-tattled to May, as Danny had to her, that Paddy considered she'd watered-down the script.

'What a sauce!' May exclaimed, but she decided to use Mr Punch's slapstick to startling effect. Although the audience gasped at the vicious *whacks* he inflicted on his nearest and dearest, it was evident from the boos directed at Punch that they realized this was part of the story and they expected him to receive his just deserts.

Not that May would countenance doing the hangman scene. That was for adults only. Jolley's was a *family* show.

'Well done!' Paddy said through the flap at the end of the performance. 'Old Red Nose was superb!'

Mr Punch replied smugly: 'That's the way to do it!' It was raining again. Smokey was braying, Toby was barking. May and her team hastily dismantled the booth and retreated.

The small theatre at the end of the pier appeared to be bursting at the seams. After a day spent mostly in seaside lodgings because of the unseasonable weather, the audience consisted mainly of visitors in mackintoshes and rubber galoshes, gently steaming in the enclosed space, but looking forward to a cheerful evening.

It had been May's and Pomona's first ride in a motor car, although May had to *shush* Pomona when she said loudly that she was too big to sit on her sister's lap.

'It's not far,' she reminded Pomona.

Now they sat in the second row, and Pomona was already rustling a paper poke bag and crunching acid-drop sweets before the curtain went up. Disembodied music began; May deduced there was a gramophone in the wings, and an energetic stage hand turning the handle. The lights dimmed, the curtain rose and a spotlight danced centre stage.

It was a varied programme. Jugglers, acrobats, a unicyclist, a stout lady singer in danger of bursting out from her tight silk gown when she hit quivering high notes; youthful tap-dancers from the local dancing school and choir boys from the church, who looked angelic but, as Pomona remarked in a loud whisper: 'They're all spotty – I could catch chickenpox!'

'Shush,' May said again. 'You've had it, remember?'

Then it was the turn of the O'Flaherty family. Pomona had to be hushed yet again when she commented: 'They're wearing *green* kilts – to show they're from Ireland, not Scotland!'

Danny, as befitted his name, sang the evocative *Danny Boy*, which had the female half of the audience wiping their eyes. Brendan played the fiddle, Brigid, seated front stage, plucked a small harp, and Paddy whistled. Each had a solo spot. Paddy whistled *In A Monastery Garden*, which was so enthusiastically received that he followed this up with something completely unexpected, *Sweet Georgia Brown*. This set feet tapping in the audience. Brendan sang the popular, romantic *Moonlight and Roses* to his wife, and she responded with the lively ditty: *Tea for Two*. The audience joined in: 'You for me – me for you – how happy we will be...'

The fiddle dominated the final number. Brendan announced it with a smile, and the spotlight lit up May's startled expression in the second row. 'This one is especially for Young May Moon, who is celebrating turning sixteen!'

'It's *June!*' a voice called. A ripple of laughter, then the music began, with clapping to the beat of the jig.

Bemused, May was nevertheless glad that she was wearing a frock, even if it was rather childish in style as Aunt Min had chosen it. Also that Brigid had taken a brush and brilliantine to her long locks and persuaded her to leave them flowing loose. Inclining her head forward, she hoped her hair would conceal her blushes.

They remained in their seats while the majority of the audience made their way to the exit, after standing to attention for the national anthem. The house lights dimmed, and it seemed they were on their own, waiting for their friends to take them back to the Swan Inn.

A hand touched May's shoulder. Startled, she turned in her seat to see who it was. '*Mum?*' she murmured uncertainly.

Then Pomona was pushing past her and was clasped in their mother's embrace. May stayed where she was, as Carmen had a companion: from his looks, a compatriot. He remained silent and aloof, but May had the uncomfortable impression that he was watching her reaction in particular.

'You used to call me *Mama,* not Mum. I suppose that is how your father referred to me. He wanted to make an Englishwoman of me, when we married, but he couldn't! I thought I would find you in West Wick, but not so soon – we only arrived this afternoon. I didn't know it would be here, tonight.' Carmen's voice was husky, heavily accented. 'It wasn't until they played that tune, and turned the spotlight on you that I realized I was in luck. I'm glad your father isn't with you, as it will be easier to make my peace, eh?'

'It won't be easy at all,' May flared. 'Dad died a few months ago. We tried to trace you, but anyway, it was too late...'

'Excuse me, is there something I can help you with?' Brendan asked politely.

'Who are you?' Carmen demanded sharply, with Pomona clinging to her arm. Her escort stepped back, but said nothing.

'I am a friend of the girls,' Brendan said. 'And you are...?'

'I am the mother of these children.'

'Is this true, May?' Brendan now addressed May. However, even in the subdued lighting, he could see the strong resemblance between May and the beautiful woman in her shiny white waterproof cape.

May nodded. 'It's all right, it's just a shock, seeing her after all this time ... she didn't know about Dad. Mum, Mr O'Flaherty and his family *are* friends, they are staying at the Swan, too.'

'This is none of your business,' Carmen said hotly to Brendan. 'Please leave us to talk.'

'I'm afraid I can't do that. We are responsible for their safe delivery back to our lodgings, and it is time to go.'

'May, Pomona, I am staying at the big hotel in the town square. Will you both meet me there tomorrow morning at eleven? By yourselves; we can speak in private, then.' Carmen disengaged herself from Pomona's clasp, and signalled to the silent man. She added 'Carlos is very discreet, I promise.'

They walked off without a backward glance.

'The family are waiting in the motor,' Brendan said, 'You are safe with us.'

As they followed him out of the theatre, Pomona whispered to May: 'Isn't it wonderful – Mum's back!'

'Let's see what she has to say first,' May said. She was still uneasy about the intense scrutiny directed at herself by the strange man accompanying her mother.

Five

The girls stood uncertainly on the red thick-pile carpet in the hotel foyer. They wore their best floral crêpe dresses as they had last night to the theatre, but the platinum-blonde receptionist with lips painted in a pillar-box red cupid's bow, gave them a supercilious look from behind the counter, before she checked the admissions book and rang through to Carmen's room.

'Mrs Jolley will be with you in a moment,' she told them. 'Please go through into the small sitting room, on the left. I will arrange for you to have coffee there.'

'I don't–' Pomona began.

May said quickly, 'Please could my sister have lemonade? She'd prefer that.'

'Certainly,' the receptionist agreed, then moved away from the window to her desk. She inserted shiny dark-blue carbon paper between two sheets of quarto white paper and rolled them into position on her typewriter. There was the clatter of keys and the noisy return of the carriage at the end of each printed line. When she became aware that the two girls were watching this procedure with interest, she gave them a look which made them move hastily in the direction they'd been told.

The tray of refreshments was placed on a low table: a tall coffee pot, jug of cream and a bowl of brown sugar lumps, with tongs. Pomona drank some of her lemonade, and crunched a couple of sugar lumps.

'Try the biscuits.' May pointed out the plate of tiny almond flat cakes.

'There's only one each.'

'You can have mine as well.'

Carmen swept in, wearing a scarlet silk frock with the fashionable 'pointed handkerchief' hemline. Draped round her shoulders was one of

42

her exotic shawls, heavily embroidered. Her black hair was pulled back from her forehead, coiled in the nape of her neck and anchored by a silver comb.

'You've plaited your hair today, it looked *much* nicer last night,' was her greeting to May. She held out her arms to Pomona, 'Aren't you going to give me a proper hug today, my darling?'

It was fortunate that May had delayed pouring the coffee, for when Pomona sprang up she spilt some of her lemonade and scattered the sugar lumps on the table. May tidied them up, ignoring the touching embrace. Then she poured the coffee and said evenly: 'Well, let's have our coffee, shall we? Then we must talk. We should be on the beach by half past one – our friends are putting up the booth and looking after the animals for us until then.' She would have to change quickly in the cramped space, into her 'disguise', she thought.

'I suppose you wish me to tell you where I have been and whom I have been with these past years?' Carmen challenged May.

'Well, the man we saw you with last night wasn't the preacher you went away with, was he?' May was emboldened by her mother's obvious surprise that her daughter was answering her back.

'No ... *that* man – we were on the boat train and about to leave for Europe, when he went out of the carriage to buy a newspaper and never returned. I certainly did not go after him!' Her dark eyes flashed.

'Why didn't you come back to Dad, to us?' May demanded.

Carmen sighed. 'Pride. Anyway, I knew it was the end of our marriage. Best for you all that I should keep away. Still, I am sad, you know, that I am unable to make amends with your father.'

'But you're back now, Mum, aren't you?' Pomona put in anxiously.

'For *you*, darling, yes. I did not forget it was your birthday, May. I shall buy you a new frock – *puff sleeves*, at your age, Aunt Min's choice, I presume. If you want to prove you are grown up you must be in the fashion. At sixteen, I suppose you can call yourself independent, eh?'

'Aunt Min is our legal guardian,' May stressed. 'Dad arranged that for us.' He wanted to safeguard us, she thought, make sure we had a permanent base.

'She does not take her duties seriously, it seems, allowing you to go off with your sister like this.'

'It was what Dad wished! For us to carry on with the Punch and Judy at West Wick. We keep in touch with Aunt Min, and she knows we are safe, staying with the Wrens at the Swan. You wouldn't want us tagging along with you. Anyway, you've been away so long...'

'Surely it is natural that I wished to contact you? I see you are as obstinate as your father was, May. I gave up my dancing to help him with his puppets – we were always short of money. I *had* to have my diversions! No, I have my own life back, and I like it, but naturally, I miss my children. Carlos and I, we will be here for the summer, like you. I hope we can all be good friends?'

Before May could answer, Carlos came into the room. He was wearing a smart, striped blazer, a silk cravat, Oxford bags (a style of trousers made popular by the dashing Prince of Wales) and spats over his shoes, which made Pomona giggle. These canvas coverings were to prevent splashes of mud from spoiling the shine. He also had a moustache which looked as if it were pencilled over his lips.

'I wish you good morning.' He nodded to May and Pomona in turn.

'I shall introduce you properly,' said Carmen, 'This is my stage partner and manager, Carlos Rivera. He is a master of dancing and puppetry, not to mention the Spanish guitar. You will see! Carlos is from Andalucia, in Southern Spain, as I am – we can both boast of a gypsy great-grand-mother and thus a tradition of flamenco. We are booked to appear in the end of the pier show from Saturday night. This is why we were in the audience last evening. I must say the acts were mostly second-rate. No doubt, *we* will be top of the bill.'

May was incensed at what she thought was a deliberate slur aimed at the O'Flahertys. 'Why aren't you appearing in London then? The only write-up you can expect here is in the local paper...'

Unexpectedly, Carlos Rivera attempted to smooth things over. 'Our real reason for coming here is simple: I convinced your mother that you would be happy to see her again. She wants an end to quarrelling, a fresh start. Will you not give her the chance to prove that to you?' He added, smiling at May, displaying perfect white teeth: 'In turn, you will show us this afternoon that you

45

have inherited some of her expertise, as well as her fire, eh?'

Despite her initial misgivings May appreciated his intervention.

Carmen cried, 'Oh, what a fool I am! I should learn to keep my mouth shut, and to hug you, instead – come here, May...'

She still smells of frangipani, May thought, as Carmen clutched her close. I missed that fragrance – I didn't realize ... we both have to learn to forgive and forget, I reckon.

'We really must go,' she said, 'We'll see you after the show.'

'Thank goodness,' Paddy said, 'We were worried you wouldn't be back in time. We had a bit of a kerfuffle soon after we arrived – Toby disappeared! Danny walked up and down the beach, calling, and eventually he spotted a boy pulling her along on a piece of string. Fortunately, he gave her up, saying she had been chasing after a ball he was throwing for his own dog. Whether that was true or not, we don't know, but she's back.'

'I'm glad you told me, it's not like Toby to run off like that. Thanks, Danny, for rescuing her – there wouldn't have been a performance without her!' May told him. 'Maybe I ought to ask you to make a Toby puppet, just in case? They used to have one in the old days, so Dad told us!'

'They're setting up the deckchairs,' Pomona reminded her.

There was another kerfuffle in the booth, the canvas sides bulged, as May struggled with her

46

change of clothes. She was startled by a roll of drums, then an excited bark from Toby.

Pomona's head appeared through the side flap. 'Hear that? Danny asked his dad if he could borrow his small drum kit! Paddy's doing the "Roll up, roll up!" routine. Brigid, Brendan and Jenny have just arrived – and *Mum's* in the front row! Hurry up, will you?'

'She must have left just after we did,' May said crossly. 'All set for curtain up...' *Fingers crossed,* she told herself.

It was her best performance yet.

Her friends hurried to congratulate her, while her mother and Carlos waited for the crowd to disperse. Jenny exchanged a few polite words with Carmen, and May guessed she was being nice to Carmen for her and Pomona's sake. After they waved goodbye Carmen came over to the booth. 'May, you have your father's touch ... it was good,' she said.

'Yes, it was good,' agreed Carlos. 'But you can learn much more.'

Learn what? May was puzzled by his enigmatic remark, but she did not ask what he meant. It had unsettled her, Carmen turning up again like this. She recalled that Aunt Min had said to her father once that Carmen was devious. Curious, the younger May had looked up the meaning in her school dictionary. *Deceitful,* she read, *Clever at getting one's own way in an underhand manner...* She had the feeling that her mother was planning something, and that whatever it was, it would involve herself.

Six

The following morning May and Pomona met
Carmen outside the exclusive dress shop in the
square. There were no puff sleeves on the stylish
frocks draped on the plaster models in the window, the designs for younger woman were sleeveless. The simple shifts did not emphasize waist or
bust, ensuring that the frocks were comfortable
to wear as well as elegant. The materials were
summer weight: georgette, silk or fine cotton.
Rigid corsetry was a thing of the past. Women
were emancipated, even if they hadn't yet got the
vote.

'Well, May, do you like what you see?' Carmen
asked.

'Oh, yes!' May agreed.

'Well, let us go inside – and Pomona, don't touch
anything, please, the assistant looks very superior!'

Some of the frocks had patterned borders to
the skirt. Others were striped or checked. Some
had a bow loosely tied around the hips or at the
neckline; there were no fussy collars. May chose
a soft green material, with a poppy patterned
border. There was a matching cloche hat, but as
the assistant remarked: 'You have far too much
hair for this model! Now, if you were to have the
new Eton crop–'

'Certainly not!' her mother cried. 'Her hair is
her Spanish heritage!' May agreed: her father had

loved her long hair. But she decided to have the Mary-Jane shoes, even though she was not keen on pointed toes.

'What about me?' Pomona asked plaintively, as the dress and shoes were parcelled up.

'You will be back at school next week, I shall buy you a new jacket in the children's-wear shop,' Carmen told her.

'Oh, pooh!'

'Thank you, Mum,' May put in quickly, 'I'm not sure when I can wear such a pretty dress, but...'

'You have a young man, I understand? He may ask you out!'

'Young man?' May blushed. She wished she could prevent herself from 'colouring-up' as Aunt Min put it.

'She means Paddy, of course,' Pomona chipped in, to her sister's further embarrassment. 'Actually, you two are always arguing, aren't you? Like Danny and me, although I usually get the better of him.'

'You are the least tactful person I know,' May hissed in her ear.

'Come along, girls; my friend Carlos will be waiting for us in the coffee shop. If you are nice to your sister, Pomona, you shall have a double helping of ice-cream.'

'Good-oh. But don't tell Jenny, May, or she'll say it'll spoil my lunch. I can't bottle this afternoon on an empty stomach.'

'So,' Carlos said pleasantly, when they joined him at a round table set in the recess of a bay window. 'You have your new frock?'

'It's green,' said Pomona mischievously, 'So, if she wants to, she can perform on stage with the O'Flahertys in their green kilts!'

'Is this what they have suggested?' Carmen asked sharply.

May managed to speak before Pomona this time. 'No, of course not!' She thought, why is Mum making a fuss about me and Paddy? I'm not ready to have a boyfriend yet. She's been away so long she has no idea how I feel. Growing up is enough to cope with at the moment.

On Friday evening, after the O'Flahertys left for the Pier Theatre, Jenny suggested that May and Pomona might like to have a bath. 'You will have the kitchen to yourselves, as Percy and I will be busy in the bar; there's always a dominoes match going on, and someone has to sort 'em out, when players get too hot under the collar. I'll get Percy to bring the tub in. I'll fill the clothes copper, so you have plenty of hot water, you can mix that with cold, can't you? Leave the tub for Percy to empty last thing – he's the expert, eh? I'll put two big towels to warm on the airer over the stove, and there's a new bar of Fairy soap, unless you prefer Pears transparent?'

They chose the Pears soap. It was a big tin tub, and took several jugs of hot and cold water to fill. There was room for the girls to sit one at either end. 'We haven't shared a bath since you were a baby!' May told Pomona. 'And don't you dare make any personal remarks!'

'I'll close my eyes until you're under water!' Pomona quipped back. She whipped up the soap flakes which Jenny had also kindly supplied, into a froth. 'Now you're concealed by the bubbles!'

'Shut up and wash your neck and feet – those are the bits you usually ignore...'

'And you can hurry up and wash yourself, because when you get out I'm going to swim from one side of the tub to the other – I bet Gertrude Ederle has a private pool! How many strokes d'you think that will take?'

'Not enough – more likely a flood on the floor!' May said.

Pomona dodged the wet sponge her sister threw at her. The sponge landed on Toby instead, as she rested her pointed chin on the rim of the bath and gazed soulfully at them. She yelped.

'Be quiet, Toby,' May warned, 'unless you fancy a bath, too!' Toby removed herself smartly.

They were sitting in their nightgowns, worn beneath thin wraparound dressing-gowns because it was summer, sipping mugs of milky cocoa, when they heard the first strains of music. Jenny was playing the piano, and the pub regulars were joining in the chorus. 'I wish we ...' May murmured wistfully. Then she had a bright idea. 'Finish your cocoa! We'll sit on the snug stairs: no-one will know *we're* singing too!'

Friday was pay day for the hard-working agricultural labourers, their night for a glass or two in the pub. It was men only, but some took home a bottle of stout as a treat for the wife. Tonight, they were joined by fishermen back from trawling herring, with coins jingling in their pockets. So sea shanties were much called for.

What shall we do with the drunken sailor, May

51

and Pomona sang with them.

They were startled when the kitchen door opened and Brigid tiptoed along the corridor. She'd guessed what they were up to.

She grinned. 'Room for me on the stairs? I gather you had a bath! The boys are emptying it, to save old Percy a job. When they've done that, Brendan will make us toasted cheese for supper. Would you like a midnight feast?'

'It's not *that* late,' Pomona said, with a huge yawn. Then, 'Yes, please! But can I have my supper in bed?'

'You go ahead,' May agreed. 'I'll bring it in a little while.'

When she followed Brigid into the kitchen she saw Paddy sitting in the rocker with Toby on his lap. Brendan was slicing bread at the table. There was already a delicious aroma of melting cheese.

'Danny gone to bed, too?' Brigid enquired.

'He has,' Brendan replied. 'Are they still singing in the bar?'

'They are ... but I'll make the big pot of tea. Though there's the glasses to wash and the place to tidy before Jenny and Percy join us. Not many landladies are as obliging as Jenny, eh? They don't let the theatricals anywhere near the kitchen!'

'Ah, she has a generous nature,' Brendan agreed. 'Especially as I have used up all the cheese!'

Brigid turned to May. 'Maybe this is a good time to ask you...'

'Ask me what?'

'Well, now we no longer have the top spot before the finale, that'll be your mum and her

52

partner. Please don't think I'm complaining, because the new acts always get a chance at that! I am wondering if we can introduce something different into our performance – you've got a pleasant singing voice–'

'Oh, no, I couldn't sing on stage!'

'Could you do a jig? To *Young May Moon,* for instance?'

'Not an Irish jig – it's more a Scottish tune, or played in a morris dance,' May said. She thought about it for a minute. 'Grandpa showed me the basic steps: *one, two, hop, then hop back, two, three and four...*' She sprang to her feet to demonstrate, but it was difficult in slippers. 'My new shoes would be better.'

'You really need the proper shoes,' Brigid said, 'but I'm sure you could do it!'

'Sit down and eat your toasted cheese.' Brendan handed May a plate. 'Then you can take your sister her share. Look, if we decide to include you tomorrow evening – after all, you'll be in the audience to see your mother's performance any-way – it must come as a surprise to everyone else, including Pomona, if the spotlight picks you out, and you are invited to join us for a special number.'

'I won't say a thing,' Paddy put in with a grin. 'Promise!'

'You've helped me with the Punch and Judy, so I'd like to do something in return for you all! I'm not sure my mum will approve!'

'She'll be proud of you,' Brigid said optimistic-ally.

Later, when sleep eluded her, no doubt due to

53

the cheese supper, May suddenly remembered her mother's sharp words earlier, about her appearing on stage with the O'Flahertys, in their green kilts. Had she been too quick to say 'yes', when she'd only known them for a week, though it seemed longer than that? Would *she* now be cast as the devious one?

Seven

The choir boys were not in evidence on Saturday evening. No doubt they were at home, their spots being dabbed with that universal remedy, bicarbonate of soda, mixed to a paste with a few drops of water, and temperatures lowered with a crushed aspirin, administered in a spoonful of jam.

The billboard outside the little theatre proclaimed:

STAR ATTRACTION!
CARLOS & CARMEN FROM
SUNNY SPAIN!

May was blushingly aware of some admiring glances, as they settled into their front-row seats. She felt conspicuous in the pretty new dress with her hair all loose, and apprehensive too. Oh, why had she agreed to perform with the O'Flahertys? Suppose Carmen made a scene? Her toes were cramped in the new shoes which also rubbed her heels. Fashion could be painful, too!

Most of the acts were the same as last week. The O'Flaherty family appeared just before the interval. When it came to the duet *Tea for Two*, May began to get butterflies in her stomach. She said to herself, maybe they will change their minds, not call me up. Then Brendan stepped forward and announced: 'By popular demand, that evergreen tune, *Young May Moon!* Once again, we have the young lady herself in the audience. Spotlight, please! May, would you care to come up on stage and take part?'

A penetrating whisper came from an excited Pomona, as her sister sat there, illuminated, but unable to speak for a moment. 'Oh, go on, May!' May stood up, the audience clapped, and Brendan came down to escort her up the steps.

The music began, and May concentrated on the basic steps – arms at her sides, raising one knee, pointing her toes; hopping on the other leg; taking three little steps back, and before she knew it, she was in rhythm with the tune and gaining confidence with each repeated sequence. It seemed surreal, like a dream. The clapping and cheers, as Brigid encouraged her to take a bow, made her realize that she had done it, performed as herself, not as the hidden manipulator of rascally Punch and company.

Back in her seat, she was patted on the back by the elderly couple sitting behind her and with the lights up for the interval, she was aware of others trying to catch her eye and waving. She could guess what would inevitably happen next, and she was right. Her mother appeared, with a cloak over her stage clothes and said simply: 'Girls, follow me.'

In the small room reserved for the top-of-the-bill acts, off the communal dressing room, they sat on a couple of hard chairs. Carmen had her back to them, seated at the long shelf below the wall mirror, which was crowded with pots of cold cream, sticks of greasepaint, cotton-wool and other items of theatrical make-up. They stared at her reflection in the glass as she powdered her face with an enormous powder puff.

Carlos was nowhere to be seen. Probably in the bar, May thought uncharitably.

'You need to enhance *your* face, May; the spotlight drains your natural colour,' was all Carmen said.

Relief washed over May. 'You didn't mind, Mum – me going on stage?'

'No. I was proved right. You have real talent, May. However, you can do so much more. Carlos and I, we would like you to join us now and then, in our own act. You would need instruction first, of course. We could arrange this so it would not interfere with your Punch and Judy time. What do you say?'

'Say yes, May!' Pomona butted in.

'I – I'm not sure. It would have to be before eleven o'clock in the morning. It's not fair if I leave the setting-up on the beach to Paddy – Pom and Danny will be at school next week.'

A bell was heard, signalling the end of the interval. Even as they rose to go, May – she didn't know why, blurted out: 'Are you going to marry Carlos, Mum?'

'I thought I made it clear: we are partners on the

stage. There is no great romance. He has, however, been a good friend to me and helped me to resume my dancing career. But I am realistic. Carlos is several years younger than me. I am already forty and the flamenco is a dance full of vigour and passion. It is inevitable, I think, that the time will come when he will want a younger partner. Why else does he look in your direction? You are like the girl I once was.' She looked ruefully at her plump upper arms and her tight waistband. 'I try to say no to the cakes, but... Hurry, now, before the lights go down. Wish me luck, tonight!'

'We do,' the girls said together.

The acrobats bounded across the stage, seemingly tying themselves into knots, then unfolded their limbs before they took their final bow.

There was a feeling of expectation, a hush in the audience, aware that the highlight of the evening was about to commence. The curtains parted and the stage appeared empty, except for a high black screen. Then the spotlight picked out Carlos, plucking the strings of the classical guitar and adding emphasis to the tune by drumming with his fingers. Then he began to sing a lament about a beautiful girl, but as it was in Spanish May could only pick out a few words. She'd been quite fluent as a very small child, and maybe, she thought, that understanding would return if her mother stayed long enough.

The spotlight shifted. From behind the screen Carmen, in full flamenco dress with a tiered frilled skirt and hand-painted shawl, emerged, snapping her fingers to the music. As she strutted in high-heeled red shoes that matched her dress, her stamping added to the staccato beat.

'Real flamenco dancers don't use castanets,' May murmured to Pomona. 'Some of them prefer fans, but Mum believes in the old tradition.' You can see Mum's gypsy ancestry tonight, she thought, and *feel* it too, through the dancing and the music. All that is missing is moonlight and a flickering camp fire. What was it Mum used to say, you must experience the *duende* – the spirit of flamenco...

When the music faded away to a few plaintive notes, and Carlos ceased singing, in his pleasant tenor voice, there was a moment or two of hush before the audience applause.

This wasn't the end of the act; there was more to come. Carmen slipped away behind the screen. Carlos bent his head over the guitar. This time the music was louder, faster, and he did not sing.

Pomona gripped May's arm. 'Look!' she whispered. Another dancer, a life-size puppet was being lowered skilfully over the screen to the stage. This figure did have jingling castanets, which were attached to her wrists. These were obviously necessary because the puppet's feet moved almost silently, although the dancing was as energetic as that of her real-life counterpart.

Abruptly the music ceased. The puppet dancer turned, beckoned to the guitar player. Now he was fully in the spotlight, his costume revealed in all its glory: matador breeches, Cuban-heeled shoes with silver buckles, a scarlet cummerbund matching the lining of his shoulder-cape. Carlos bowed to the puppet, inviting her to dance with

58

him. This time there was no musical accompaniment, just the sound of the castanets and his heel-tapping. They danced side by side and the effect was spellbinding.

At the end of the dance he bowed to the audience and the puppet dancer sank down in a graceful curtsey. She remained in that posture as the lights went up and Carmen emerged from behind the screen, smiling and waving to the crowd. They took a final bow, supporting the puppet between them.

'Did Mum *really* pull the strings behind the screen?' Pomona exclaimed. 'Wasn't it wonderful?'

'Wonderful,' May agreed. She thought, Dad didn't like Mum performing after he came home from the war. He thought her place was to be with us, supporting him. I can understand now why she wasn't happy, she needed the *duende* – to be a free spirit. We have to accept that she won't change.

They knew the way backstage now. They met up with the O'Flahertys, who were full of praise for the new act.

'We'll wait while you congratulate your mother,' Brendan said.

'You must be very proud of her,' Brigid added. 'As she should be of you.'

That night, back at the Swan, there was a lot to tell Jenny and Percy. Except, of course, that neither of the girls mentioned what Carmen had said about Carlos, or his interest in May.

'You're hobbling, darling,' Jenny said, concerned. 'Take those shoes off and let me see your heels. My, what a blister!' She fetched her tin of Zambuck, the soothing ointment.

Eight

The school was five minutes' walk away from the Swan. It was a typical Victorian building, with high windows to deter children from looking out, and Gothic-style oak doors which matched the ones on the nearby church, which had founded the school. There were other schools, privately run, nearer the sea, including a girls' school where the pupils wore smart uniforms and straw boaters with a ribbon in the school colours, but the free church schools provided a sound education for most.

Big changes had taken place in the local school over recent years. The two big rooms had each originally been divided into two sections to accommodate much wider age-groups. Boys and girls still studied together, but there was not such a range of ages, which made it easier for the two teachers to cope. One class catered for the six-to eight-year-olds; the other, the nine- to eleven-year-old pupils.

There was segregation in the playground: one side for the girls and the infants, the other for the boys, who played more vigorous games. The latrines were outside, of the bucket-and-drain variety, and drinking water, with a dip-in tin mug, was available in a pail, under the shade of a tree. This was tepid in summer, as Pomona discovered, and you were limited to half a mugful. A monitor was in charge to see that this was observed.

There were qualified teachers for the older children, but the infants, in a smaller room, were in the charge of a supplementary teacher, a young woman who had no formal teaching training, had not long left school herself; but was both intelligent and kind. She taught the little ones by rote, which was how she had learned herself: words were pointed out on a cloth which was rolled down to cover the blackboard, and the children recited these obediently after the teacher. A pupil from the top class sometimes helped the slower readers.

The population had increased since the end of the Great War, and now the church school took children up to eleven. At the beginning of the century, children often left school at that age, but education now continued until they were fourteen. So a new school was built, out of town for the older students, who were provided with bicycles, by the local authority, to get there.

Pomona and Danny were in the lower school. The old slates had been replaced by exercise books and pencils for handwriting practice; there was ink in the wells in the desk tops, and scratchy metal pen nibs to scatter blots on copy work. There was a large globe of the world, with plenty of pink patches for the British Empire, which could be swivelled on a stand. Less daring children looked at it wistfully, wishing they could spin it like one or two of the bolder ones did, when the teacher temporarily left the classroom. The cane, a few swipes on the hand, was still the punishment if you were caught.

The blackboard had a white film of chalk where the rubber had been carelessly applied. The teacher of the top group had an unerring aim with stubs of chalk, to sting the unwary behind an ear, when heads were turned to whisper to a neighbour. To Pomona, surveying the classroom apprehensively on her first day and separated from Danny, who was in the other class, it all seemed very old-fashioned. Some girls even wore starched frilled pinafores over their dresses, just as their mothers had done. However, many now had their hair bobbed, as she had insisted upon for herself. It was bad enough being dubbed 'Freckles', without having long plaits pulled, or wound round rulers by the sneaky type behind you, she thought.

She was in for a pleasant surprise later. Soup, made from vegetables grown by the boys in the gardening club, some of whom had escaped scripture lessons, which had been their motive for joining the club originally, was served every day for lunch. Because of the current high level of unemployment, tradesmen helped the needy. The local baker provided yesterday's bread for free, and the butcher gave meaty marrow bones for the basis of the soup. Volunteers from the top class chopped the vegetables and tipped them in to a big cauldron, which simmered on an old oil stove for most of the morning. This nourishing food was particularly important for the children from outlying villages, who had already walked a long way to school, some without breakfast. There was no dining hall, so the children had their soup sitting at their desks. Empty plates were taken to the pump and rinsed before play was allowed.

Pomona managed a few words to Danny over the fence which separated the boys from the girls.

'How did you get on?' he asked, after cautiously checking that the teacher on duty was not near by.

'All right,' she fibbed. In fact she had failed an arithmetic test – well, what did she know about fractions? They hadn't been tackled at her school.

'I got on all right too,' he said, but he didn't sound too convincing either. It was unsettling, attending a new school near end of the term. 'It was good soup,' he said.

'I could have done with more bread,' Pomona said. 'But someone told me, the teacher will be bringing round a basket of windfall apples shortly – hope she does!'

While Pomona and Danny were settling in at school May was on the pier by ten o'clock, meeting Carmen in the empty theatre. The cleaner had already been and gone, having gathered up crumpled paper bags and orange-peel, and wiped the tip-up seats with disinfectant. The curtains were pulled apart for their practice.

May had thought she would be shown how to manipulate the dancing puppet, but she soon discovered that she was in fact being taught the first steps of the flamenco.

'I will lend you a pair of proper shoes, but not today – with that sore heel of yours!' Carmen said, wincing as it was revealed.

'Harden your feet with surgical spirit,' she advised. 'Wear your father's boots!'

It was not altogether a successful session, Carmen was not the most patient of tutors. She was also unaccustomed to such an early start. 'Of course,' she said, 'I learned to dance as soon as I could walk. When you were with Aunt Min during the war and I was on tour, she did not encourage you, like me.'

'You can't blame her for that; she's not a dancer! She never followed Dad into the world of Punch and Judy either! She got married young and helped her husband on his parents' farm. When they died, she inherited the farm. She's worked hard all her life, and given us a home when we needed it,' May reminded her mother.

'Am I wasting my time?' Carmen demanded. 'Will you please concentrate!' It's hard without music, May muttered to herself. But as she watched Carmen displaying the basic steps, there was a rustling of the back curtain and Carlos appeared, yawning, with his guitar, and seated himself in a shadowy corner. Now May felt the urge to follow, faltering at first, in her mother's footsteps. When they paused briefly, Carlos called to Carmen, 'It will take much time, but the girl is worth it.'

Just before eleven the session was over. 'Carlos and I will return to the hotel for breakfast,' Carmen announced. 'Think about what you have learned this morning. Come again on Wednesday.'

May felt hungry too. She hoped that Paddy had remembered to bring sandwiches for their lunch!

Paddy was waiting on the beach. Smokey was tethered and enjoying a nosebag of hay. Toby was on a long lead, which Paddy had looped round

64

his ankle as he soaked up the sun on the sand and watched the waves ebb and flow. There were not yet many people about, but some of the beach-hut doors were open.

May unfastened her boots and cooled off her feet in the shallows. 'Ooh, that feels better!'

'I reckon most of the Whit week visitors have gone home,' he observed. He opened his rucksack. 'Hungry?'

'I certainly am,' May said, accepting an egg-and-cress sandwich. 'Hope you made a flask of tea, too!'

Paddy was right, there was only a small straggling audience at the first show of the afternoon. It could be another month before things picked up, she thought, and it was obvious from what the papers said, and listening to the crackling wireless when she took her turn with the headphones, that tough times were ahead for the country as a whole, and that holidays would not be a priority for most folk. As if he could read her thoughts, Paddy said, as he unwrapped the buttered scones, 'Maybe you should have gone home after all, and come back in August.'

'What about you?'

'Actually, Mum and Dad are talking about giving up the wandering life after this season. Dad has been offered his old teaching post, to start next September. Danny could complete his education there, and maybe I could get an apprenticeship in furniture making – my grandfather could pull a few strings in that respect. We'd have to move in with him, to begin with.'

'And your mum?'

'Mum could take private pupils, when we find a permanent place to stay.'

'But you're not going yet?' May asked anxiously.

'No, we'll be here, like you, until the end of August. Don't worry, I'll be your assistant until then!' He didn't add 'unpaid' for he had insisted, from the beginning, that he was happy to help out for free. He'd deduced that May's earnings in July, before the main holiday, would only cover the girls' board.

She smiled. 'Good!' She hoped that they would be friends for ever. To think that she hadn't liked him when they first met! She needed someone on her side – she was understandably wary of her mother's interest in her future. 'Promise me, you'll keep in touch after the summer,' she added.

Nine

'You need cheering up,' Paddy said to May after the Punch and Judy had played to an audience of four, one windy afternoon on the beach. 'Let's pack up, go back to the Swan, give the animals the rest of the afternoon off, then suggest to Mum and Dad that we meet the young 'uns from school and go to the second house at the pictures. It would fill in the time before the evening on the pier.'

'Sounds like a good idea,' May agreed. 'What film is on?'

'*The Navigator* – Buster Keaton. It came out

last year.'

'We promised Jenny to hold the fort here, as she's out today. You might get a glimpse of her in town,' Brigid said mysteriously. She would not divulge anything further, but added: 'Why don't you two go on your own? The children need a run around after school, not sitting down again in the pictures. They can throw a ball for Toby and maybe groom old Smokey. He's looking rather shaggy.'

'He's getting ancient – this could be his last summer season, I suppose, before he retires,' May said regretfully. How could she return to West Wick then?

They'd had their packed lunch on the sands, so now they had time to change their attire for going out. May hesitated for a moment, thinking it wasn't really a special occasion as nowadays a cinema seat cost only sixpence, if you didn't mind sitting in the front row and tilting your head back to view the screen. Then she slipped into the green dress her mother had bought her, and the now comfortable Mary-Jane shoes. However, she re-braided her hair, mindful of Aunt Min's warnings: 'You never know what might hop off the back of the seat on to your hair, in the cinema.' The very thought made her scratch her head. She'd escaped being lousy by bearing that in mind, she thought. Who wanted to smell of paraffin, the treatment for itchy scalps, or to have the fine-tooth comb plied to remove nits?

The cinema here was actually a modern, well-run place. The management insisted on good quality films, so the picture did not wobble on the screen or break down frequently as in the aptly

67

named flea-pits in poorer towns. Lighting was good, and local advertising helped towards a full house at most performances. Aunt Min would certainly have approved of the West Wick Palace cinema. May and Paddy, arriving early, were shown to the best seats in the centre of the third row.

The Navigator was a full-length film. Both May and Paddy were familiar with Buster Keaton's short features so they looked forward to a story with more of a plot.

'I think I prefer Buster Keaton to Charlie Chaplin,' May whispered to Paddy. She received a prod in the back from the person behind her to remind her to be quiet.

'I agree,' Paddy dared to whisper back. 'That dead pan face, and all the acrobatics – he's a genius.' It was his turn to be prodded.

They had read about the film when it first came out: of how when Buster Keaton learned that a once-great passenger liner was about to be scrapped he bought at a bargain price the ship, which had been a troop-carrier during the war, to use as a giant prop. He had invented a story around it.

There were two main characters, Rollo Treadway (played by Keaton), a rich, idle playboy, determined to marry spirited heiress Betsy O'Brien, who was equally determined not to marry him. Somehow, after a series of comical misunderstandings, the two found themselves alone on the abandoned ship *Navigator,* not aboard the luxury cruise liner on which both, by coincidence, had booked passages. *The Navigator,* the subject of

68

mistaken identity, was then set adrift in the fog by a 'foreign power' to be destroyed at sea.

Despite the implausible plot the audience was engrossed by the desperate survival tactics of the two players. May was unaware that she was gripping Paddy's hand when Keaton attempted to open a solitary can of meat with a chopper. Later, they were due to be on the menu themselves when they came upon an island populated by fierce cannibals...

Although the film had no soundtrack the accompanying stirring music on a piano situated below the screen made them thrill to the unfolding picture story.

At the end of the hour-long film, when Rollo had proved that he could be brave and resourceful rather than shallow and selfish, and so had won the girl, the lights went up and the pianist took a bow while the audience applauded her skilful playing.

'It's *Jenny Wren!*' May exclaimed, wondering if their friend had spotted them. She realized that she was still clutching Paddy's hand. 'Oh, sorry.' She blushed, 'I got over-excited!'

Paddy smiled at her confusion. 'I must say I didn't mind.'

The girl who had beamed her torch along the aisles when they arrived was now playing a different role. She had a tray suspended on cords round her neck, laden with small tubs of ice cream and tiny wooden spoons. She stood at the bottom of the centre aisle and a queue formed in front of her.

'My treat. You paid for the seats,' May said,

giving a precious shilling to Paddy.

The lights dimmed and the advertisements were shown on the screen. Then there was a newsreel, followed by a short film of a car chase causing havoc in a sleepy town. The subtitles were full of exclamation marks. The national anthem signalled the end of the show, when the audience all rose to attention as one.

May and Paddy resumed their seats while the audience left the cinema, then went to congratulate Jenny on her performance.

'You never know, they might ask me again. It makes a nice change from standing behind the bar, particularly now folk make one drink last all evening, as funds are low! Don't wait for me – I have a bit of shopping to do before I come home. The regular pianist will be here this evening. Tell Percy I'm on my way.'

They emerged into the late afternoon sunshine, blinking at its brightness.

'Better hurry back,' Paddy said. 'I'll have to leave again soon for the evening show. I imagine Mum is cooking supper, as Jenny is filling in here. Did you enjoy yourself, May?' It seemed natural now for her to link her arm in his as they walked along in the wake of other cinema-goers. 'Oh, I did!' she said happily.

It was fortunate that they only had eyes for each other, because they were under intense scrutiny from the other side of the road.

Carmen had been shopping. The parcel she had tucked into her handbag contained a box camera, a present for her daughters. They could record the Punch and Judy as much as they liked,

70

for Carmen was determined that this would be their last season on the West Wick sands...

Even the fact that Pomona was having a fit of the sulks because she had not been invited on their outing couldn't spoil May's euphoria. She thought: I suppose Paddy is my young man now, and it's a good feeling, it really is.

Ten

'Fancy a tasty piece of smoked haddock for supper?' Jenny asked on the last day of the school term. 'A celebration meal for our scholars! The good news is that our friend Bobby Blowers has taken over the old smoking huts that you can see across the estuary from the bridge. Ever been over that side?'

May shook her head. 'I can't swim,' she said cheerfully, 'even though the water is clear at that point.'

'My dear, you can take the ferry from the harbour, then walk back along the river path. Paddy's keen to make the trip, why don't you go with him this morning?'

'It's supposed to be my practice today,' May said.

'Ring your mother up – say you've got something better to do,' Jenny advised.

'Oh, I can't do that, I'd never hear the end of it.'

'Look,' Paddy put in, 'I don't mind waiting while you have your lesson. Then, why don't we

71

give the Punch and Judy a miss until Saturday, when the visitors will begin to arrive? You're bound to be busy from then on, especially with the August bank holiday coming up on the third.'

'You don't need to ask me twice!' she told him.

Paddy sat where he was told, some way back in the little theatre. He had been warned by Carmen to be quiet. There was no dancing spotlight on stage for rehearsals, but the house lights were on. The guitar strumming began. May, to her mother's disapproval, was not dressed for dancing. She wore a pair of faded blue box-pleated shorts which Jenny had sorted out from a collection of clothes destined for the next jumble sale, deeming these suitable for a boat trip, and her old school blouse. Her hair was tied severely back. May followed her mother's instructions.

Paddy observed how May had grown in confidence, but with that hairstyle, he thought, she looks very different from when we first met.

'You will soon be ready for your debut – the audience here will not realize you are a novice. You have the hair right, anyway,' Carmen said, at the end of the hour.

'Debut...?' May sounded uncertain. 'Well, thank you for the lesson, anyway. We have an errand to run for Jenny now.'

'Wait a moment, I have a gift for you and your sister. Can you use a camera?'

'Yes, Dad's old Brownie. He showed us how to make good pictures. Unfortunately, Pom dropped it one day and the film is jammed inside. Aunt Min said she'd get it mended–'

'That won't be necessary now. But you should be the one responsible, not your clumsy sister.' Carmen handed the box to May. 'This has a film, ready to use.'

'Thank you.' I can take photographs to record our summer season, May thought, pleased. She said aloud, to please Carmen, 'I must get a picture of you in costume on stage.'

The trip in the rowing-boat across the river was quite an experience. A chain ferry would soon be in place to transport freight as well as folk, but meantime the town was reluctant to lose its ferryman, the last of a long line, with his shaggy beard, twinkling eyes, if rheumy from the wind, ancient cap and fisherman's smock. The swish of the oars as the boat headed for the far side, the cries of the swooping gulls overhead, the breeze whipping May's hair free of its constraints, was exhilarating. The boat was packed with passengers, and as they sat shoulder to shoulder on the plank seats, Paddy was able to watch May's expressive face at close quarters.

All too soon the boat arrived at the mooring, and old Noah, despite his great age, leapt nimbly out and helped them ashore. There were people waiting for the return journey.

'Back in a while,' he called, as he made ready to row back.

May and Paddy strolled along to the huts and joined a queue of people with baskets to fill.

Bobby Blowers had a ruddy face, a shock of silver hair and an explosion of a laugh, which caused his big belly to wobble.

The smoked fish looked like washing hanging

73

on lines, and Bobby had a fine selection. 'On the bone – or does Jenny want me to fillet some for you?' he asked.

May had to back tactfully out into the fresh air outside the hut while Bobby wrapped the haddock in newspaper. The smell of fish was overpowering, she thought. Paddy lingered to buy some sprats, too, which were packed in a barrel with crushed ice. There was a glut of these tiny fish this summer.

'Fresh caught early this morning,' Bobby beamed.

May suddenly recalled the camera in her bag. 'May I take your picture, Bobby?' she enquired, producing it.

'Of course you can, my dear – there won't be no smell to that! The local photographer took one yesterday, and he says he's going to print my face on postcards and sell 'em to the tourists! Make sure you get the sign in the picture, eh?'

Others followed suit with their cameras, and Bobby enjoyed his moment of fame.

When they arrived back May exclaimed, 'Oh, I must get one of Noah now! I want to remember this summer for ever!'

Noah seemed pleased to oblige, but it was difficult to focus on him, with passengers stepping ashore, and others waiting to get on the boat.

'I probably included some extras,' May remarked ruefully to Paddy as they crossed the road to the cinema, to glance at the forthcoming attractions advertised on the billboards outside. 'A camera attracts people who want to be in the picture.'

'It will add to the atmosphere,' he observed. 'Like the cannibals in *The Navigator!*'

The haddock was served with a poached egg on top. With new bread, warm from the oven and spread with pale golden butter, this was indeed a feast.

'Smile please!' was repeated often over the next few days. Jenny, rolling an empty milk churn; Percy scything nettles in the paddock; Pomona and Danny peering out from the branches of a tree; Paddy whittling a piece of wood; Brigid hanging out washing and trying to hold down her skirt in the breeze, and Brendan polishing the bonnet of the car. These were all spur of the moment snaps.

Carmen, on the other hand, insisted on elaborate poses. Somehow, Carlos always seemed to be lurking in the background, which was disconcerting, but May could hardly say that to her mother. Toby was grumpy and out of sorts on bank holiday Monday. 'She's getting stout – but how can I tell Jenny not to give her titbits?' May worried. 'She's so kind to us all.'

'Maybe it's nearing the time for Dog Toby to retire, too, like old Smokey,' Paddy suggested. 'I'm still willing to have a go at a wooden Toby, but Mum could probably do a better job sewing a glove puppet for you, to use as a stand-in.'

'I could handle that – easy!' Pomona put in quickly.

'We'll see how it goes today, eh?' May said, thinking wistfully: why can't things go on for ever, in the same old way?

Despite all the gloomy predictions in the press,

the general worries about the country's financial state, the bank holiday crowds appeared as jolly as ever and determined to make the most of their time by the sea, even though it was a cloudy, breezy day. August had not got off to a good start, but when they looked back on it years later, they would recall that 1925 was actually one of the driest on record.

All the deckchairs were taken for the Punch and Judy show. 'Hold on to your hats, ladies!' advised the irrepressible Pomona.

'Is my mum out there?' May asked, when Paddy peeped in to the booth to see if she was ready to begin the show. He shook his head. She added: 'Would you take some pictures for us?' He nodded this time. She passed him the camera.

May wanted a record of this special date, because she accepted that this might be their last summer season for quite a while. She didn't yet know what the future might hold, but at least she had carried out her father's last wishes, she thought.

Eleven

Pomona had been bubbling with anticipation for days; preparations were well under way for Miss Gertrude Ederle's attempt to swim the English Channel. She was pictured in all the newspapers. It made a nice change to see her smiling face rather than the grimmer photographs of protest marches of the unemployed, she thought. She was swimming on most days herself, Danny wisely didn't try to compete, but borrowed his father's pocket watch to time the lengths she managed when the pool was not too full of visitors.

On 18 August, May agreed they would take the day off from the Punch and Judy. Pomona and Danny passed the headphones back and forth as they listened to the commentary on Jenny's wireless in the Swan kitchen. Toby snoozed and snored in her box by the stove, obviously appreciating a lazy day, too.

After eight hours and forty-three minutes, Miss Ederle had battled for over twenty-three miles in turbulent water and was showing signs of sea sickness. Her swimming coach, Jabez Wolffe took the decision to pull her out of the freezing Channel into the accompanying boat.

'He shouldn't have touched her – that means she's disqualified,' Danny said.

Pomona burst into tears herself, while her heroine's sobs faded as the broadcast was curtailed.

'She's a brave young lady, and she won't give up, I reckon. She'll have another go.' Brigid said, trying to cheer them up. 'Did you read in the paper that she's suffered from increasing deafness since a childhood illness? She was advised to stop swimming, but she refused. She's very determined. Like you, Pom!'

Later, in an interview with the press, Gertrude Ederle insisted that when she next attempted to break the record, she was not to be taken from the water however distressed she might appear. She later added that she had no complaints about her coach's action. 'I am not a person who reaches for the moon as long as I have the stars...'

Those words made a lasting impression on the young Pomona, and May.

'There's always next year,' Jenny said comfortingly, as they drank their bedtime cocoa.

Sometime after midnight Jenny tapped on the girls' bedroom door. May had only just managed to get off to sleep due to Pomona's laments about the failed Channel swim. The tentative knocking didn't disturb her sister from her slumbers.

Yawning, May tiptoed to the door, opened it. She took in the fact that Jenny was still in her day clothes, having only just finished her evening chores after the pub closed.

'Can you come, dear? Your little dog seems to be in distress.'

In the kitchen Toby was panting and scrabbling at the old jumper in the orange box which Jenny had provided for her bed.

'What's up, d'you think, Jenny?' May asked, in alarm.

'Why, I believe she's having pups. Didn't you know?'

May shook her head in disbelief. 'We thought she must be too old for breeding. That's why Dad thought she was perfect to be Dog Toby. The one we had before, kept running off.'

'Didn't you say, oh, it must be a couple of months ago now, she went off with another dog along the beach?'

'I wasn't there, but Paddy got her back, thank goodness. D'you think...?'

'Seems likely, doesn't it,' Jenny said. 'Now, what do we do? Shall I fetch Percy? Though he'll probably say, let nature take its course.'

They were startled when they heard the latch being lifted on the back door. 'It's only me,' Paddy said reassuringly, as he entered, torch in hand. 'I noticed the light was on in the kitchen, and thought something might be wrong.' He spotted Toby, now growling uncertainly in her bed. 'Oh, what's up?'

May clutched her old robe round her. She thought, I must look a sight! She said, 'Jenny thinks ... Toby's about to have pups!'

'All right, old girl,' Paddy said gently. He bent over the little dog. His hands gently felt her distended stomach. The growling ceased, and Toby licked his fingers. 'Is it her first litter?' he asked.

'I'm not sure,' May floundered. 'We were told she was past ... that sort of thing. Dad rescued her from a cruel owner; we don't know anything about her early days.'

'You look as if you know something about the process,' Jenny addressed Paddy. 'So how about I make you both a nice mug of tea, and leave you to it – you can always give me a call if there's any complications. I don't think it's fair to crowd round the poor creature, eh?'

'It might be a long night,' Paddy said to May, as they sipped the hot tea. 'D'you want to put something warmer on, while I hold the fort?' He'd hastily dressed, pulling on a heavy jumper over his short-sleeved shirt. It might be August, but, after all, they were near the sea, which made for chilly nights.

'I'll borrow the knee blanket from the old chair,' May replied, 'and put that round my shoulders.' She added, 'Jenny's right; you do look as if you know what's what.'

'My grandfather keeps a pair of collies, I helped with a litter last time we were staying with him. Don't interfere unless necessary, but be there, that's what Grandad says. It's just occurred to me – are you squeamish? I mean...'

'You mean,' she said, sounding sharp and defensive, as she had when they first met: 'Have I seen an animal give birth before? Well, of course I have, being brought up on Aunt Min's farm!' She wasn't going to tell him she'd not hung around to see the house cow drop its calf, but had rushed to fetch her capable aunt. She'd only been about Pomona's age at the time.

'Shush,' he advised her. 'We ought to whisper.'

'I am whispering,' she returned crossly. 'You started the conversation!'

There was a sudden upheaval in the dog's box, Toby was panting and whimpering alternately.

May poked Paddy in the ribs. 'Go and see!' she hissed.

'Nothing happening as I far as I can tell,' he reported. 'There might be a big pup causing the hold-up.' He stroked the dog soothingly, and moistened her mouth with a drop of water from her bowl. 'Pass that old newspaper, May – she needs to be doing something.'

May watched as Toby shredded the paper with her teeth and rearranged it to make a cosy nest. All was quiet now, apart from the loud ticking of the kitchen clock. The hands were moving on to two o'clock.

Almost an hour later the first pup arrived, but was instantly rejected. 'I'll move that one away,' said Paddy tactfully. Then in swift succession, came two smaller white pups, with distinctive black and brown markings, which Toby accepted.

May and Paddy were joined by a sleepy Pomona, who had been alarmed to find herself alone in the bedroom. Jenny reappeared behind her.

'Why didn't you call me?' Pomona demanded, put out. Jenny sat down in the rocking-chair and invited Pomona to sit on her lap. 'You'll catch cold, dearie – where's your dressing-gown?'

'I was – *abandoned!*' Pomona said, glaring at May.

'Sorry – but haven't you noticed what Toby has in her box?' May replied. 'Stay where you are. Toby doesn't want any fuss.'

Pomona rested her head on Jenny's shoulder as May and Paddy tidied up. 'If there's a girl pup, I'll call her Gertie,' she murmured.

'How I would have loved one like you,' Jenny said softly, cuddling her close. 'Now, shall we all go back to bed? Toby's cleaned the pups up, and they've snuggled down together. It'll be time to rise again, before we know it.'

Paddy tugged gently at May's long plait, which was hanging over one shoulder. 'Goodnight, May. See you at breakfast.'

A substitute Toby, a joint effort by Brigid and Paddy: a wooden head and cloth glove, danced on stage.

'You see,' Paddy said to May, 'we make a good

81

team, don't we?'

May had to agree, they did. Tucked in her pocket was a little poem, another secret between them both, called – what else? *The Punch and Judy Lady*.

At the end of the show, Pomona called boldly: 'Three cheers for Young May Moon, Professor Jas Jolley's daughter!'

The audience clapped and cheered as May poked her head shyly through the curtains. There was a clicking of cameras, including the girls' box Brownie. It would always be Jas Jolley's show, but May, emerging to take a bow in her green dress and Mary-Jane shoes, was definitely in charge.

Twelve

'I see you made the front page of the local paper,' Carmen remarked to May at practice a few days later. She sounded displeased.

May blushed. 'It wasn't my idea – I didn't contact them.'

'Your so-called friends, I suppose!'

'Mum, the reporter mentioned you. Said I was the daughter of the fiery Spanish dancer Carmen Maria Rivera, now dazzling audiences at the end-of-the-pier show. Why did they use Carlos's name?'

'There's nothing Spanish about *Jolley!*' Carmen flashed back. Then she gave a conciliatory smile. 'It was a good picture of you, though. One for my scrapbook. How is your photograph album coming along?'

'I am collecting the first prints today from the chemist,' May said proudly.

Carlos emerged from his corner, carrying his guitar. 'I meet you back at the hotel for breakfast,' he said to Carmen. He gave his customary nod to May. 'You were at your best today,' he complimented her. 'Your big moment will soon come.'

'Don't hurry away,' Carmen said to May, after he had gone. 'I have something I must tell you.'

May had a feeling that she knew what this might be. Her mother had mentioned the fact that she had spoken to Aunt Min on the telephone recently. Did Carmen intend to get custody of Pomona, and to take her back to Spain? At the beginning of September their summer season would be at an end. Pomona was due to return to her old school, and they'd be home with Aunt Min and Grandpa. It would also be the parting of the ways with the O'Flahertys, whose contract with the little theatre was almost over. There would be no more shows until Christmas. Carmen and Carlos would be on the move, too.

'I must get ready for my show soon,' she reminded Carmen. 'And as I said, I have my snaps to collect first.'

'Aunt Min will not allow me to take Pomona back with me. Perhaps it is just as well, because I have not the time or patience for one so young. It is different for you. You may decide for yourself. You have the chance to make a good career from dancing, although you have a great deal still to learn. You would be the young Carmen, not the young May Moon as your father called you,

83

against my wishes.'

'Do I really have a choice?' May demanded. 'How can I ... abandon my little sister, she'd never forgive me!' Unconsciously, she used the word *abandon*, as Pomona had, dramatically, the night the puppies were born.

She expected a spirited response, but was taken aback when Carmen's eyes filled with tears, which she furiously blinked away, smudging the kohl she had used to enhance them. 'May, I thought of you both every single day, while I was away.'

'Why didn't you contact us then?' May demanded.

'Your father would not allow it. My letters were returned.'

'I didn't know that.'

'He was bitter, and I cannot blame him. I was not a good wife. I was a reluctant mother. But I did – oh, I *do* love you! I thought I could make it up to you. What future is there for you here? The economy of the country is in decline. What qualifications do you have – only those of the Punch and Judy. This is fun in the summer, but what do you do in the winter?'

This was the conclusion that May herself had reluctantly come to. 'I intend to go back to school – like Pomona! Well, to a secretarial college, if I can. Dad left us fifty pounds each; he wanted us to be as independent as possible. I'll be allowed to use that to pay for training now that I'm sixteen.'

'You would prefer to be a typist, rather than a dancer?'

'I didn't say that. But I need to be able to

84

support my sister. *She's* clever enough, I think, to go to university.'

'Then my plea falls on deaf ears?'

'Oh, Mum, no! It means a lot to me to know you didn't forget us. I think I can understand and forgive you now. You and Dad – you weren't suited; you made each other unhappy. Neither of you was to blame for that. One day, I'll visit you in Spain, I promise! Dad never encouraged us to think of ourselves as half-Spanish, but, of course we are. We must keep in touch from now on, will *you* promise that?'

'Come here,' Carmen cried, holding out her arms. 'I promise, I really do!'

May ran from the chemist's shop to the beach, clutching the folder of photographs – she hadn't had time to look at them yet.

'I was wondering if something had happened to you!' Paddy had been anxiously keeping an eye on the time.

'I had to sort something out with Mum. Sorry!'

'Did you quarrel?'

'We actually came to an understanding. Don't worry, all's well.'

'You smell very nice!' he exclaimed, as she brushed past him into the booth.

'It must be Mum's perfume – frangipani. She gave me a real hug!' She still felt a warm glow inside from that.

The puppets were in place, Smokey had been given a nosebag, Pomona and Danny were putting out the deckchairs.

'Time for a quick sandwich – I'm starving!'

May said. 'Then we'll look at the photographs. I can't wait until tonight!'

They sat in a circle on the sand, and passed the snaps from hand to hand. Some of the action ones were slightly blurred, especially those of Pomona: she couldn't hold a pose for long! The best prints were those May had taken of the ferry-boat trip to the smoke houses and on the quay. However, she couldn't help noticing a familiar figure on the edge of these particular pictures. *Carlos!* Staring unsmiling into the camera lens... May gave an involuntary shiver. She thought: he must have been following me, spying on me!

The audiences were dwindling towards the end of the summer. The doubtful weather didn't help. Folk didn't sit around in deckchairs when it was chilly. They packed up early. 'I shan't bother tomorrow,' May decided. 'I feel like a day off!'

'We can spend the morning training the pups,' Pomona told Danny. They had duly named one Gertie, and the other Bertie. It was agreed that one pup was for Jenny, and the other for Danny, when they were old enough to leave Toby.

'They haven't got their eyes open properly yet,' he pointed out. 'Toby won't like it, if you take them away from her, they're too small.'

'Oh, why do you know it all? Well, we can have a day at the swimming pool.'

'I might have known you'd suggest that,' Danny said ruefully, with an exaggerated shiver. There was a chill wind today. 'I think I've had enough of watching you swim this summer!'

'Seems like a good time to ask you to come with me to the amber gift shop in town,' Paddy whispered to May. 'Remember the piece I found after the storm?'

'You never showed it to me!' She'd thought it was mean at the time.

'We weren't good friends then!'

'Are you hoping to sell it?'

'Wait and see,' Paddy said mysteriously. 'We won't take those kids, anyway!'

May always enjoyed gazing at the window display in the gift shop. Even on an overcast day, she thought, there was a golden aura emanating from the beads and brooches arranged on velvet cushions.

'It's amazing to think the amber found here on the east coast has probably come from under the North Sea; could be millions of years old,' Paddy observed.

'Some of it is darker in colour, but I prefer the lighter pieces. I read somewhere that amber is always warm to the touch, unlike most stones,' May said.

'Then you'll approve of my lucky find, I think!' The bell jangled as they entered the shop; they went down a few steps.

It was like a cave of jewels, May thought as she took in the sumptuous displays. She also noted a price-ticket or two, which made her gasp. Paddy unrolled a square of cloth which he had wrapped around the chunk of amber. A solemn-faced man examined it with the help of an eyeglass. He turned the amber this way and that, rotating it slowly between thumb and finger.

'You wish to sell this?' he asked at last. 'Or to

have an item of jewellery made, perhaps more than one? Because it is a fair size, if not top quality?'

'I was wondering,' said Paddy boldly, 'If it could be divided into two, and if you would care to keep one piece in repayment for a pendant made from the other?'

'Mmm... There would still be the cost of a silver chain to consider.'

'How much would that be, please?'

'I believe I could provide one to suit your pocket,' the man replied. 'The pendant will be ready for collection in ten days. Let us shake hands on the deal.'

As they walked away from the shop May said impulsively, 'Your mother is a very lucky lady!' She assumed that the pendant was a gift for Brigid.

He smiled. 'I hope she has a guinea to lend me!' he said.

Thirteen

The billboard outside the pier theatre proclaimed:

FINAL APPEARANCE TONIGHT
OF OUR STAR ACTS!
DON'T MISS CARLOS & CARMEN!
OR THE VERSATILE O'FLAHERTYS!

On Saturday evening, Jenny and Percy posted a notice on the pub door.

CLOSED – FOR ONE NIGHT ONLY.
WE HAVE BEEN INVITED TO
A SPECIAL PERFORMANCE
AT THE PIER THEATRE.
BUSINESS AS USUAL TOMORROW!

Earlier, on the beach, May and Pomona, with Paddy and Danny, had packed up the Punch and Judy outfit after their final show. The puppets were looking slightly shabby after all their handling.

'Mr Punch needs his nose painted!' said Pomona. She pointed out the worn patch to May.

'Mmm,' May agreed. She thought, maybe it's time *he* retired.

There were not many people about, and few coins rattling in the bottle. The girls would be returning home the day after tomorrow. 'You look very solemn,' Paddy said softly to May.

'Well, I don't like saying goodbye,' she admitted.

'To anyone in particular?' he prompted her.

'To all of you – dear Jenny and Percy, Brigid and Brendan, Danny and – you!' May's words came out in a rush. She added: 'Mum, too – despite everything. That's in the past. She and Carlos are leaving later this week, like you.'

'Is she still on about you joining them later in Spain?' Paddy wanted to know.

'No, but Carlos tried to persuade me again after our last rehearsal. He got me in a corner and grabbed my arm. I shouted out *Ouch!* so Mum could hear, and he let go. He's afraid of her

89

when she's in a temper! He can't stand up to her tantrums, like Dad did. I wanted to say it was none of his business, but I thought she'd be cross with me then. Carlos doesn't seem to realize that I don't like him, and that I never will! I certainly don't have ambitions to be his dancing partner.'

'When your eyes flash like that, you look very Spanish!' said Paddy. 'You ought to visit the place your mother came from, one day. I know I want to go to Ireland sometime, to find out why I am as I am. It must be the same for you.'

She didn't answer that, but instead said softly, 'You didn't say, you know, that *you'll* miss me...'

Paddy glanced over at his brother and Pomona, who were intent on popping the little bladders on a smelly piece of seaweed which had been washed ashore. 'Little pitchers have big ears, as Mum sometimes says, eh? You know I will. I might even write to you—'

'What d'you mean, you *might?*' she demanded.

He grinned. 'One thing is sure, I won't forget this summer, or you, Young May Moon, presenting the Punch and Judy show.'

They had front-row seats in the pier theatre this time. Percy and Jenny sat on either side of Pomona, and Jenny took charge of the bag of jelly babies, which she'd recommended because Pomona couldn't crunch those. May was opposite centre stage, not only because it was the best vantage point, but also because she needed to be near the steps up to the stage for a special reason. The little theatre was packed.

The lights dimmed, the chattering ceased, and the show began. There had been a few changes in the cast over the summer. The opening turn was a rather inebriated ventriloquist, with a dummy whose bulbous red nose rivalled that of Mr Punch. Pomona watched intently for any twitching of the ventriloquist's lips. She wasn't disappointed.

'Don't be daft,' Percy said in a gruff whisper. Jenny gave them both a dig in the ribs.

Next was a thin man who played tunes on a line of glass jugs, containing varying amounts of water, which affected the ringing sound. He was followed by a couple who blew amazing soap bubbles in rainbow hues.

The O'Flahertys were the penultimate act before the interval – Carlos and Carmen were to round off the first half.

The audience expected to hear the old favourites. *The Rose of Tralee* and *I'll Take You Home Again, Kathleen* brought tears to the eyes, those wistful songs so often sung by homesick soldiers during the war prompted heartfelt singing-along.

Then Brendan sprang his surprise. He came front stage, looking down on the upturned faces in the front row. The spotlight wavered, then illuminated a startled Jenny.

'You all know Mrs Jenny Wren, I'm sure, from the Swan Inn, who sometimes plays the piano at the picture house. Stand up, Jenny, and take a bow! Will you sing for us?'

Jenny, rosy-cheeked and crowned by her Sunday hat, rose to the challenge like the old trouper she was. She allowed Paddy and Danny to escort her on to the stage, and waved away the offer of a microphone. Before she could ask, 'What would you like me to sing?' a piano was wheeled on from the wings and she was invited to accompany herself. A whisper in her ear, and her voice soared to the beams above: *My old man said foller the van, and don't dilly-dally on the way!* Maybe she wasn't as mesmerizing as her idol, Marie Lloyd, but the applause was deafening. Jenny was a star!

She blew a kiss to Percy, who was grinning proudly.

'How do we follow that?' Brendan asked, as Jenny rejoined her companions. But they did, and brought the house down. It was, after all, the grand finale for the O'Flaherty family.

Carlos and Carmen gave their usual dazzling performance, leaving the audience wondering whether they could surpass that in the second half.

During the interval May slipped quietly away, as prearranged. 'Change behind the screen,' Carmen told her.

Carlos was seated at the long mirror, arranging his hair. As May glanced at his reflection, he said only, 'You have come, then.'

'Yes. To make Mum happy,' she said firmly.

May recognized the costume which her mother had hung over the side of the screen. It smelled a little musty, for it had not been worn by Carmen since she had put on weight. The ruffled skirt, the slightly faded peacock-blue material: this was the dress her mother had brought with her when she arrived in England from her native country as a girl, around May's own age. As a small child, May had been allowed to try on the dress just once, when Carmen was in a mellow mood. Now, it fitted her perfectly. She slipped her feet into Carmen's spare pair of dancing-shoes. They both took size four.

When she emerged from behind the screen Carmen indicated a stool behind the long counter. 'I will see to your hair, and your make-up. Carlos, you can leave us now, but mind you do not be long at the bar.' She took up a brush, swept May's hair away from her face, pinned it back firmly, then draped a towel around her shoulders. 'Sit still, do not move,' Carmen commanded. 'No comment!' she added, as May opened her mouth to ask that she go easy on the greasepaint.

Close up, the finished effect was startling and May bit her lip. She thought: oh dear, I don't look like me at all!

'It will appear good from a distance; to the audience you will be the beautiful young Carmen,' her mother said firmly.

'I would rather have my hair loose, even if it has to be combed back off my forehead,' May returned. She was aware that Paddy liked her hair in that style.

Carmen removed the restraining pins. 'You can wear it so, because you are young.' As a final touch she decided on a pair of small glittering combs. 'Sit still a little longer, while I fasten these!'

Someone knocked on the door. Startled, they both looked round.

'Whoever is that?' Carmen said sharply. 'I asked that we be not disturbed. You need to be quiet before you go on stage.'

The door handle turned, and Paddy was revealed. He had obviously overheard Carmen's remarks. 'I will only be a minute, I promise, I just want to give May a good-luck token,' he said.

'Please, Mum, let him in,' May put in quickly as she took in Carmen's exasperation at the interruption.

Carmen sighed, moved aside. 'Come in then, but be quick.' She went behind the screen to tidy up.

Paddy fastened the silver chain with the drop amber pendant round May's neck. He gently stroked her hair back into place. The stone nestled in the hollow of her throat, warm against her skin. So it is true what they say about amber, she thought. For a brief moment he rested his chin on the crown of her head, his hands on her shoulders, as together they gazed at their reflections in the glass. It almost seemed as if they were embracing. The moment passed; he stepped back.

'I thought ...' she faltered.

'You thought it was for my mother – well, I was going to give it to *you* when we say goodbye, then I decided I would do it now,' he said.

'It's lovely, Paddy. Thank you. I'll keep it for ever!'

'Good luck,' he told her. 'Well, I'd better go – the minute is up!'

Carmen re-emerged with an armful of clothes to hang over the screen.

'Look, Mum – isn't this a special gift?' May said tentatively to Carmen.

'From a special young man, I think,' Carmen said unexpectedly. She quickly composed herself. 'To remember him by. These ... youthful affections, I must tell you, rarely last for long.'

I'm not going to argue with her, May decided.

94

Not tonight.

May waited in the wings, trying to compose herself, while Carlos and Carmen repeated the performance they had given to such acclaim on their first night on the pier. After the puppet bowed to the assembly and was then manipulated to float silently upwards and over the big screen, it was May's cue to move into the spotlight, on stage. A banner unfurled the length of the screen: INTRODUCING YOUNG CARMEN.

In the shadows Carlos bent over his guitar, and the dancing began. May knew that her friends must be watching with bated breath, willing her to do well, but she did not look directly at them, for fear of missing a step.

It was like a dream, unreal, but she concentrated on what she had learned over the past weeks from her mother. All she was aware of was the music, the stamping of her feet, the swish of her skirts.

Tonight, she *was* Young Carmen, not Young May Moon.

She took three curtain calls, the first two by herself, the final one flanked by her mother and Carlos. May looked down at the first row of seats then, and saw her friends waving and smiling. Pomona was on her feet, clapping her hands over her head in her excitement.

'You see,' Carmen whispered in her ear, 'you were born to dance, like me.'

'I didn't know... I didn't realize,' May whispered, but she knew her success would not alter anything. They were going home to the farm; she would keep her vow to look after Pomona, to provide a stable background for her and to work to provide for them both.

They were driven back to the Swan in Percy's motor. Pomona hugged her tight and breathed, 'You were wonderful!'

Later, while May was supervising Toby's nightly run around the meadow, without the pups tagging along for once, she was joined by Paddy. He slipped an arm around her waist as Toby disappeared in and out of the bushes, sniffing hopefully for rabbits in the moonlight.

Paddy asked softly: 'D'you mind if I kiss you, May? This is probably our only chance – with my brother and your sister always around, eh?'

'I thought you'd never ask!' May answered. She might sound bold, she thought, but she felt nervous at the same time. She guessed, rightly, that it was the same for him.

'Are you still Young May Moon?'

'Of course, I am,' she said as she closed her eyes and waited for him make the first move. That kiss was a bit hit and miss, which actually caused them to relax, giggle, and then to try again.

'Was that better?' he asked.

'I like the taste of your toothpaste!' she joked, to dispel the intensity of her feelings. She hoped she didn't sound out of breath, but that was the effect on her of their lingering kiss. She wondered if he knew that this was a new experience for her.

'I'm glad you wiped your face clean of all that paint,' he returned, 'or the imprint of your red lips would have given the game away!' He hoped she didn't realize that he was inexperienced, too.

Toby barked. Time to get back to my family,

they interpreted. Paddy kept his arm around her as they walked back to the house.

What a special day it had been, for both of them.

Fourteen

There was an autumnal nip in the air, and that chill mist off the sea, known as a fret, when May and Pomona waved goodbye to their good friends at the Swan, at just after 7 a.m. on Monday morning. They were leaving behind one member of the Punch and Judy show, Dog Toby. She was staying with Jenny and Percy until the pups were weaned.

'We'll drive over with Toby and Bertie to the farm in a couple of weeks' time,' Jenny promised. 'Then we'll take the pup back with us. Gertie should have been collected before that by her new family.'

'I can't wait!' Danny was holding the wriggling puppy in his arms.

'We have to get Grandpa's permission – not that that will be a problem, but let us get settled in first!' his mother reminded him.

'Mum might have come along and wished us a good journey.' Pomona was disappointed that Carmen had not put in an appearance. 'But I suppose it's too early.'

May had been thinking the same thing, but she made excuses for Carmen on this occasion, as she didn't want Pomona to feel hurt.

'Well, we said all we needed to say, on Saturday

evening, when you were waiting for me in the dressing-room while Mum was cold-creaming my face and wiping off all the greasepaint, eh? She's promised to keep in touch from now on, that's the main thing. Anyway, if she'd made the effort to be here this morning, no doubt Carlos would have insisted on coming along too!' I hope we've seen the last of *him*, she thought.

Smokey brayed reproachfully. He wasn't used to an early start these days.

'He's telling us to get going,' May said regretfully.

'Safe journey! See you again soon!' Then they were turning out of the yard, not left, as the donkey had become accustomed to do, but right, towards the bridge.

The river had recently been dredged, but there were still trails of slime clinging to the footings of the bridge. May made ready to step down from the trap. 'Whoa! Smokey,' she commanded.

Then they spotted the large black taxicab blocking the road at the other end of the bridge.

'That wasn't there a minute ago!' Pomona cried. 'One of us will have to back up to let the other through.'

The door of the taxi opened, and Carmen stepped out. She hurried towards the trap, arms outstretched. 'Oh, I am in time!' she declaimed dramatically. She had obviously left the hotel in a great hurry, for they could glimpse her nightdress hanging below the hem of her white mackintosh cape.

It was Pomona who scrambled down to meet her, to be enveloped in her hug.

'I have something I forgot to give you, May,' Carmen said, over Pomona's shoulder. 'Please come and take it from me.' She waved a parcel in one hand.

May climbed down, then stood holding the donkey's collar. 'Thank you, but we must get on, Mum. Please ask the taxi to move back to where the road widens.'

'You disappoint me,' Carmen said. She kissed Pomona, then gave her the package. 'You take it to her, she spurns my embrace!'

'It's just that I didn't expect to see you...' May began, when the cab door was flung wide again, and Carlos appeared.

'What is the problem?' he shouted. 'I ask your mother to come, so I can persuade you that your future is with us, May. You must join us soon and carry on with your training.'

May returned to the driving seat. She hoped she was out of reach there. 'Go away, Carlos! Mum, I'm sorry I was short, but I did tell you my plans, didn't I? I'm not going to change my mind! Pomona, get back in the trap. Mum, please speak to your driver now.'

'Carlos, *no!*' Carmen yelled instead. Carlos was hauling himself up on to the parapet, looming above the two girls in the trap.

'I don't come down, until you agree with me!' He looked ridiculous in his red brocade dressing-gown over silk pyjamas, the legs of which were flapping in the wind. Incongruously, he wore his spats.

'Help!' Carmen called to the taxi driver. He joined them reluctantly.

'You'll have to pay for all this wasted time, madam.'

Carlos stretched out a wavering hand, clutched at May's shoulder as she sat in the high driving seat. 'You are the young Carmen; you and I, we will be the new partners in the dance!'

'Rubbish!' May said angrily. 'How dare you cast off my mother like that! She is the one with the real talent – there must be plenty of better guitarists in Spain! The flamenco is a dance for a *woman*, it needs years of practice, I'm only a girl and I'm not nearly good enough, maybe I never will be. Look how she handles the puppets – she's a *real* artiste! Let me go!' She nudged him to make him release his grip.

Later, May would say that what happened next, was rather like a sequence in a Buster Keaton film. Carlos wobbled, arms flailing, lost his footing and plummeted down into the river below with an enormous splash.

Carmen was screaming hysterically, and Pomona said urgently to May: 'Let me jump in and save him – I'm the only one of us who can swim!'

May found her voice at last, 'No need for that, Pom! See, Bobby Blowers is just downriver in his boat – he's been to the harbour for the early morning catch. He's spotted Carlos and he's rowing like mad to get to him.'

'He's not coming back in my motor,' the taxi driver said. 'Nor are you, madam. I'm off. Don't bother about the tip!' He reversed the taxi, turned and drove off in the opposite direction.

Carlos was brought, dripping, out of the water by Bobby's boathook and laid, floundering, among the fish in the bottom of the boat. Bobby waved to the watchers on the bridge. 'You'll have to return to the harbour to collect him. I'll row back now. I'll cover him with a tarpaulin! He's all right, he's cussing in some foreign language!'

'Make room for Mum in the trap,' May told Pomona. 'I'll drop you off at the Swan. Ask Jenny to ring Aunt Min and tell her we'll be later than we said.'

'How can I smuggle him back into the hotel, dripping like that?' Carmen worried.

'You can borrow Smokey's blanket to put round him,' Pomona said cheerfully. 'It needs a wash and smells of donkey, but Carlos'll want a bath anyway, won't he?'

They didn't turn into the Swan's drive, but watched Pomona hurrying off, then they continued on down to the harbour.

Bobby Blowers was just unloading his unexpected catch. 'Here you are then! I must get back, I'm running late. He's been ranting all the way; he ain't lost his voice, anyway.' He waved away a proffered coin from Carmen. 'Keep it, missus. Done my good deed for the day!'

They wrapped the smelly blanket round Carlos's shaking shoulders, and Carmen pulled a strand of nasty green river vegetation from his oiled black hair. 'Shut up!' she hissed to him, as they made their way towards the hotel's tradesmen's entrance. 'Thanks for your help,' she called belatedly to May. 'Keep in touch, as you promised!'

May thought, with a smile she couldn't suppress, that the squelching of Carlos's shoes and the ridiculous spats would alert the hotel staff to his arrival.

Back at the Swan she was welcomed as if she had been away for some time, not just an hour or so. There were big mugs of steaming tea, and scones, split and buttered. 'It must seem a long time since your breakfast, my dears,' Jenny said. 'Give us your version of events -your sister's good at elaboration, as we know.'

May caught Paddy looking at her. He was smiling broadly. She could tell he was pleased to see her again so unexpectedly.

'What did Aunt Min say?' she asked Jenny.

'Oh, she took it in her stride. Said, why not stay another day?'

'I was hoping she'd say that!' May was honest as always.

Later, back in their little room, she opened her mother's parcel. It contained the precious dress Carmen had loaned her for that special performance. *Keep this with love* was written on the accompanying note.

'I will, oh I will,' she said aloud.

Fifteen

Kettle Row, September, 1925

After a few days back at the farm it was as if they had never been away, as if the summer season in West Wick had been a dream. May looked back on the experience as her transition from a child to an adult. The reconciliation with her mother had been unexpected, but she was glad it had occurred. She hoped that their friendship with the O'Flahertys would survive the parting of ways and the distance now between them, but her priority must be her headstrong little sister.

The trunk containing Punch and his companions was stored away in the spare room, which had been Jim's bedroom. Aunt Min draped the trunk with a flowery curtain. 'There – no one would guess what is inside!' She was in her mid-fifties, for there had been a ten-year gap between herself and Jim, her only sibling. She was rather abrupt in her manner towards strangers, but fiercely protective of her family. She had a wiry frame, straight up and down, with her sleeves rolled up, whatever the weather, to reveal muscular forearms from all the humping of sacks and boxes. Min was not so keen on housework. The old house was shabby, inside and out, but the girls thought of it as home.

Grandpa was in his early eighties and spent his days roaming restlessly around, as he had been doing since he recovered from a mild stroke some years ago. May could remember him as full of fun when he toured with the show, his lively fiddle-playing, and how he'd taught her to dance a jig, but Pomona was too young to recall any of that.

'Glad you girls are back,' Aunt Min told them. 'You can run faster to catch him when he goes a'wanderin' than I can.'

They were soon immersed in the familiar routine: Pomona went off to school, reluctantly at first, wanting to be out in the orchard with Aunt

Min and May, picking the early eating-apples and pears. Smokey might have retired from transporting the Punch and Judy, but was still needed to take the produce to the local market. They had the usual stall by the gate, and Grandpa greeted the occasional customer with, 'Helloo, there!' while Toby, home again, barked to alert the pickers that the services of one of them was needed to weigh the fruit in the scales with the brass weights, and to take the money.

The tall trees had been planted half a century ago by Min's late in-laws. Min pruned them as best she could, but a ladder was needed to reach the topmost fruit. May was not too keen on heights, but she climbed the rungs to save the strain on her aunt's arthritic knees. There was not an abundance of apples this year, but it still seemed an endless task – more of a chore May thought, once the excitement of plucking the first ripe fruit was over. It had been sausages and mash for supper most nights for a while, but now they were in for a treat.

The fire crackled, spitting out a few smouldering twigs, which made them jump. The trees were in shadow. The smell of apples mingled with bonfire smoke and the compost heap behind them.

The girls wore old, patched dungarees with wellington boots and shapeless jerseys knitted long ago, which had stretched and sagged in the laundering. If Paddy saw her now would he recognize her, May wondered? She realized, with a start, that this was the first time she'd thought of him, all day. She'd written twice to him, but he hadn't found time to write back.

'I must wash my hair before Monday,' May said. She could do with a bath, too, but was too weary to contemplate that tonight.

'You ought to put it up, to look the part of a lady typist,' Aunt Min told her. 'Or have it shorn, like me. The barber is cheaper than a ladies' hair-dresser.'

May grinned, thinking: the barber's too fond of the clippers. She said: 'I'll try plaiting it into *earphones*. I can't afford a permanent wave. Anyway, I don't think it would suit me, do you?'

'Earphones are *ugly!*' Pomona, crunching away at a toffee apple, added: 'I like the lump of dark toffee at the top, where I pulled it off the tray.'

Grandpa had to suck his, having lost his teeth. Brown dribbles ran down his chin. He dabbed at them occasionally with a sleeve.

'You'll get all stuck up,' Aunt Min said with a sigh. She had most of her own teeth which she attributed to 'all them apples'. She usually had one 'on the munch' as she put it, in her apron pocket. Toby watched out for the cores, held them between her front paws like a prized bone.

They were startled when Grandpa began to sing. He'd once had a tuneful voice, but now it sounded rusty. 'Show me the way to go home, I'm tired and I wanta go to bed...'

'Now where did he learn that ditty? Has he dodged down the pub lately without me knowing it? I ain't heard that before – must be a new 'un... Come on, old dear, rise up and we'll go indoors,' Aunt Min said. 'You girls watch the fire 'til it dies down. Have another toffee apple.'

Before 1914 most secretarial and clerical positions in large firms were the prerogative of men. Due to the shocking loss of young males in the war there were many women, destined to remain single, entering the workforce. Being in service no longer appealed to this better-educated, ambitious new generation. Women had taken on responsible jobs, proved their worth throughout the war years. Now, in a time of recession, many ex-servicemen found it difficult to secure even menial or repetitive factory work, for this sector employed more females, who were paid less than the men. It was an ugly fact that there were now beggars in crowded city streets just as there had been in what were referred to as 'the bad old days'.

However, in the nearby market town, Kettle Row, on the Suffolk/Norfolk border, there was a general feeling among the local traders of pre-war prosperity, the reassurance of growth. The struggles of those in the surrounding rural areas were much the same as they had been for generations. Kettle Row itself had expanded from a hamlet with a so-called kettle pond which had been a source of clean water for a modest row of dwellings. The pond, railed off, was not dipped into with kettles nowadays but had a colony of colourful, sometimes quarrelsome ducks. It was the bus stop and main gossip area. 'Meet you at the pond,' was a familiar expression.

The Central School, which May had attended from the age of eleven until she was fourteen, had a recent addition, a commercial and business studies block. Shorthand and typing were now included in the curriculum for the older pupils, and for adults, during the day, or at the evening classes, which were subsidized. There was also instruction in the use of the comptometer, that wonderful arithmetical machine. On her introductory tour May was amazed at the speed of the flying fingers of the lady instructor, who said proudly that all her pupils were expected to aim eventually for around 50,000 strikes on the keys per day! Somehow, May could not visualize herself as a comptometer operator. You couldn't use your imagination, she thought, as you could when handling puppets.

Learning to touch-type, as she shortly discovered, was a slow process and frustrating at times. She began her morning session in a room with rows of long tables at which sat young women, heads down, concentrating. Each typewriter had a cover positioned over the keyboard to ensure they couldn't see the letters on the keys; a metronome on the teacher's desk indicated the speed at which they were required to type. The students' gaze must be directed at their copy sheets, at the simple exercises, not the print which appeared on the paper slotted in the machine.

May was left standing in a corner until the teacher called for a break. Then she was ushered to a seat in the front row. She felt conspicuous in her summer frock, worn with a cable-knit cardigan and the 'earphones' which muffled what the teacher was saying. Most of her fellow typists had shingled hair.

She positioned her fingers carefully on the hidden keys, silently reciting the sequence to herself:

'a s d f g *pause*' as she pressed her thumb on the space bar. The click of the metronome and hammering of the keys were the only sounds, apart from the satisfying ping of typewriter carriages at the end of each line.

It seemed an interminable time before the next break, when their work was scrutinized. Remarks were more encouraging than critical, which was a relief to May.

May bought a typing manual from the pile on the teacher's desk. She would need to do quite a lot of studying at home, she realized. Pomona might help her make a dummy keyboard.

On to the room where shorthand was taught. Here, May joined a small group of new pupils, with pristine notebooks and newly sharpened pencils. A larger group, including two earnest-looking youths, were taking dictation at the far side of the room, while the teacher with the novice group stood by a blackboard to explain the first simple strokes. 'Thick and thin' were now the key words.

The point snapped on May's pencil. She couldn't stop to sharpen it, and she hadn't a spare. A replacement was rolled along the desk top to her by the girl in the seat beside her. She didn't have time to say thank you until lunchtime. She tapped her neighbour on the shoulder as they left the room 'You saved my bacon – thanks!'

The girl paused, smiled at May. 'Have you brought a packed lunch?' She wore gold-rimmed glasses and, like May, had plaited her hair in an unbecoming style, but the dimples in her cheeks were attractive.

'Yes, I have.'

'I thought I'd go into the park and sit on a bench there – care to join me? I'm Bea Wright, by the way.'

'Oh, I would! I'm May Jolley. This is my first day.'

'Mine, too. We moved to Kettle Row in July, when I turned sixteen and left school. I've got my school certificate, but all the office jobs appear to require shorthand and typing, so my parents enrolled me on the course.'

'I finished school two years ago. I'm sixteen, too.' May confided.

'You've been at work already?' They passed through the main doors and stood blinking in the sunshine outside.

'Yes.' May wasn't ready to divulge more at the moment. They needed to get to know each other first, she thought.

As they walked along to the park, which was at the end of a cul de sac off the main street, May spotted the new municipal swimming-baths, which had been built since she was at the school. A cluster of children emerged, clutching soggy towels, socks at half-mast after hasty dressing.

'My sister will be pleased. It won't be so far to come for a swim!'

'The village schools round about, all have sessions here. D'you like swimming?'

'Not much,' May admitted, 'I prefer dancing!'

'So do I. Maybe we could go together to a local hop?'

'Maybe.' They found a vacant bench, and opened their lunch packs. Aunt Min and Bea's mother obviously had the same idea. As they munched on their cheese sandwiches with thick slices of Spanish onion, Bea remarked: 'We'll have to sit beside each other this afternoon, too, as we'll both have strong breath!'

'Tomorrow,' May said, 'I'm going to tie my hair back; my sister was right, I look like an old fogey with these earphones.'

'I shall ask Mum to let me have an Eton crop. I'm really glad to have met you, May. I was dreading today.'

'So was I. Still, it's nice to be called Miss Jolley.'

They brushed away the crumbs, threw a crust to a hovering pigeon, then went back to tackle the amazing green machine, the comptometer.

Sixteen

There was a lot going on in Kettle Row of which May had been unaware before she embarked on her training in office skills. Bea, she soon discovered, despite her studious appearance, was a sociable girl and keen to introduce her new friend to societies and clubs which flourished in town. Best were the ones which offered free membership or reduced subscriptions for those not yet earning their living. There were the earnest debating societies, who provided weak tea and soft ginger biscuits; the church and chapel social evenings, where the tea was stronger and there was the lure of substantial rock cakes; the bellringers, who demanded dedication and muscles; and a recently formed group, the Singing Kettles. May had not yet confided to Bea her unusual background, but she liked the name, for a start. Pomona was keen to join the Brownies, but May and Bea considered that they were rather old to become first-time Guides.

Min raised no objection to May's going out one evening in the week, so long as she was assured of a lift home afterwards. 'I'm not having you wandering the lanes in the dark, young May Moon.'

'Oh, Bea says she'll arrange an escort,' May said airily.

May enjoyed her first visit to Bea's home, and meeting her family. Bea's sister, Selina was nineteen. She didn't go out to work as she suffered from asthma, so stayed at home to help her mother. They had an older brother, Henry, who'd gained his degree this summer after three years at Cambridge.

'I see the Singing Kettles are having auditions soon. I'll put our names down – they left a list in the church porch,' Bea told May. She glanced at Henry, but he seemed oblivious to the chatter at the tea table. Bea murmured: *'He's* a member already but he didn't tell *me* about the audition, of course.'

There was also a clever twelve-year-old, Terence, much indulged by his sisters, who instantly reminded May of Pomona. The family lived in the rectory, for their father had taken holy orders after his army service, and was now rector of the church on the outskirts of town. The congregation was much diminished from pre-war days, but the Reverend Osmund Wright was determined, in his quiet way, to turn things round. He was particularly aware of the needs of the young as well as the old in the community.

May soon realized that the Wrights were just as hard-up as her own family, but were generous in welcoming friends to their table. They appeared to eat a great deal of soup, chunky with vegetables but not much meat. Emma Wright, whom Bea much resembled, had an inspired touch with herbs and seasoning: the bowls were brimming, and the bread basket full of large, crusty chunks torn from a new loaf. 'The staff of life,' the rector observed. Grace was recited, however humble the meal.

On May's first visit the family were indeed concerned about how she would get home that evening, as there was no late bus. Henry, who was aloof from his siblings now that he was twenty-one, surprised May by offering her a lift home on the back of his motorcycle. He usually had his nose in a book, which precluded conversation with younger visitors.

'Oh, yes please,' May exclaimed. She was embarrassed by the general amusement at her response. Fortunately, Henry didn't appear to notice, but merely turned another page in his book. No-one remonstrated with him for reading at the table. It was that sort of family. As with the O'Flahertys, she felt like one of them.

Henry, however, was nothing like Paddy. He was not very tall, was slightly built, pale-faced, with spectacles which slipped down his nose. He was not the stuff of young girls' dreams.

'Henry,' Bea said casually, 'as I may have mentioned, is a founder member of the Singing Kettles. They're putting on a pantomime this Christmas.'

'That doesn't mean I can influence the others regarding your possible membership,' he said, without looking up from his reading.

'We'll get in on our own merits,' Bea flashed back. She grinned at May. 'I expect you're glad you've only got a sister, eh?'

'You haven't met Pomona yet,' May said with feeling.

May's first pillion ride was both exhilarating and frightening. She clung on to Henry, arms round his waist, face pressed against the rough tweed of his jacket. As she didn't have goggles her eyes watered each time she ventured to look where they were going. When they came to a corner, she was convinced she'd be thrown off; she was conscious that her skirt was riding up above her knees and that she'd laddered her stockings. However, by the time they reached the farm track, she was more relaxed and loosened her grip, despite the bumping over the ruts.

It was nine o'clock, the time she had promised to be home. There was still a light showing in the kitchen and a lantern hung in the porch. No electricity here, but there was the pervasive smell of oil lamps.

The motorcycle engine cut out. Henry dismounted and helped her to alight. He looked comical to May, in a close fitting leather cap that buckled under his chin, and goggles pushed up on to his forehead. He adjusted his glasses, cleared his throat. 'Not so bad, was it?' She shook her head. She was still shaking a bit. 'Well, goodnight, then.' He grasped her hand, his was still encased in its gauntlet.

'Goodnight, and thank you,' May replied. She waited while he wheeled the motorcycle back to the gate, which he closed behind him.

The door opened, and Aunt Min stood there, peering beyond May. 'Why didn't you invite your young man in to meet me, May?'

'He's not my young man! We've only exchanged half a dozen words so far!' She was cross at Aunt Min's assumption. She thought: I suppose I felt the same when I met Paddy, and Jenny and Brigid were keen to pair us off, but I soon realized I liked *him*. However, I'm not attracted to Henry at all!

'You'd better set to and darn them stockings before you go to bed,' Aunt Min said in her usual forthright way. 'Money don't grow on trees, despite Pomona being named for a goddess. Though if it did, you could buy a dozen new pairs.'

The Singing Kettles met in the church hall on Friday evenings.

'Don't be intimidated by Imogen, the producer,' Bea advised May, 'Her grandfather was a Shakespearian actor, so she thinks she knows it all. Her father's the local bank manager and she went to an exclusive boarding school. She was head girl there, and she's still bossy. I met her when she came over to ask Henry to write the panto script. She said they've got some good singers, including Henry.'

114

'Oh,' May responded, not sure whether she believed that Henry could sing.

'It seems they're all very earnest types and older than us. They can do with a bit of stirring up!'

'I'm game for that!' Shades of Punch, May thought.

Imogen reminded May of the hotel receptionist in West Wick. Imogen had ash-blonde hair; rouged cheeks and lips; she wore a knitted jumper suit, belted round her narrow hips with a wide black patent leather belt with a silver buckle.

She stared long and hard at May and Bea before she drawled:

'What experience have you had in the performing arts?'

'School plays,' Bea volunteered, 'Don't you remember me? Henry's sister.'

'I suppose you imagine that that will sway my judgement? Can you sing – can you dance – can you *act?*'

'I'm told I can. Anyway, you can teach me, can't you?'

Imogen actually smiled. 'Why not? I like your attitude. Beatrice, isn't it?'

'Bea.'

'And you are?' Imogen turned her attention to May.

'May Jolley.'

'Is that your real name?'

'Yes, but my family call me Young May Moon.' May thought: why on earth did I tell her that?

'That's a jig, isn't it?' Imogen said unexpectedly. 'Does that mean you can dance?'

'Yes. My mother is a professional dancer.'

115

'Good. You sing, too?'

'Well, yes.'

'Any stage experience?'

'Some... I – well, I've worked with puppets.'

'You didn't tell me that!' Bea interjected.

'My father was Professor Jas Jolley, the Punch and Judy man.' The sudden break in the surrounding conversation meant that others were listening in, May realized.

'How exciting!' Imogen sounded as if she meant it. 'Did you assist him?'

'Actually,' May said diffidently, 'I took over from him this past summer season, but I am now training as a shorthand typist.'

'Welcome to the Singing Kettles,' Imogen said graciously. 'The auditions will take place after singing practice – go to the end of the line-up. We've appointed your brother choirmaster, Bea.'

Henry put down his notebook, in which he had been industriously writing, picked up a baton, and waited for the clearing of throats to cease. As an accomplished singer himself, he was listening intently for any signs of real talent. Any wobbly high notes made him visibly flinch. However he kept his comments to himself until after the practice.

'Too many would-be sopranos – and that includes the fellows,' he began, with a sigh, then followed that with: 'But that can be remedied.' He spoke to each one in turn. 'Bea – you're good with harmonies, I know. May – nice tone, but you forced the top notes. Pat, good range, but not much expression. Imogen, excellent breath control. George, pleasant baritone. Vera, a genuine soprano – your singing lessons paid off.' Last of

116

all he came to a young man who'd arrived late. 'Denzil, we could do with you in the church choir, as I keep telling you in vain. Will you all practise your scales during the week, and we might manage a song or two next time. Thank you.'

Imogen took May and Bea backstage. 'Easier to talk to you here. Excuse me, while I find out if refreshments are on offer.'

It was musty in the cramped space which served as a dressing-room. May could picture it on performance days, with actors reprising their lines anxiously, and costume changes taking place behind the screen. It reminded her of the pier at West Wick. Still ruffled by Henry's remark, she said to Bea: 'You say that Henry is writing the pantomime script. He doesn't seem very humorous.' Bea grinned. 'You could be surprised! May, you're a dark horse, too, not telling me what an interesting life you've led!'

'I – thought – you, being a vicar's daughter, might not approve!'

'Well, you must realize by now that we're very irreverent in some ways! I know you lost your father early this year, and that must be awful for you. Have you always lived with your aunt?'

'Yes, except when we were at West Wick, each summer. My mother is Spanish; she moved back to her birthplace a few years ago, while Pom and I remained with my father. She's a dancer, as I told Imogen – a flamenco dancer, in fact. Her name is Carmen. Before you ask, we saw her this summer and our relationship is easier now.'

'Here you are, a cup of tea and a soggy biscuit – sorry, I'm not good with trays.' Imogen placed it on a card table. 'Now, let's talk. May, you first. What do you think you can offer the Singing Kettles?'

'Well, I imagine you're really keen on Gilbert and Sullivan.'

'We are. But we're not good enough for that, yet.'

'I suppose you could say that appearing on the End-of-the-Pier show and Punch and Judy shows is like pantomime, at times!'

Bea butted in: 'Same as coming from a big family, jostling for attention and trying to make yourself heard!'

May and Bea went in turn through the door leading to the stage. Someone had pulled the faded curtains, and it was time to walk front stage, aware of the row of chairs below and the expectant faces. The exception was Henry, who only shifted his gaze from his notebook when May began to speak.

She prayed that the single sheet of paper wouldn't tremble in her hands. She'd chosen her piece with encouragement from Bea, but didn't feel confident enough without the prompt, even though the words were familiar ones she'd recited at school. She tilted her chin. '"You are old, Father William, the young man said..."' She'd been trained by her father, after all, to project her voice.

To her audience, she looked rather like *Alice in Wonderland*, having changed at the rectory into her best frock, and been persuaded by Bea to let her hair hang long and loose, swept back from her forehead by a band borrowed from Selina.

The applause was warm. May focused on one smiling face in particular. Denzil, who'd arrived

late and to whom she had not yet been introduced. He waved, when he caught her eye. She
blushed.

'Your enunciation is excellent,' Imogen said,
'though you suppress your body language. You're
rather rigid.'

The criticism didn't surprise May, after all, she
was used to acting unseen by an audience, the
puppets being on stage. She'd only shed that self-
consciousness when she danced as Young May
Moon, and then Young Carmen at West Wick.

The stage steps were not in place. Two young
men rose from their seats to give her a hand
down. The languid Henry, surprisingly, was
quicker than Denzil, which disappointed May.
However, she found herself sitting between them.

Bea had done her homework; she memorized
the extract from *The History of Mr Polly*, by H.G.
Wells. Without her glasses, as she said she pre-
ferred to view the audience as a blur, her eyes
seemed larger, luminous. She had a gift for acting, May realized; for Bea, on that empty stage,
conjured up the dingy room where Mr Polly
contemplated escape from a dreary marriage.

'Bea, there will definitely be a role for you in
the pantomime,' Imogen informed her. She
hadn't said that to May.

'Would you like a lift home?' Denzil asked May.
'My motor is parked outside.'

She hesitated, 'Well, I usually go on the back of
Henry's bike.'

'That's all right,' Henry said, as if it was of no
importance to him, 'I can vouch for Denzil.'

'Oh...?'

'We were at Cambridge together,' Denzil enlightened her. 'Anyway, I live not far from you, at the Moat House. D'you know it?'

'I've ... seen it, of course, from a distance.' It appeared to be a ruin of a place, neglected for years, she thought. Rather spooky. The Twistleton-Pikes had lived there for generations.

'When you're ready then.'

'Before you go,' Imogen called out, 'we shall need some young members of the cast – for crowd scenes, singing, dancing, so bring any suitable children to our next monthly Saturday afternoon meeting.'

'Pomona would love that!' May exclaimed.

'So would Terence. Time they met!' Bea agreed.

Seventeen

'I'd rather have ridden on the back of your Henry's motorbike!' Pomona exclaimed, disappointed to hear from May that Denzil was collecting them in his motor for the Saturday afternoon meeting of the Singing Kettles.

'Before you think of calling him that, he's not *my* Denzil, either!'

'Wear your woolly hat and scarf, dear,' counselled Aunt Min. 'You'll get the wind in your hair in that open-top motor. Don't he feel the cold? It's getting on for November, not many leaves left on the trees.'

'He's used to draughts, I reckon; the old Moat

120

House looks as if it could do with a new roof,' May said. Both she and Pomona were keen to see inside the house, but so far had not been invited to do so.

'Well, he inherited it from his grandfather while he was away at Cambridge. He lost his father in the war, as you know, and I reckon he's taking his time wondering what to do with the estate. Why is he cavorting on stage when he ought to be balancing the books?'

'Bea told me that Henry thinks Denzil would rather be an actor,' May said. He was dashing enough, she thought, to be in films, being so tall, athletic and self-confident. That rich, deep voice sent a pleasurable shiver down her spine whenever he spoke to her. He certainly wasn't a snob. He would be aware that he must buckle down to work soon and get on with restoring his run-down family estate. It didn't seem likely that he would be a Singing Kettle for long, and he was the best-looking man there. May certainly wasn't the only one bowled over by his charm; as Bea remarked to May in private, 'Imogen sticks to him like glue! Mind you, she's older than he is. Rumour has it she's getting on for thirty, but her family are rich, and I heard his mother expects him to marry well!'

'You have to give up fancy ideas and do what needs doing.' Aunt Min looked at May, jolting her out of her reverie: 'That's so, ain't it?'

May nodded. She means, like me giving up Punch and Judy. 'Toby's barking,' she said. 'Denzil has arrived.'

121

Pomona wasn't in awe of the senior Singing Kettles, but she and Terence studiously ignored each other. He was a weedy boy with a shock of hair; he was myopic, like the rest of his family, with the bridge of his glasses mended with tape, following a tumble from his bicycle. Two other youngsters brought along by one of the members were well-behaved at present, but Pomona thought that the older of the pair, who'd made a face at her when she thought her elder sister wasn't looking, had possibilities. In return, Pomona pulled out the corners of her mouth with her thumbs and grinned hideously. The other girls giggled.

'You can sing?' Imogen enquired sharply.

'I've got a loud voice as you can hear,' was Pomona's cheeky reply.

'You won't be a soloist,' Imogen said crisply. 'Can you dance?'

'My aunt says I've got two left feet. I like swimming better.'

'No swimming scene in *Cinderella!* What can you do?'

'I can get an audience going. I like playing a part – and I can do acrobatics. Ask May!'

'I have. She says you're a natural performer.'

'She usually calls me a show-off.'

'In other words, you're an extrovert. I'm hoping your sister will take you kids in hand and show you a few simple dance steps.'

Pomona shrugged. 'Mum tried to teach *me*, but she got fed up. May's different. She could have been a flamenco dancer, too, you know, but she gave up her dreams to look after me.'

'Pom!' May was embarrassed. 'Flamenco isn't

expected in pantomime.'

'Perhaps not,' Imogen said. 'However, I'm sure we can make good use of your talents, May. So much to do behind the scenes.'

May couldn't help smiling to herself. Obviously, I'm not going to be Cinderella, even though I feel like that, at times.

Bea whispered in her ear: 'Only room for one leading lady here – and it's obvious who *she* is.'

The pantomime was no longer just an idea, it was becoming a reality. The Kettles teamed up with a local musical trio: elderly ladies, accomplished in piano, violin and flute. Terence brought an African tom-tom drum from home and demonstrated that he could enhance the beat. Pomona was relieved, as she'd thought she might be landed with him as a dancing partner. Henry was responsible for the script. He arranged for a friend to be in charge of the footlights.

May found herself involved with sewing costumes, along with the other girls, and making props, mostly fashioned from cardboard. She also, at Henry's diffident suggestion, penned some catchy rhyming lyrics, which he then put to music. She found that fun to do. It reminded her of the scripts she and her father had written for the Punch and Judy shows. The whole cast had a hand in painting the backdrops, on sheets, spread out on newspaper on the floor and then pegged out to dry. May also taught the children, whose numbers swelled week by week when word went round the school, how to dance a jig.

'Can I borrow your dancing shoes?' Pomona wheedled. 'My feet are nearly as big as yours now, May. I'm nine years old, remember.'

'Not until January, you're not. How can I forget, when you keep reminding me? Oh, all right. But don't scuff the toes, will you?'

At last the scripts were typed by Bea and May on the rector's antiquated typewriter, and the final casting took place.

Bea could hardly believe her ears – had she really got the main part: Cinderella?

'Don't cut your hair before January,' Imogen told her.

'But it's all straggly–'

'Just right for the early scenes! You can wear a wig to the ball!'

Imogen read out the rest of the list: 'Baron Hardup, George. Baroness, Pat. Fairy Godmother, myself. Vera will be Buttons, she's good at learning lines... The Ugly sisters, I think you will all agree that Henry and Denzil are a good pairing. They'll be quite unrecognizable with plenty of greasepaint, and frightful wigs. Prince Charming, a small part though an important one, requiring a pair of shapely legs, goes to Young May Moon! Terence, you can be the Prince's page.'

Now they're all looking at my legs, May thought, embarrassed. I wish Imogen wouldn't call me Young May Moon – she sounds rather mocking when she does. It's the *family* name for me, after all.

Pomona whispered to Terence: 'May won't be the only one wearing tights – *you* will be, too!'

Terence muttered, 'Don't rub it in.'

'I'll do it, if you don't want to,' offered Pomona. She hadn't been offered a part; she was only in

124

the crowd scenes. 'You can be my understudy.'

'No thanks! You sounded just like Imogen then. You can ask her. I'm not going to get a clip round the ear.'

'She wouldn't – would she?'

'She doesn't have any brothers or sisters, she can't abide children. We're a necessary evil she says, in a pantomime.'

Imogen's response: '*I* do the casting!' had their ears ringing from her exasperated shriek anyway.

She continued in a more moderate tone: 'May, I've had a bright idea about how we could fill the intervals during the change of scenes. Could one of your puppets appear through the gap in the closed curtains and entertain the audience? No script needed, just ad lib. *You'd* be unseen, of course.'

'Of course.' May did not intend to sound ironic. Not Punch, she thought, he needs refurbishing, but the substitute Dog Toby that Paddy made for me, would do.

'It wasn't her idea,' Terence whispered to Pomona, 'it was Henry's. He thought your sister ought to have a bigger part. Imogen's jealous because May has more acting experience than she has herself.'

'Ready to go home?' Denzil asked when Imogen declared the meeting closed.

They didn't drive past the Moat House on this occasion. 'My mother said she'd really like to meet you,' Denzil said. 'What d'you say?'

'Ooh, yes please!' Pomona spoke for both of them.

The moat was almost devoid of water, but there

was a plank bridge across to the old house. Denzil drove over it at speed. May screwed her eyes up tight but Pomona, emitting a shriek of excitement, didn't want to miss a thing. They drew up outside the entrance to the house. The walls were smothered in ivy, some of the windows were badly cracked, and the bell push on the massive oak doors didn't work, as Pomona soon discovered when she tried it.

The door was opened anyway, not by a maid, but by Denzil's mother herself, wiping fingers sticky with dough on a voluminous apron.

'I thought you might like a bit of company, Mother,' Denzil said, ushering them into a large, empty hall. 'Let me introduce you: this is Young May Moon as we call her. She's one of the Singing Kettles – our most talented member in my opinion, and this is her sister, Pomona. They live with their aunt, Mrs Jarvis at Orchard End. Ladies, my mother, Mrs Twistleton-Pike, who prefers to be called plain Mrs Pike.'

'Your father kept quiet about the Twistleton when we first met in London, so I followed suit. He'd fallen out with his father after his mother died, and he decided on an army career, instead of managing the estate. We didn't move here until after I was widowed, and Denzil's grandfather finally asked to meet his grandson because he was now his heir. Come into the kitchen, the warmest place in the house.' Mrs Pike led the way. 'I've only recently taken up cooking,' she continued. 'Since our cook-housekeeper packed her bags, Denzil and I have been left to cope on our own, apart from a woman who cleans the

126

rooms that we inhabit. But you are welcome to try one of my scones when they are ready.'

'I'll make a pot of tea,' Denzil offered.

It was a cavernous kitchen, with rows of copper pans hanging from hooks on the whitewashed walls. Some of them, May couldn't help noticing, were festooned with cobwebs. They were evidently not in use, now that there were only two persons in residence. There were several sizes of mixing bowls stacked on the shelves, but Mrs Pike had obviously mixed her scones in a pudding bowl, which had been to hand. She flapped a tea cloth over the table to remove spilled flour. 'I won't say take off your winter wrappings, or you'll soon be shivering ... Denzil, give the stove a riddle, will you? I'll get the scones out of the oven first, though. Now, tell me about yourselves. I understand you have a theatrical background?'

'Not exactly. Our father was Professor Jas Jolley – he was a professor of Punch and Judy, in case you're wondering–'

'If he was a *real* professor,' Pomona finished for her embarrassed sister.

'How marvellous!' Mrs Pike sounded as if she meant it.

'Mother is rather bohemian herself.' Denzil filled the teapot with water from the kettle on the stove.

'Oh, do you think so, dear? My father was an artist, my mother was his model. We lived in Bloomsbury, but not in a garret. Father actually made money from his painting; nudes are always popular.'

'I'd rather you didn't show them those particular pictures,' Denzil smiled.

127

'Why not?' Pomona demanded. She could guess, of course.

'Pomona, it's rude to talk with your mouth full.' May thought that Denzil must have noticed her blushes. She added: 'We mustn't stay too long, as Aunt Min will wonder where we are. The scones are lovely, Mrs Pike. Thank you.'

'Thank you for coming. I do hope Denzil will bring you to see me again soon. I'll entertain you in the drawing room then; there are plenty of pictures in there.' Mrs Pike had a twinkle in her eye. She was older than May had thought she would be, probably in her fifties; still upright and handsome, like her son.

Pomona rushed indoors to tell Min about their unexpected visit, while May said goodbye and thank you to Denzil at the gate. It was almost dark; time for their six o'clock supper. She held out her hand to him. He took her by surprise, pulling her towards him and cupping her face between his hands .The next thing she knew, he was kissing her.

She murmured. 'Please, Denzil, don't...'

'You wanted me to kiss you, didn't you? I wouldn't dream of taking further liberties, but there's no harm in a kiss between friends. You're a very attractive girl, May, and in a few years you'll have been much kissed. Am I the first?'

She didn't answer. She didn't want to think about Paddy just now. She gave an involuntary gasp as his lips brushed her closed eyes. 'Have I sent you to sleep?' he teased.

Then came the call from Aunt Min: 'Don't

stand out there and freeze, May, supper's ready!'

'Goodnight, Denzil,' she said firmly. He released her without another word. She was quivering, but not because of the cold.

Eighteen

Mid-December was the Singing Kettles' Christmas party. 'Fancy dress – no exceptions,' Imogen said firmly. 'We will provide the entertainment ourselves. My parents have kindly agreed to buy the food and drink. Fruit punch for all. No alcohol in the church hall!'

Pomona and May discussed what they would wear. Aunt Min sat knitting busily in her chair by the living-room fireplace, unaware that the cat was playing with her ball of wool which had rolled off her lap to the floor. 'What about the dress your mother bought you, May?'

'I've worn that green frock so often. It's not fancy dress, is it?'

Pomona had the answer. 'How about Mum's dance frock?'

'I'd be expected to perform the flamenco then!'

'Well? Henry plays the guitar. He could accompany you.'

'Maybe. I'm tired of sewing; my fingertips are sore when it comes to typing.'

'You should wear a thimble.' Aunt Min's needles clicked.

'I've decided to go as an apple,' Pomona

announced. 'I've worked it all out: two circles of cardboard like a billboard, back and front, I'll just slip it over my head after I've sloshed on plenty of red and green paint, and add paper apple-leaves in my hair, as the only ones left round here are all wrinkled and brown.'

'Terence could go as a pear–'

'I know what you're thinking – we'd be a *pair*, then! No thanks. The invitation says, you are welcome to bring a guest. Shall we invite Danny and Paddy?'

'Oh, Pom, they couldn't possibly travel all this way just for an evening out. I wish you could come, Aunt Min, but I know you can't leave Grandpa.'

Aunt Min was picking up a dropped stitch with the aid of a crochet hook. 'I might be able to bring him to the pantomime – *that* could catch his attention.'

Pomona sighed. 'I don't suppose we'll see the O'Flahertys again.'

'One day we will,' May said, but she didn't believe it herself.

It was the party night. It had been a grey, cold day and, when it came to it, the girls were reluctant to leave the warmth of the living room with the fire burning bright. There was never a shortage of wood, which they gathered most days from the orchard and its surrounds.

'Don't stand about outside, waiting for the car,' Aunt Min advised. 'Toby'll let us know when Denzil arrives, and no doubt he'll honk that dratted horn. Look, take the rugs from the sofa

130

and drape them round your shoulders. I don't need to have you go down with *poo-monia*.'

'Red-checked one for me.' Pomona seized it.

'That leaves me with the blue one with the frayed fringe. That's the one Toby curls up on at nights; it smells doggy and you can see all the white hairs–'

'Stop arguing, you two. Just think you're lucky it's not raining, or worse, snowing,' Aunt Min scolded.

Toby's ears pricked up; she rushed to the door at the loud knock.

'Thought I should escort you to the gate,' Denzil said. 'To make sure you didn't slip up in the dark. I understand they've been invited to stay the night at the rectory, so I'll deliver them there after the party, Mrs Jarvis. Hang on to me on either side, you two.'

Pomona had a brown-paper parcel containing her apple billboard under one arm. May was wearing her costume and would have been shivering without the blanket. She bent to pick up their overnight bag. They were excited at the thought of spending the night with Bea.

'Allow me to take that.' Denzil took the bag from May and they set off down the track. He was wearing a dark old-fashioned cloak which, they guessed, was a relic of his grandfather's youth.

'Have a good time!' Aunt Min called after them.

The hall was brightly lit and transformed with paper chains and other homespun decorations. Denzil removed his cape and revealed his outfit. 'King Charles the Second!' exclaimed Pomona as

131

he donned a dark wig. 'Where's Nell Gwynn?'

'I'm here,' said a familiar voice. Imogen had a wig too, with tumbling curls and a basket full or oranges. 'Denzil, my parents are waiting to speak to you.'

'Excuse me, please,' Denzil said to his companions.

May helped Pomona adjust the apple boards, then fastened the leaves in her hair. It had been too much to expect, she thought ruefully, that he would stay with us...

'She should have stuffed a couple of those oranges down her front,' Pomona said, loudly. 'She doesn't have enough bosom for Nell Gwynn, does she?'

'Shush, Pom.' May thought, those two have obviously hired their costumes. My outfit looks well-worn, which it is, and it smells fusty from being in the trunk. But at least it's genuine. I hadn't realized it would reveal my cleavage, too, but now I have more to show off than I did only a few months ago, even though I probably smell doggy from the blanket and of carbolic soap. I wish Aunt Min would buy soap that smelled nicer. I wish Paddy was my escort this evening. She fingered her pendant. The glowing amber was warm against her skin.

'I couldn't make up my mind what to come as, until the last minute,' Bea said as she joined them, to their relief. They'd been wondering where she'd got to.

'What are you?' Pomona asked tactlessly. Bea appeared to be wearing her mother's unfashionable clothes and hat.

'A suffragette – look, read my banner: VOTES FOR WOMEN!'

The stage curtains parted, and Henry, who had borrowed his friend's cape and wore a deerstalker cap which looked as if it was a left-over from a jumble sale, was revealed as Sherlock Holmes, with a pile of records on a chair and a gramophone on a small table. His assistant, Dr Watson, complete with false moustache, was his young brother.

'We'll start with a lively number to break the ice: The Charleston. Don't say you can't do it: Imogen and Denzil will demonstrate how.' Henry used a megaphone to gain the party goers' attention.

'I'm not sure I can dance in these boards,' moaned the apple.

'I won't need my castanets,' said Young Carmen. 'Let's get behind the others and follow what the front row do.' They shuffled sheepishly round those who were eager to join in. This was followed by the Paul Jones. May and Pomona joined the circle. The music stopped and she found herself opposite Denzil. He smiled. '*Señorita,* may I have the pleasure of this dance?'

May felt the pressure of his hand on her back as he guided her in the waltz. She nodded when he asked if she was enjoying herself. The music changed; she was swept back into the circle to grasp Nell Gwynn's hand on one side and Bea's on the other.

After they had enjoyed a splendid buffet it was time for the entertainment. There was some clumsy conjuring involving a top hat and a toy rabbit; a duet, and a couple of lengthy monologues. Then Henry picked up his guitar and announced: 'Young Carmen.' May flashed an indignant glance at Pomona, who'd obviously told him after all that it was the odious Carlos's name for her. She hoped Henry had practised the music beforehand and that she could remember the sequence of steps. Her mother's dancing-shoes would help.

The spotlight was on her, the lights dimmed in the hall. May was suddenly confident: Carmen would have been proud of her performance. There was silence for a brief moment when she finished dancing and the music died away, then the clapping and shouts of 'encore' began. May seemed frozen to the spot. Henry came to her rescue; he put down his guitar, moved beside her, his arm around her shoulders. Together they bowed. Then he led her off stage.

'Well, *you* stole the show,' Imogen told her. She made it sound like a reproof.

'She certainly did,' Denzil agreed. 'You were *wonderful*, May.'

The party was over.

The bed May shared with Pomona in one of the smaller bedrooms in the rectory, felt cold and clammy. The hardy Wright family did not have hot-water bottles to alleviate the initial shock of jumping under the covers.

'It was a lovely party. I had two of those cream horns,' Pomona confessed. She actually snuggled up to her sister. 'I wish you didn't have such cold feet.'

'So do I. Let's put our rugs over the bedclothes,

134

even if they do pong a bit.'

'Aren't you lucky? Two young men after you. If old Imogen had thought to bring her fairy god-mother wand along, she could have waved it and transformed you into a mouse!'

'I felt like a mouse beside her. Two young men? I didn't notice–'

'Don't fib! Denzil and Henry. Bea told me Henry is looking out for a sidecar for his bike, so *he* can take us home in future.'

'And don't you be so silly! They're good friends, not rivals! I like them both.'

'Yes, but you keep blushing when Denzil talks to you. Just like you did when Paddy was around, in West Wick last summer. I s'pose you've forgotten *him?*'

May placed the palm of her hand over the amber on her pendant. It still meant a lot to her. 'No, of course, I haven't. Go to sleep, Pom, do.' She lay awake for some time herself after that. How can I be so foolish? As Denzil said, it was a kiss between friends. That was all.

Nineteen

They woke on Christmas morning to a pow-dering of snow. It actually felt warmer, but there was the threat of a heavier fall to come. It was a Friday this year, so Boxing Day was on Sunday, which would make the break seem longer.

The girls were soon up and dressed and downstairs by the fire to open their Christmas sacks which they'd filled for each other. Grandpa was intrigued by his clockwork novelties, sending them across the floor where they toppled over when they came into contact with the rag rug. He took a childlike pleasure in winding them up and hearing them whirr. May and Pomona's gift to him, a tin donkey covered in grey felt, with a whizzing-round tail and ears, was already a favourite. He set this one off on the kitchen table, where it collided with the salt-pot: Aunt Min rushed to scoop up the spilt salt and to throw it over her left shoulder, a superstition they all followed.

Aunt Min unwrapped her new pinny, patterned with sprigs of holly with oversized scarlet berries. She put it on: 'Thank you girls, very festive – just what I needed.' The box of chocolates was placed out of Grandpa's reach. 'We'll open those later, eh? What have you got?'

'The lovely slippers you made for us, of course – thank you!' May said quickly, having noted Pomona's disappointment at the khaki wool-and-cardboard soles. They should have known what to expect when Min drew round their feet on cardboard, and cut round the pencil outline.

'I'm going to start my diary right away. There's a blank page before the new year,' Pomona told them. 'You're not to look in it, May, because diaries are private. Or you, Aunt Min.'

'I ain't got time for reading rubbish,' Aunt Min returned. 'What have you got there, May? I would have thought Carmen could send you both something this year.'

'She must have posted our presents off too late;

her card said to expect the postman to call. This is a present from Bea. Look, such nice writing paper and lined envelopes!' She'd write first to Brigid, she decided, to thank her for the Christmas card she'd sent them, enclosing a long letter from herself and notes for May and Pomona from Paddy and Danny. They were settling into their new life, Brigid said, but hoped to see them in the summer, for they had been engaged by the pier theatre by popular request for one week only at Whitsun.

More a holiday! We will stay with Jenny of course. Any chance you could join us? If not, we'll hope to visit you...

It's a long time 'til then, May said to herself with a sigh. Still, there's the pantomime to come in the new year. I'm not looking forward to it as much as I was because Imogen seems suspicious that Denzil and I... How ridiculous! Why would he be interested in me? But she couldn't help remembering that unexpected kiss.

'I need a volunteer to do the sprouts. I went out into the cold and picked 'em, so one of you can have the pleasure,' said Min. She sighed. 'Bit of a "bread and pullit" Christmas, I'm afraid, girls. Getting harder to make ends meet...'

'Oh, Aunt Min. As soon as I can I'll be working and able to pay for our keep,' May exclaimed. 'I never thought... Dad didn't leave much, did he?'

'He hadn't got much to leave, my dear. I told him it was more important to make sure that you two had something to help you on your way.'

'But that wasn't fair to you, Aunt Min!'

'Look, I ain't going to argue about it, 'specially not today. I don't need rewarding for what I do; you're my family.'

'Anyway, it *smells* like Christmas in the kitchen!' Pomona cried. She flung her arms round her aunt's skinny frame. 'I like chicken better than turkey!'

'So do I,' May said, hoping that Pomona would not notice today that the old rooster was no longer crowing. She decided that her new year resolution must be to find a weekend job, to add a few shillings to those already in the old teapot used for depositing the fruit- and egg-money. Nothing much was discarded in this house: the spout leaked, but the teapot was still useful.

It was a quiet Christmas this year, their first without Jim. They took a holly wreath to the churchyard on Sunday to lay on his grave, and then went into the church for the morning service to sing all the joyful carols.

The next time the postman called the girls were overjoyed that Carmen had kept her promise. May had a soft leather green handbag, with draw-string top and a matching purse inside, and Pomona had a brightly embroidered cambric blouse. Aunt Min and Grandpa had not been forgotten; each had a silk handkerchief: Min's was peacock blue and Grandpa's was scarlet.

'You mustn't blow your nose on it, Grandpa,' Pomona told him. 'It's for show!'

'I'll pin it in your best jacket pocket,' Min promised him.

The dress rehearsal on Friday 8 January was a disaster. Bea was the only one who knew all her words. Pomona was hastily substituted for Terence as the page, an outcome she had been hoping for all along. Terence, declaring his relief, flung the despised tights at her and joined the musicians with his drum.

It was not a speaking part, but Pomona was determined to be noticed. She wasn't too sure about wearing the tights after Terence, but Imogen, who was shrieking by this time, told her there was no time to wash them. There was much fluffing of lines; only Cinderella escaped the producer's wrath. As Imogen was in her fairy godmother's costume and waving her wand so fiercely that it was in danger of snapping, there was muffled laughter from the nervous cast.

'You're not ugly enough!' Imogen shouted at the Ugly Sisters. 'George – when are you going to shave off your moustache? It doesn't match your false beard.'

'I have,' he replied indignantly.

The ripe pumpkin for the transformation scene needed careful handling; Pomona gave it a prod and juice oozed out. She moved away quickly, hoping no-one had noticed. This scene needed the most rehearsing, but eventually they got it right. The cardboard coach, presenting its one side to the audience, was walked along by Cinderella and the flunkey, each with a hand through the cut-out windows. The wheels concealed their feet. However, the pantomime horse between the shafts lumbered along displaying two sizes of black wellington boots.

The musicians sighed and surreptitiously passed round a silver hip flask of brandy. The violinist poked Terence with her bow. 'Mind your p's and q's, boy!'

Pomona wished she could have doubled up as back or front of the horse, but competition for this had been fierce, and the prize part was awarded to two boys who were too boisterous to be in the team of dancers.

When it came to a romantic scene between Cinderella and Prince Charming in the palace gardens during the ball, Terence was in charge of the moon – which slowly appeared above their heads and wavered on the string, which Terence was pulling from the wings. He stood on a step ladder to do this, and Pomona, waiting for a cue as the Prince's page, was instructed to hold the steps steady. She couldn't resist making it wobble, but didn't mean to leave him dangling, clinging to the rafters, while the moon dipped and fell at the couple's feet. The backing singers faltered in their rendering of *Moonlight and Roses*. The great Count John McCormack, who sang it so beautifully himself, would have been disappointed at their feeble effort.

Imogen was furious. She rushed on stage to confront Pomona, and then came a shout from Terence, 'Hey, what about me?'

'Get back to your drum!' she yelled, when he descended. 'You, Pomona – stop playing tricks!' She was actually crying by the time they called a halt to the disastrous dress rehearsal. Denzil offered to take her home; he could see how upset Imogen was. 'I'll come back for May and Pomona.'

'Don't worry, I can take them home. Pomona can try out the new sidecar on the bike,' Henry said immediately.

'I'd rather go on the pillion!' Pomona put in, 'but I know you'll say I'm not old enough! I won't even be a Singing Kettle after the pantomime.'

There was a sudden burst of singing from those still in the hall: *I'll see you in my dreams...*' May blushed yet again, for Denzil was deliberately winking at her.

'I'm ready and waiting,' Henry said in her ear. 'It'll be all right on the night. It always is.'

Twenty

January 1926

Fortunately there had been little snow since Christmas, but it was still very cold and the days were short and gloomy once the festivities were over. The pantomime was just what the inhabitants of Kettle Row needed to raise their spirits again.

The girls, together with the rest of the cast, arrived well before the matinée scheduled for 2 p.m. Aunt Min and Grandpa intended to travel to town by bus in good time for the early performance, and would be home in time for tea. Imogen made it clear that Denzil and his mother were invited to dinner at her parents' house after the evening show. 'We prefer a private celebration,' she said smugly. 'I'm sure you can make other arrangements for a lift afterwards, May.'

'Don't worry about us,' May returned. 'We're having supper at the rectory and Henry will take us back home.' They had actually been invited to stay overnight again but they knew Aunt Min would want to talk over the exciting events that night.

In the hall kitchen there was a deep sink, and also a counter on which were placed ready a big teapot and crocks. The gas stove heated the water in the pair of whistling kettles. The players took their turn at being made up at the table, where the boxes of greasepaint, cold cream and powder were arranged, together with a swing mirror borrowed from someone's dressing-table. Denzil's mother, having come from an artistic background, volunteered to apply the actors' make-up. She was assisted by Bea's sister Selina. Mrs Wright was in charge of the refreshments. She hadn't had time to remove her hat: the one Bea had borrowed when she was a suffragette at the Christmas party. The appetizing smell of fresh-baked, crumbly cheese scones in haphazard shapes, (for Mrs Wright hadn't time to bother with a cutter either), mingled with a waft of perfume emanating from the person of the elegant Mrs Pike.

Backstage, in the dressing-room, costumes were being donned. The young dancers were told to sit still on the row of chairs against the wall and not to distract those who, as they disrobed behind the screens, muttered their lines repeatedly.

'The orchestra is tuning up, but Terence is not allowed to bang the drum yet,' Pomona reported

142

in great excitement. 'All the seats are taken! I spotted Aunt Min and Grandpa in the front row.'

'Terence has been practising drum tattoos since dawn,' Mrs Pike said ruefully. She fingered Bea's lank tresses. 'The wig will transform you later in the Ball scene. Pomona, *please* don't touch it. Bea, you're done – you can both join Buttons in the wings.'

'I'll come with you,' May said. 'I don't need to be in costume until after the interval.' Between scenes, only her glove puppet would appear through the gap in the closed curtains.

The curtains slowly parted, the audience ceased chattering, the lights dimmed in the hall but the footlights illuminated the stage; the opening music faded away.

Cinderella was on her knees, poking the coals of the fire under the black pot suspended over the range that was depicted on the backcloth of a dungeon-like kitchen. She rose, sighing, wiping grubby hands on her ragged skirt. The opening lines came loud and clear.

'I am little Cinderella, and oh, I wish I had a feller,
to take me out at nights, you know, to see the sights...'

Cue for Buttons to appear. Vera, that rather plain little bookkeeper, now entered, in a trim uniform with glinting silver buttons and pill-box hat perched on a page-boy bob. Buttons gave Cinders a bun filched from the pantry, and commiserated with her. He understood, he told her, because of the way the Baron, his wife and her awful

143

daughters treated him, too. *If only I could be, the one to set you free...* The soaring soprano voice made those listening in the wings, quiver with relief.

Buttons took Cinderella's hand as she sang her lament:

*'Who rises early, brews the tea
And never has a moment free?
Who gets bath water piping hot–
Who stirs the porridge in the pot?'*

'Cinderella!' roared the audience

In the wings May relaxed her grip on Pomona's hand at this rousing response. Imogen's stern instructions to May had been: 'Hang on to your sister!' The pantomime had got off to a good start.

The Ugly Sisters, Ag (Henry) and Pru (Denzil) shrieked and quarrelled throughout their scenes and were greeted with much laughter and ribald calls. Their pompous stepfather and spiteful mother were also a good double act. When the sisters heard that they had been invited to the Prince's ball, the shorter, well-padded-out Ag came downstage to display her new gown to the audience. As she preened, there was the shout: 'Look behind you!' Her taller sibling stepped forward and delivered a scathing comment:

*'Your frock does nothing to camouflage flab,
In that pink you look like an overdressed crab!'*

In the ensuing tussle, Ag's skirt was ripped from the bodice and her baggy, spotted bloomers were revealed. This should have prompted

144

laughter, but instead the horrified expression on Ag's face resulted in a concerted sympathetic, '*A-ah!*' from the audience.

On rushed the baron to castigate his step-daughters.

'*Grizzle, grumble, groan and grouse – am I not master in this house?*'

He was booed off stage.

At each change of scene, the dog puppet appeared to entertain the audience. Because May was using the swazzle, his voice was that of Mr Punch. It was fortunate that May couldn't see the audience, for two were missing from the front row.

'When you've got to go, Min, you've got to go,' Grandpa hissed in his daughter's ear. Apologizing, Min propelled him along the seats and towards the WC off the hall.

Min waited outside the door, but became anxious when the music began for the next scene. She tapped on the cubicle. 'Grandpa, hurry up – we've missed May's turn and now they're singing again...'

She rattled the doorknob. The door was locked. 'Shoot the bolt back, Grandpa...' Then she heard muttering.

'Can't. It won't budge.'

'Hang on, I'll get help.'

It took the caretaker a good ten minutes with a screwdriver to open the door. Grandpa was bewildered. 'What happened?'

'Can't talk about it now,' Min said, 'Let's creep back to our seats.'

May took a deep breath, Pomona gave her a push. The Prince and his page were revealed resting on a fallen log in the forest. Pomona had complained at the last minute that her tights were wrinkling round her ankles; May was more concerned that hers were too revealing – she thought her tunic was on the short side. When she'd dared to say so to Imogen in the wings, she'd been poked with the Fairy Godmother's wand, which was now slightly bent, but fortunately hadn't snapped in two. It was rather disconcerting to be wished 'break a leg' by the two Ugly Sisters.

'The King says it's high time to wed,
In his opinion I'm too easily led.
That's the reason for the Ball,
But I don't want to go at all...'

This, unfortunately reminded Grandpa that *he* did... This time, May was aware of the shuffling around in the front row of seats.

She couldn't recall her next line, despite frantic hissing from the prompt corner. Pomona came to the rescue, improvizing:

'Let's practise the waltz, I know the beat,
Though 'tis said, I've two left feet!'

Terence seized the opportunity for a drum roll, and the musical trio hastily joined in on piano, flute and violin.

The Fairy Godmother turned the pumpkin into a

146

coach, the small dancing mice disappeared with Cinderella in a puff of smoke and the pantomime horse trotted on stage, this time in matching wellington boots. Cinderella's change of clothes was a miracle of good timing. The golden wig covered her tousled locks. She reappeared in a beautiful ball-gown, sparkling with scattered sequins, with silver slippers in lieu of glass on her feet. The Fairy Godmother waved her wand again:

'You shall go to the Ball, my dear! That's your right,
But leave you must, at first stroke of midnight...'

Cinderella entered the coach and waved to the audience. The curtain closed. It was time for the interval and refreshments, and a big scene change. Lights up, much blinking, and Grandpa spilled his tea.

The curtain rose again to reveal the Palace ball-room. Downstage left, on two gilded chairs, sat the Ugly Sisters, discussing the merits or otherwise of the male guests as they arrived and were announced by a footman. Ag waved her fan vigorously to attract attention, and Pru flicked her dance card. Both wore wigs to match their gowns: Ag's was emerald green, and Pru's shocking pink, Cinderella having repaired the torn frock. Ag wore the family tiara; Pru, a band of feathers.

A fanfare, and the Prince swept in, followed by the page, with a nervous jerk at the waistband of his tights. The dancing was about to begin when a late arrival was announced: 'The Honorable Ella!' Cinderella had arrived. The Prince regarded

147

her for a moment, then bowed and requested the first dance.

The pantomime was almost over, but there were some magical moments still to come, before the spell was broken. Cinders was back in the kitchen, after fleeing the Ball just in time, but leaving a slipper behind. Her stepmother was railing at her for slacking and not providing enough bath water. 'Now every bath is wallowed by three!' she shrieked, just as Buttons ushered in the Prince and his page, who carried a silver slipper on a velvet cushion. Panting behind were the Ugly Sisters.

'Ma,' Pru cried indignantly, 'that little toad says my feet are too big!'

'He ain't a toad, he's more a pig,' asserted Ag.

'What's all this?' demanded the Baroness.

'*Didn't you hear the proclamation?*' Buttons asked boldly. '*This shoe was found after the Ball, when all had gone to bed. It belongs to the girl the Prince intends to wed.*'

'*Let them try,*' the prince said with a smile. Buttons moved a stool for the sisters to sit on in turn. Despite their efforts, they could not force the silver slipper on their too-big feet.

Then it was Cinderella's turn and of course, it was a perfect fit.

The final duet between Prince and Cinderella, '*If you were the only girl in the world– And you were the only boy,*' was fervently echoed by the audience.

The curtain calls were over, following the second performance, when Imogen came forward with Denzil, both still in costume, to make an announcement.

'It is a happy ending for us too, we are about to celebrate our engagement with our parents! Thank you all for coming. Goodnight.'

'Just a minute, May,' Henry said, when she and Pomona were about to enter their house. She gave Pomona a nudge. 'You go ahead...' When the door closed, she turned to Henry. 'It all went so well, you were right about that, Henry. Didn't Bea play her part well? She really ought to go on the stage, I think.'

'I know you must be upset,' he said softly. 'You and Denzil, I thought you felt the same way about each other. I should know, because I wish you could feel that way about me.'

'Oh, Henry!' She gave him an unexpected hug. 'I suppose you could say, well, we all expected it, didn't we?'

'He's marrying her for her money, so he can restore the manor–'

'To be fair, Henry, I think she loves him, that's why she's so jealous. She's good at making things work – look at the panto.'

'I'm saying goodbye to you tonight, May.'

'I – I don't understand...?'

'I have been offered a job, oh, not what I really want to do, but it's a start. I owe it to my parents to help out where I can, not expect them to keep me at home. I am off to London next week. You need space and time to grow up, May, but I promise you I won't give up! May I keep in touch with you by letter?'

'Of course you can.' She reached up and gave him a peck on the cheek. 'Henry, I won't be

149

sobbing in my pillow all night, you know.' It's not the first time my heart has been broken, she thought. Paddy soon put me out of his mind. I have grown up a lot since last summer, but Henry's right, I'm not quite there yet.

In the kitchen Min passed her a cup of cocoa. She didn't ask why May hadn't come indoors immediately.

'Pomona told me about the special announcement,' she said casually. 'I'm afraid I've got one of my own. I've had an offer to buy this place, and if I agree, there'll be enough in the kitty to rent one of them new little houses in Kettle Row – much more convenient for you girls to go to school and college. We'd have to retire Smokey and find him a home, but Toby can come with us – and Grandpa, of course. I don't want him thinking he's off to the workhouse!'

'We'd be in civilization,' Pomona made it sound like paradise.

'I'll finish my course at Easter,' May said. She thought, I won't be going to West Wick, that's made my mind up for me. 'I'll get a job. You can enjoy your retirement too, Aunt Min. So long as we're together, that's enough for me.'

'And me!' added Pomona.

PART TWO

Along Worple Road
to
Wimbledon and beyond

Twenty-One

1935
Autumn, nine years later.

May was sorting out the contents of the house near the pond in Kettle Row. She'd waited until after Pomona was settled in at Cambridge University. She was very proud of her sister, and was glad that Min had known of Pomona's success before she passed away in the spring.

This is what Min said I should do, she thought, as she looked around her at the stacked boxes – this lot for the church jumble, these to be stored at the Rectory until she had a home of her own – but when would that be? Min wanted me to be free to pursue a career, but I'm not sure, at this moment, that I know what I want in my new life.

She looked around the kitchen, saw Grandpa's old cap hanging on the hook on the back door; he'd been gone eight years now, had died soon after they moved here. Dangling below this was a dog's lead, Toby had not been replaced by a new puppy, despite Pomona's pleading. 'You'll be grown up and gone before we know it,' Min told her, 'and who will have to look after a lively young dog, then?'

May folded the cap and rolled the lead into a ball. She placed these in what she called her memory box. Also in there was Pomona's first bathing-costume, which seemed impossibly small, for her sister was now quite an Amazon, with a muscular frame due to all that swimming; Min's faded apron, the one the girls had proudly presented to her nine years ago on Christmas Day, nestled next to a parcel containing the flamenco dress her mother gave her at West Wick, before Carmen returned to Spain and her daughters to Kettle Row. May hadn't worn that, or danced, since the Singing Kettles days. At the bottom of the box was the bundle of cards she'd received for her sixteenth birthday at West Wick, including the home-made one by Paddy and Danny. The short poem written by Paddy, *The Punch and Judy Lady*, was tucked in the now shabby green handbag. Correspondence with the O'Flaherty family had lapsed over time. She still wore the pendant Paddy had given her; this day it was unseen beneath her blouse. The amber was warm against her skin. It was a link with the past, even though she believed she wouldn't see him again. As for Denzil, that had just been a flirtation on his part.

May sighed. There was no recent news from Carmen, which was worrying because of newspaper and wireless reporting on the likelihood of a civil war in Spain. There were two opposing factions, she'd learned: Republican and Nationalists, the former were in government. She hoped that Carmen was in a place of safety. The unpleasant Carlos had left her years ago, and Carmen had become a solo artiste. The promised reunion with her children hadn't materialized.

May turned from the memory box, to the old

trunk, still festooned with cobwebs, which she had brought down from the loft. She brushed them gently away, but she didn't lift the lid, because she knew exactly what was inside: her father's battered straw hat and the Punch and Judy puppets on top of the striped canvas of the booth. Pomona had her own mementos in Cambridge, including Grandpa's old fiddle.

I'm sorry, Dad, that I couldn't carry on, she thought, but she was aware that it wasn't the same at West Wick nowadays. Jenny and Percy weren't around any more; the Swan was a private house, and the depression had affected even the end-of-the-pier shows. The town too, had changed, had become what Min called 'gentrified'. Rich people had holiday homes there now; they arrived by train and car at weekends throughout the year and Norland Nannies wheeled prams along the promenade. The charabancs and paddle steamers no longer spilled out day-trippers. The open-air pool had been abandoned, and as well as new swimming-baths, there were tennis courts and a golf course. The fishermen were having a hard time, some of their sea front cottages had signs advertizing bed and breakfast.

She felt in need of a cup of tea, but where had she put the kettle? Even as she glanced around there was a knock on the door. Henry was here to fetch the remaining boxes. When they'd loaded his car, she must sweep up, lock up, and wait for him to collect her. She was spending the night at the Rectory. The next day Henry was driving her to Raynes Park, near Wimbledon, where she'd been invited to stay in his house until she found a job and somewhere she could afford to rent. Bea, she hoped, would be there to greet her, for she lodged there when she was not on tour with the repertory company. Her success in the pantomime had been the start of a stage career.

When Bea left Kettle Row May took the first job offered. She was the only female employee at the local estate agents. The men were all kindly, but over fifty years old. She missed the fun, the girlish giggles, the companionship of a true friend; her social life was almost non-existent.

'I must drop the keys off at the office,' she said now to Henry, as he stowed the boxes on the dicky seat of his small car.

'They will be sorry to lose you. How long have you been working there?'

'Ever since I finished my commercial course; you know how long that is,' she retorted. 'You keep reminding me, after all, that I should have made my mind up by now about marrying you.'

'I realized it wasn't possible until Pomona was independent and your aunt, of course, needed your support in her later years.'

He looked at her thoughtfully before starting up the engine. She was conservatively attired in a V-neck bottle-green cardigan over a beige blouse, a calf-length skirt, salmon-pink rayon stockings and rather clumpy court shoes. She still wore her glossy black hair in a knot in the nape of her neck, which gave her an old-fashioned air. She was twenty-six. Bea was the same age, and she wasn't married either, or ready to settle down yet, but she certainly led a less conventional life than May. 'Do you really intend to take the Civil

156

Service exam?' he enquired.

'Why not?' she returned. He smiled at that. Some things hadn't changed. May was a determined young woman. He was thirty years old with a responsible job in a London bank, he had a mortgage, a second-hand motor car and he played the organ in the local church; but, he thought ruefully, there's no romance...

'I'll be back in half an hour,' he said.

'I'll be ready.'

Emma Wright hugged May close, the following morning. 'I can't believe you're leaving Kettle Row, too. I haven't got used to Terence not being around – the place is far too quiet and tidy! But it's nice that he and Pomona are both in Cambridge, isn't it?'

'They might not see as much of each other as you think,' Henry reminded his mother. 'Especially as Pomona is in a women's college.' Terence had decided against applying to university himself, but secured a job at W.G. Pye in research. 'He was always experimenting, seeing how things work,' Henry had said when he heard this news. 'Look what he did to my motor cycle.'

'He put it all back together eventually,' Emma said in his defence.

'You've got Selina's baby to look forward to,' May said. Shy Selina had surprised them all by being the first of the family to marry. A young curate came to assist at the church and was offered lodgings at the rectory. Within a year an engagement was announced, followed by a wedding six months later, and recently the good news of

157

Selina's pregnancy. The couple had their own quarters at the rectory, where Emma could help out if her daughter had an asthma attack, but fortunately, these were now infrequent. 'Selina is *serene*,' as her mother happily observed. 'Marriage suits her, unlike Imogen and Denzil.'

'He knew what he was taking on,' Henry said wryly.

May said nothing. It was a shame, she thought, that Imogen had not continued organizing the Singing Kettles. Within a year or two of the pantomime they'd disbanded; she might be autocratic, but she'd been the force behind the group.

'I'll look after the family in the churchyard,' Emma whispered in May's ear. 'Remember, we are always here for you if you need us, Young May Moon.'

No-one had called her that for ages.

Henry parked the car outside the house. 'We don't leave cars in the Street; after I've seen you indoors and unloaded your boxes I have to drive along to the garage where I keep it. I only use the motor in the summer months, and lay it up for the winter, as there is plenty of public transport – the trolley bus runs along the Worple Road to Wimbledon, and there's a good train service to London.'

They were in a short residential street, which linked with busier roads with shops. Henry's house was the end one of a row of substantial late Victorian villas, with walkways between each pair. The houses were built of mellow yellow bricks, with contrasting red bricks round the bay windows of the sitting room, and the largest bedroom above. The small front gardens were enclosed by neat privet hedges, which also marked the divisions between the houses. These had been intended for white-collar workers, but without provision for servants, though most housewives employed a daily help on busy days.

The late-afternoon sunlight streamed through the stained-glass panel above the door. May stepped inside the long hall and smelled lavender polish.

'Everything shining, in your honour!' Henry said. 'I told Mrs Hemsley, the daily, that you were coming!'

The sitting-room door was opened with a flourish and she was ushered inside. Waiting with outstretched arms was Bea.

'Oh, May, it's wonderful to see you again! You haven't changed a bit.'

'You have,' May murmured. Bea was still tall and skinny – no longer awkward but elegant in a shirt and slacks, as the wide-legged trousers were called. Her bobbed hair was now blonde and she wore spectacles with tinted lenses.

'Hello, May, remember me?' May realized that there was a young man in the room, and she instantly knew who he was: the bright red hair was unmistakable.

'Danny?' He towered over her. She had last seen him when he was ten.

He smiled. 'I can't believe you're not surprised! I must have grown a bit.'

'Quite a lot, actually. It's ten years since West

159

Wick, Danny.'

'You two know each other, that's obvious,' Henry said. 'Introduce us, Bea.'

'Sorry! Danny was at a loose end, too, now that the current tour is over, and I said you wouldn't mind if he tagged along with me for the weekend here. When I mentioned May he said he'd always wanted to see her again. Danny, meet Henry. Henry, this is Danny.'

They shook hands. Then May said to Danny: 'Were you really hoping to see my sister? Pom's at Cambridge, Danny.'

'I'm not surprised. Though I expected to see headlines in the newspapers one day, with a photo of her, celebrating swimming the Channel.'

'You catch up on all the news, and I'll get some tea, while Henry is disposing of your luggage. I hope you don't mind sharing a double bed with me, May, for a couple of nights? I could always shift into the small bedroom and Danny can sleep on the settee in here – he's used to that!'

'No, of course we can share a room, Bea – we've lots to catch up on,' May assured her.

'I'm not earning much as understudy to the leading man,' Danny said frankly. 'I haven't slept in a proper bed since I left home.'

May had been hoping to follow Henry upstairs, to have a wash to freshen up, before changing into a cotton frock. She felt hot and sticky in her travelling clothes, but she sat down obediently in a chair opposite Danny, as the others left the room.

'How old are you now, Danny?' she asked, for something to say.

'Almost twenty-one. I've already asked Bea about you. I know you're about the same age as Paddy. I'm sorry he never kept in touch with you, because he was really smitten at the time, you know. Am I right when I say I think it was the same for you?'

'You're just as nosy as you were when you were ten!' She couldn't help smiling. 'We've all grown up.'

'Has Pom still got freckles and is she just as fierce?'

'Yes, to both your questions. She's very superior now, too, and I suppose you'd call her a bluestocking.'

'I reckon I could soon get round her,' Danny said confidently.

'Danny, did things work out for your family as they hoped?'

'Did they for you?'

'Not exactly. I expect you already know from Bea, that I'm a shorthand typist, not a flamenco dancer – nor a Punch and Judy lady.'

'Well, it was like that for us too. My parents lived in my grandfather's house, Dad returned to his old school, Mum stayed at home and taught music there in her spare time, but she's busier than ever now, looking after her granddaughter...' he broke off, then continued, 'Paddy's child. He married young, he was only my age when he started his own small joinery business. It wasn't a good time; he went bust, like many others in the early thirties. His wife left him to struggle on, and she left the baby, Cluny, too. Paddy had no alternative but to go home with her.'

161

'What does he do now?'

'He works from our grandfather's old work-shop, repairing and restoring old furniture. He takes any job he's offered; he's making farm gates at the moment.'

'But *you* became an actor – keeping up the family tradition; that must please your parents,' May said, still trying to take in the news about Paddy.

'Tea and cakes!' Bea pushed a loaded trolley before her. She looked keenly at her friend's flushed face and wondered what the two had talked about.

So did Henry, who came in the room behind her.

'What d'you think of him?' Bea asked, as she climbed into bed.

'Danny, I presume? He's grown up very nicely! Bea – you're not – you know...?' May floundered.

'Lovers? Of course not, he's far too young for me, but he's good company and I suppose he reminds me of my cheeky young brother. Are you still pining with unrequited love for Denzil?'

'I got over him years ago.'

'I gather you and Danny's brother were close when you were in West Wick?'

'Perhaps – but that was even more years ago.' She fingered the amber at her throat.

'Did *he* give you that?'

'Stop asking questions! But yes, he did. We were far too young for a serious commitment then. Goodnight, Bea, sleep well.'

'I shall be awake now, wondering what you haven't told me, May,' Bea said, as she switched off the bedside lamp.

Twenty-Two

The following morning, Saturday, May was awake before Bea. She looked around her, smiled at Bea's white slacks which she'd flung haphazardly on to the chair, and which dangled to the floor; her friend was as untidy as ever. This was the biggest bedroom, with the bay window, and there was a fireplace opposite the bed – it must be cosy in winter to lie and watch the flames flickering in the dark, she thought.

There was sun streaming in through the curtains where she had parted them last night, to look at the stars. She glanced at her watch, it was already 7 a.m. May turned back the covers on her side of the bed, and lowered her legs to the ground. The linoleum was cold to her feet. She found her slippers and dressing-gown, noted that Bea was still fast asleep, and went quietly out to the bathroom opposite.

She put down her rolled towel and toilet bag on the edge of the bath, marvelling at the depth of it, standing on clawed feet: so different from the tin tubs of country life, and the narrow hip bath in the small bathroom in Kettle Row. The WC had been off the kitchen there; here there was a throne in a cubicle next to the bathroom, with gleaming tiled walls and proper lavatory paper. Min had always provided cut-up newspapers hanging on a nail on the wall: old habits died hard. May tried

163

the hot tap over the basin. The water gushed out, but it was cold. Did she need to boil a kettle in the kitchen, and bring a jug upstairs, she wondered?

A polite tap on the door startled her.

'It's only me.' It was Henry's voice.

She opened the door and there he was, clad in a thick, checked, woollen dressing-gown with a knotted girdle. His hair was ruffled and, without his glasses, his myopic eyes were large and luminous, as she recalled Bea's were when she was on stage.

He took in her appearance, too: her hair long and loose, which instantly reminded him of Young May Moon when she danced on stage while he strummed the guitar. She'd been so vulnerable in those days, he thought, but he had been too shy to presume that she might be attracted to him, as he was to her. Maybe it was too late now, as she obviously valued her independence. Despite the proposals, he'd never progressed beyond a brotherly hug and a kiss on her cheek.

'I'm sorry, I forgot to tell you that you have to put a match to the geyser over the bath – be prepared for a loud pop! But it soon runs nice and hot. Shall I do it?'

'Please.' May moved aside to permit him to enter the bathroom. He had a box of matches in his pocket. 'We don't keep them in here, as they get damp and then you can't strike 'em,' he said.

He demonstrated how to turn the geyser on and off. 'It's not a problem in winter, because there is a back boiler in the dining room downstairs which heats the water when the fire is lit. Well, I'll leave you to it. Why don't you have a bath, before my sister takes over the bathroom? She never used to bother with her appearance when we lived at home, but *now*... I must start on the breakfast.'

'Oh, I expect you wanted to use the bathroom first. You'll have to tell me the rules of the house!'

'There aren't any. I want you to treat this as home, May, while you're here. I washed earlier – in cold water – too lazy to light the geyser then! Join me downstairs when you're ready.' He paused for a moment. 'Leave your hair loose, I – I like it.'

Later, Henry said ruefully: 'Seems it's just thee and me for breakfast – maybe just as well – I burned the toast.'

'I could tell you had, as I came downstairs,' May said. 'I'm surprised Danny didn't wake up and think the house was on fire.'

'I think he and Bea are both late risers, they don't get to bed until the early hours after an evening performance, I gather. We'll eat here in the kitchen, if you don't mind?'

'Of course I don't. Well, what's on offer, Henry?'

'Rubbery scrambled eggs and well-scraped toast.'

'Didn't you add any butter to the eggs?'

'I'm a typical bachelor, May. I just whisk the eggs, shake in pepper and salt, and a dash of milk – then scramble away with a fork.'

'I don't mind doing the cooking while I'm here,' she offered diffidently. 'I learned a lot from Jenny Wren when we were at West Wick. Aunt Min was more your style of cook!'

'I accept your offer with alacrity,' he said. He took down a couple of odd plates from the dresser. 'Sorry, I should have put these on the rack above the cooker to warm. Would you care to pour the tea?'

'I would,' she replied. She wondered where he had acquired the china cups, and the teapot with a chipped spout. She looked in vain for a tea-strainer.

'Any crumbs left for a hungry chap?' They looked up from the table to see Danny lounging in the doorway, grinning at them.

'Eggs and bread; help yourself, if you don't mind cooking your breakfast,' Henry said amiably. 'I'll need to go shopping later on,' he added to May. 'I haven't much left in the cupboard.'

'You didn't count on having an unexpected visitor,' Danny said cheerfully. He sawed at the heel of bread and put a thick slice under the grill. 'I won't bother with the egg. I'm not conversant with the gas cooker. Any tea left in the pot?'

'Just a trickle.' Henry gave an almost imperceptible sigh, then rose to refill and boil the kettle. The telephone rang in the hall. 'Excuse me,' he said, 'I expect that's my mother, wanting to know we arrived safely.'

May made a fresh pot of tea, found another cup but without a matching saucer, and took these to the table. As she bent over the pot, to stir the contents, the locket on her neck swung forward and Danny instantly recognized it. 'Paddy gave you that, didn't he?'

'Yes.' She tucked it back into place.

'As a symbol of eternal love...?'

166

'We were too young for that,' she said primly, passing his cup.

'It was Pom's letter, you know.'

'What letter?'

'She wrote to me about the pantomime – the Singing Kettles – and she mentioned that you were madly in love with someone called Dennis.'

'Denzil, actually. It was nothing really, certainly not on his side. He married someone else. I – I just liked him a lot, that's all. I suppose you showed the letter to Paddy?'

'He demanded to see it, in case there was a message for him from you. You broke his heart, May.'

'Oh, don't be so dramatic – and you're as hopeless as Henry; you've burned the toast too.' It was a tactless thing to say, because Henry, coming into the kitchen, must have overheard her remark.

He said merely, 'Bea's calling out to you.'

Bea was seated before the dressing table, concentrating on pencilling in her eyebrows. She paused for a moment, seeing May's reflection in the mirror. 'You're shocked, I know, to think I could pluck my brows and replace them with artifice!'

'It seems a shame,' May ventured, 'to do so – but I understand why you wish to follow the latest fashion. I'm way behind the times.'

'Despite the fact that you're the one who comes from a theatrical background, eh? You're still Young May Moon, you know, but you seem to think you're middle aged. Come here.' Bea rummaged in her vanity case. 'Don't bundle your hair up again. Yesterday I was reminded of those hideous plaited earphones, the day you and I met. Allow me to brush the top and side hair back from your face and secure it with this hair comb. There, that's much prettier!'

'I'm not against powder and paint, Bea, but I suppose Aunt Min discouraged it. Pom, now, took no notice and did as she liked, from the age of sixteen. Well, you were calling for my attention?'

'Won't Danny have something in mind? I'm going to offer to do the grocery shopping for Henry. He doesn't seem to have much idea...'

'Oh, Henry needs a wife! I'll come, if you like. Danny's not one for shopping.'

'You haven't had your breakfast yet.'

'Breakfast? Since I escaped the family gruel I haven't bothered.'

'No wonder you're so thin,' May worried. Over the years she'd only seen Bea on her flying visits home and had not taken in the changes to her appearance. However, their old rapport was still strong.

'Danny agrees with you: not much of me to clasp, he says.'

'Oh – I thought you told me you were just good friends!'

'Did I? Please don't say anything to him, will you, but I can't help myself. He may be too young for me, but...' She broke off, noting May's expression. 'He'll be our leading man in the new show. It's a musical, and he's an accomplished singer.'

'He was, even as a boy.' May recalled the treble voice and the show-stopping rendition of *Danny Boy*.

168

'While I, dear May, am a character actress. My Cinderella days are gone, but I still get to dress up.'

The Royal Arsenal Co-operative shop was an imposing, double-fronted building, just a short walk away along the Worple Road, a bustling thoroughfare with a variety of other shops. One shop was displaying baskets of mismatched crockery in straw, half-blocking the pavement, with handwritten cardboard notices: NOTHING MORE THAN SIXPENCE. So that was where Henry bought his crockery from, May thought. There was no need to venture further unless you wished to go into Wimbledon on the whining, clanging trolley bus, which was considered a treat in itself to the many children who were about on a Saturday morning.

'I do find the names of roads hereabout intriguing,' May observed. 'Pepys Road, for instance, I wonder if it is connected with old Samuel who wrote diaries?'

'I asked Henry the same thing – but I might have known he would have delved into the history of the area before he moved here. It became Raynes Park in the 1870s because the land around here was originally owned by the Rayne family, as simple as that. Pepys Road was named after Charles Pepys, Earl of Cottenham – there's a Cottenham Park, apparently. The locals pronounce it 'Peppis', so now you know... Got your list ready?' They entered the brightly lit interior of the shop with its marble-topped counters and cheerful, white-coated assistants.

'Just look at those boxes of biscuits!' Bea exclaimed. 'I've never seen so many different sorts. Now I feel hungry.' They studied the contents of the boxes through their gleaming, glass lids.

With a ten-shilling note in her purse from Henry, May was seduced by all the good food on offer.

Crumbly cheddar – a wedge was cut with wire, by an obliging assistant. 'Here, dear – or a little more?' A flitch of bacon was inserted in the machine and streaky rashers fell one by one on to greaseproof paper. Sausages, hanging in glistening necklaces from a hook were cut free, and then deftly parcelled up. Bread was tapped to show it was fresh, then wrapped. Butter was patted into shape: sugar was poured into a bag fashioned before their eyes, from a piece of coarse blue paper and made into a cone shape. Eggs were placed carefully in a brown paper bag. May's basket was filled to the brim. Then Bea requested a bag of broken biscuits. 'Bourbon are my favourites!' she said, with a winning smile. As well as a handful of small change, they received the tokens which were issued according to the amount spent in the store.

Satisfied, they strolled up the road to see which film was showing at the Rialto. 'King Kong!' Bea exclaimed. 'I've seen it. Have you?'

May admitted she had not. 'I don't think it would be my cup of tea.'

'It might do my bashful brother good to hold you in the palm of his hand, like that great ape does with Fay Wray – well, you know what I'm getting at, don't you?' Bea took a bite from a broken Bourbon.

'You can forget the matchmaking, Bea. But thank you for letting me know how stuffy I'd become – I needed that,' May said, meaning it.

Twenty-Three

On Monday morning May was woken by a light tap on the bedroom door. Bea and Danny had departed late the previous evening, for rehearsals were due to start for the new production today, so it could only be Henry, she thought; unless it was his daily help; it was washing day, after all.

She sat up in bed, but pulled the sheet up under her chin as Henry entered with a tray. 'I brought my cup too, hope you don't mind if I sit on the side of the bed?'

'Of course not,' she said, letting the sheet drop from her clasp, as she positioned the spare pillow behind her head. 'You're spoiling me, Henry. I only expected a call to remind me to rise and shine because I ought to be job-hunting in earnest from now on.'

'Not today, or tomorrow,' he returned. 'I'm taking a couple of days' leave, and we'll go out and about, because I'm hoping to persuade you to stay on here. At least you'd have a friend to talk to in the evenings, I know from experience how lonely it is living on your own.'

'So long as you understand...'

'I do understand. Let's see how we get on, shall we?'

171

'Well, you've made a good cup of tea, used the tea-strainer from the Co-op!'

As she raised the cup to her lips she was aware that one shoulder strap of her flimsy nightgown had slipped down her arm and that he had tactfully turned his face away from the sight of an exposed breast. She surprised herself by exclaiming: 'Don't tell me you are *repelled* at seeing more of me than was intended. It would be more flattering if you were *excited!*'

'You have no idea how I feel, that's obvious.'

'I do! And it's most frustrating!' Tears welled in her eyes. 'Maybe I made a mistake coming here. You – you don't know how to woo a girl, Henry! D'you want to know why I almost succumbed to Denzil's charms that time? It was the element of danger. He wasn't worried that I was too young, too innocent; in fact that was what made me attractive to him. You've never even – touched me. You're the kindest person I know, but...'

He took her empty cup, 'Here, give me that.' He placed it on the tray. Then he was leaning over her, his hands firm on her bare shoulders. 'Stop talking for a minute, and I'll show you exactly how I feel.' He kissed her parted lips before she could protest. His arms encircled her and he hugged her tightly. His voice was muffled by her hair. 'When I saw what you were unconsciously revealing earlier I was reminded of Young Carmen in that tight dress you wore when you performed the flamenco and I accompanied you on the guitar. I thought you were beautiful and desirable. I still do, but then I was dumbstruck. Where do we go from here?'

'Down the Worple Road to Wimbledon,' she said demurely. 'But first you might have a shave!'

She wore a new frock, lettuce-green cotton, chosen because it reminded her of the pretty one Carmen had bought for her when she was sixteen. It was too outmoded to wear now, but she'd kept it, thinking she could sew table napkins from the skirt. The new dress had short, butterfly sleeves, an exaggerated, pointed white collar, a snug waist and an elegant skirt with a flared hemline. She'd mastered the art of fixing her hair back with the comb that Bea had given her; she didn't have a hat, but she pulled on short, white summer gloves. It was warm enough not to need to wear a jacket, though she carried one folded over her arm.

May enjoyed every minute of the day out on the common, but first there was the ride in the trolley bus. The high-pitched whine made conversation difficult, so she gazed, entranced, through the window at a bustling new world.

They walked for miles, it seemed, for there was so much Henry wanted to show her. The hill up which the heavy horses lumbered with their loads, and the drinking trough where the animals slaked their thirst. 'There's a fountain for mere mortals,' Henry said, smiling, as she slipped her arm in his, and they went to find it, for they too were looking forward to a long draught of cool water. They walked round the imposing drinking fountain and read the Biblical texts engraved on all four sides.

'Seventy-five years ago, washerwomen brought

173

their damp linen to the common, fixed lines between the trees, or dried smaller garments on the bushes,' Henry told her. 'It really was common land, then.'

They ate their lunch at noon by the boating pond, where, on the sunlit water, small boys and energetic grandfathers sailed boats, to be caught in the reeds on the far side. Henry pointed out the slippery edges to the pond, where the grass was worn away, and warned May not to get too close to the water. They sat on a wooden bench and unwrapped thick slices of Co-op bread, cut when new, with cubes of cheese and a red apple apiece.

'I should've worn a hat,' May remarked ruefully as the sun blazed down on her unprotected head.

Henry lightly touched the crown of dark hair. 'Your hair is thick enough to protect you from sunstroke, and long enough to cover the back of your neck. However, you are welcome to borrow my cravat.'

She looked up at him, mischief glinting in her eyes. 'I gather you have decided I'm not averse to you touching me, eh? Thank you, I accept your offer of the cravat.'

He pulled the silk scarf from under his collar and passed it over. May tied it gypsy style, knotting the ends under her hair at the back. 'I'm not too sure navy blue with white spots goes with green, but I feel very Spanish today.' The silk smelled faintly of bay rum, she thought, with a little smile curling the corners of her lips. It reminded her of Jim, who had slicked back his unruly hair with the same lotion.

'And I feel cooler without it, even though passing ladies may look disapprovingly at my lack of a tie!'

'It was a good day,' she sighed contentedly, when at his suggestion she put her feet up on the sofa that evening, after they'd eaten their fish-and-chips supper. She wriggled her bare toes, having slipped off her stockings while he was washing up in the kitchen. 'I'm feeling the effects of all that walking, though.'

Henry sat down at the end of the sofa, and said diffidently: 'I'll give your feet a rub, shall I? That should help.'

The soothing massage caused her to relax, close her eyes and doze. He gazed at her for a few minutes before he woke her with the words: 'Time for bed, I think. Off you go. See you in the morning.'

Pomona was feeling decidedly homesick. She sat at the small table by the window in her room to compose a letter to her sister. First she needed to fill her Waterman lady's fountain pen with ink. She squirted a jet of blue-black on to the pink blotter, considering what to write. She couldn't admit to being unhappy, knowing how hard May had worked to help her reach her goal of university, and here she was, at Cambridge, feeling like a fish out of water. She sighed, shaking her head, then fingered her honey-coloured fringe from her eyes. They might call me Mona, she thought wryly, but at least I'm not Sandy, as I was at school. Thank goodness my hair darkened as I grew up. Here I am, a student of English, finding it difficult to

175

express my thoughts.

Dear old thing,

Every day is a challenge here! But I am keeping my head above water (just) regarding my studies. The young ladies here (you don't think of them as 'girls') are very confident and I don't think most of 'em know what to make of yours truly. I'm not Pom here, but Mona – if only I was Harriet or Elizabeth! We wear our gowns even for dinner, which is a very formal affair. However, most of us are keen on sport, which is good – hope to carry on swimming, and to get involved with rowing.

You asked if I have seen Terence. So far, our paths haven't crossed. We weren't pals, you know, like you and Bea – more like rivals! What about you and Henry? Fancy you meeting up with Danny after all those years! Has Paddy been in touch?

Good luck with the job hunting! Why don't you take a holiday first? How about Spain? Have you heard from Mum?

Tutorial coming up – much love from Pom x

She looked pensively out of the window. Far below, tiny figures in black, some with mortar boards on their heads, hurried by. 'So this is life in a stately pile,' Pomona said aloud. She slotted her letter into an envelope, sealed it, and wrote May's address on the front. She'd post it later. Reluctantly she gathered up her books, and ventured outside her room into the echoing long corridor.

'Two letters for you, and the electricity bill for me,' Henry informed May.

176

She flipped the eggs over in the frying pan. 'There – you haven't laid the table yet, and breakfast is just coming up! Two letters – one from Pom, I hope. Who sent the other, I wonder?'

'Don't ask me, I haven't got X-ray eyes. Thanks, that looks good. Eggs without frizzled edges, just right for dipping my fried bread in.'

May read her letters when she drank her tea; Pom's first. 'Oh dear, I think she's realized that she's no longer top of the class, as she was at school, and that she has to work harder than she ever has before.'

'She can do it,' Henry observed, wiping his plate clean with the last slice of bread and butter. 'Well, open the mystery letter, then!'

May did so, but didn't immediately enlighten him as to the content. She read the single sheet of notepaper twice, then poured more tea before she satisfied his curiosity. 'If you must know, the letter is from Danny's brother, Paddy. I told you about him, didn't I?'

'You didn't, but Bea dropped a few hints. A former boyfriend, I gather?' His tone was light, and he smiled at her.

'I suppose you could call it young love. It didn't last, of course. I was only sixteen. I actually *was* Young May Moon then.'

'I wish I had met you then,' he said softly. 'By the time I did, you were no longer the Punch and Judy lady, but had given it all up for shorthand and typing.'

'Didn't you, Henry, ever have a youthful infatuation like mine?'

'I have to admit, I did not. I was rather a solitary scholar at Cambridge. That doesn't mean I didn't ... well ... hope to meet the right girl in time. When I did I was too unsure of myself to do anything about it.'

'Are you talking about me, Henry? I liked and respected you from the moment we met, but you seemed so much older, and often aloof...'

'I'm only five years your senior,' he reminded her.

'Henry, I'm very fond of you – I've got to know you so much better since I came here – but you must be patient still.'

'Are you going to tell me what he says?' he asked diffidently.

'Paddy? He tells me he is separated from his wife, that he has a little girl named Cluny, that he has never forgotten me. He doesn't ask if we can meet, or even if I will reply to his letter; he just says that he was glad to have known a girl like me. That's all, Henry.'

'Nevertheless, will you reply to his letter?'

'I don't know, I really don't. He's still married, after all. Don't look so ... stricken, Henry. Let's just enjoy getting to know each other properly, eh? Today, I have my first job interview! It was a good idea of yours to place an advertisement in the *Standard* and a pleasant surprise when I received such a prompt reply! I'll meet you afterwards at lunchtime, outside the bank, as we arranged.'

Twenty-Four

Bloomsbury. The little May knew about the area came from occasional articles in the press about the colony of artists and writers who'd lived there at the turn of the century. They were known as the Bloomsbury group and were freethinkers. Denzil's father, she recalled, had been a painter of nudes; she smiled at the thought of her blushes at the mention of this. When Denzil married, and his new wife embarked on the restoration of the old manor house, his mother soon decided to leave. There were rumours that she had re-married, but she never returned to Kettle Row.

Mary's prospective employer was a potter of some repute, who had signed her letter with her first name, *Tatiana*. She certainly didn't live in a garret, but in a mews house with an attached studio. The surviving members of the Blooms-bury group, now middle-aged or elderly but still unconventional, mostly lived, it seemed, in rural isolation and decorated old houses with colourful murals.

May skirted a large, leafy plant in a pot and a bottle of milk on the doorstep. A newspaper pro-truded from the letter box. Her appointment was for 11 a.m.; was Tatiana a late riser?

Even as she hesitated before giving a second pull of the bell, the studio door opened and a petite lady, less than five feet tall, emerged. She

179

wore a creased, faded blue smock with smears of clay and paint. The hand she held out in greeting was bony and blue-veined, but her grip was strong.

'I do apologize, I lost count of the minutes ticking by. You must call me Tatiana; my other name, which you may have deduced is Russian, is unpronounceable, so I'm often told. And you are May, which is easy to say. Let's go in to the house and we will talk and take a glass of tea.'

The drawing room was so crowded with ornaments of varying sizes that May had to wend her way between tables and cabinets to sit in an upright chair with an embroidered tapestry seat.

The tea kettle on the spirit stove on a low table was brought to the boil and tea, without milk or sugar but with a slice of lemon, was indeed served in glass cups held in elegant metalwork containers with handles.

'My parents brought these with them, not much else, when they left Russia during the revolution. I was already here, studying in London, living with my godmother. She inspired me to become an artist; this house and studio I inherited from her. Like Olga, I didn't marry. Your good health!' Tatiana raised her glass.

Bemused, May looked at her over the rim of her glass. Tatiana, she surmised, was probably in her early forties. With those high cheekbones, almost almond-shaped dark eyes under arched eyebrows, the sleek, improbably black hair severely restrained by a wide band, no-one would take her for an Englishwoman.

'You like what you see?' Tatiana asked in amusement. 'Well, so do I; despite your name I think you are also an exotic flower.' This was said without irony.

'I am half-Spanish, yes. Would you like to see my references? Certificates?'

'If you wish. Your personality is of more interest to me than your qualifications. This is not just a secretarial job which I offer; I need someone who will look after the business matters, but also assist me generally.'

'In the pottery, do you mean?'

'Your interests include the artistic, I believe?'

'Well, yes.' Did her expertise with puppets count? May wondered.

'Then I believe we shall suit each other very well. More tea? Then I shall show you my work, and explain everything,' Tatiana said.

There was colour everywhere in the long studio. Shelves of pots and bowls gleamed with gold and silver and jewel colours, like ruby and sapphire. Some of the designs were oriental, others had a religious theme; a section was devoted to ethereal, fairy-tale picture plates.

'You see what it is I strive to do?' Tatiana asked, as May paused by the last section.

'Oh yes,' May whispered in awe.

'You know that this is lustreware?' May nodded. 'It is a very old art form, which has its origins in Persia and Moorish Spain in the thirteenth and fourteenth centuries and spread to Italy in the fifteenth century. It was introduced into Europe by the Dutch traders who brought it from the Orient. I expect you are aware that Spain still produces much lustreware?'

'I've never been to my mother's country,' May admitted, 'but I can remember a lovely bowl which she kept on her dressing-table. My sister and I were not allowed to touch it. I – I don't know what happened to it, after she left, when I was twelve.'

'We will not discuss our past history today, I think. You would like to know more of the process involved in the making of lustre? To put it simply, I use the original reduction-firing method. Clay is combined with silver and copper salts and then the design is painted on the surface of a plain glazed pot. It is fired again but without oxygen this time and the fine layer of colour mingles with the glaze. Like the rainbow produced by oil spilled on water, you have this iridescence.' She gestured expressively with her hands.

'Are there many other lustreware makers in this country?'

'We have grown in number since the Arts and Crafts Movement, but it remains a specialist process. You would like to be involved? I don't mean with the manufacture of my pieces, but with the cataloguing, the exhibitions from time to time, and the selling to my clients?'

'I would like that very much indeed.'

'Well, let's go back in the house and discuss the formalities, and shake hands,' said Tatiana.

'This is very good news: your first interview, and a successful outcome,' Henry said warmly. They were sitting in a small café round the corner from the bank. He had ordered coffee and a sandwich for himself, and a Bath bun and a glass of lemonade for May, at her request. She was too excited to want more. 'I'll make us a special dinner tonight,' she promised. 'Cottage pie, your favourite.'

'Just one thing: won't you stay on with me at Wimbledon? It seems to me we have a mutually agreeable arrangement.'

'I've been thinking – why not? But you must let me pay my share of expenses.'

'When you receive your first pay envelope, I'll hold out my hand!'

'Oh, I *do* like you, Henry!'

'Good. Then that's settled.'

Bea was stretched out on the sofa in the hotel bedroom, with her head in Danny's lap, while he idly stroked her hair. 'Your roots need a touch of peroxide,' he said.

'Would you prefer me as I was – plain, mousy Jane?' she joked.

'Don't talk nonsense. You are you – and I love you as you are.'

'Do you mean that?' she demanded.

'Of course I do. And don't argue that I'm too young to know my own mind; age doesn't come into it. If our ages were reversed, would that make any difference? Of course it wouldn't. My brother was married and a father at my age.'

'But Danny, that didn't last, did it?'

'They weren't right for each other, but you couldn't tell him that when he was nineteen. And he wouldn't be without little Cluny. How do you feel about me? That's what I need to know.'

'Right now, I don't want to say goodnight, I

183

don't want you to go.'

'You didn't answer my question.'

'It might take me all night to do that. I've been struggling with my feelings ever since we met. It's my upbringing, I suppose, even though my parents are never judgemental.' She sat up, swung her feet to the ground. 'I love you Danny.'

'I won't let you down,' he promised solemnly. 'Ever.'

Their letters crossed in the post. Bea wrote to her best friend:

Dear May,

I'm not sure you will approve, but you could say that I have thrown caution to the winds! Danny and I are now a couple. Yes, we have anticipated marriage, and are blissfully happy, but we will tie the knot when we are ready... You can confide in Henry, though I guess he may be shocked, but I would rather tell our parents myself after they have met Danny, which should be soon, after Selina's baby arrives and we all get together for the baptism!

Hope the job-hunting proves successful. Our new show is going well – I must admit I am jealous when the leading man gets the girl in the final scene, and it ain't me! We may even get to a London stage, you never know.

Much love from Bea.

Henry regarded May across the breakfast table. 'Any message for me?'

'I'm not sure.'

'What d'you mean?' He grinned, to show he

didn't mind too much.

'Bea and Danny, well...'

'They are engaged?' he suggested.

'Not exactly.' May floundered.

'Ah...' he said. He folded the newspaper. 'Well, you don't want to be late on your first day. We'll leave the dishes to soak. I'll get the car – you powder your nose.'

'Oh, I thought we were catching the train.'

'Not today, I shall deliver you to the door.'

'Thanks, Henry.'

He turned at the door, 'I suppose you think I am seething with disapproval? The fact is, I wish it could be like that for us. See you in ten minutes!'

She thought about what Henry had said as she combed her hair and checked the contents of her bag. She didn't want to follow in her mother's footsteps, but she was aware that the passionate side of her nature, long suppressed, was ripe for release. But was Henry the one to help her shed her inhibitions? She came to a decision: she would reply to Paddy's letter; she'd do it this evening after work.

Dear Paddy

It was a nice surprise to hear from you after all this time. What a lot of changes in both our lives. I recognized Danny immediately despite the years between, I wonder if it would be like that if you and I were ever to meet again? We have a lot of catching up to do! Mr Punch and Co. are tucked away inside the old trunk, and I haven't been back to West Wick for more than ten years. As for flamenco, I gave that up, too.

185

I am about to start a new job as Assistant and Secretary to a Russian potter who makes the most beautiful lustreware. I am fortunate to have somewhere nice to stay here in Raynes Park, with a friend, Henry, from Kettle Row. His sister Bea is in the same theatre company as Danny, Pom is at Cambridge, but she hasn't swum the Channel yet!

Please remember me to your parents, I have never forgotten how kind they were to two young girls on their own. I am sorry your marriage didn't work out, but glad you have your daughter with you. She must be very special to Brigid and Brendan. I am afraid Pom and I rarely hear from our mother, Carmen, who is still in Spain.

I hope we can meet up again, in the future.

Yours, Young May Moon.

'Paddy,' Brigid reminded him as he sat there, letter in hand, thinking about his first love, 'Cluny is waiting for you to take her to school.'

'Sorry, Mum. I didn't expect to hear from May, although of course I hoped I would. But was I right to contact her at all?'

'Dear boy, you acted on impulse. It's not always a bad thing, you know. Your divorce is going through; it's good to remember happier times. May's not married?'

He shook his head. 'No. But she's living with Danny's girlfriend's brother Henry. That's how she and Danny met again, through Bea.'

'Don't jump to conclusions, and hurry up, Cluny hates to be late for school.'

Twenty-Five

Pomona was home for the Christmas vacation. She was thinking: home is where May is, so it's Raynes Park now. We'll join the Wrights in Kettle Row on Christmas Day, but it won't be the same as it was in the old days, with Min and Grandpa, and earlier than that, Jim and Carmen ... and Mr Punch.

'I'm looking forward to seeing Terence,' she informed Henry as he assembled their suitcases in the hall on the morning of Christmas Eve, prior to driving to Suffolk. 'We haven't met since we both went to Cambridge; he's probably forgotten I exist.'

'I shouldn't think that's possible,' Henry said mildly. Pom had breezed in on the previous Saturday, leaving her sister to pay for the taxi she had taken from the station, and surprised him with a hug and a warm kiss on the lips. 'That's for being so nice to May and now me,' she said.

'My pleasure.' The cheeky little girl was now an attractive young woman.

'I wish you'd kept your motorbike and I could ride pillion! I was so-o jealous of May, because she had that privilege.'

Henry grinned. *You* would have been far too distracting, I think. We'd have probably ended up in a ditch. Anyway, I can picture you tearing round the countryside on a bike yourself, one

187

day – as modern girls do.'

Now, she took the opportunity to put a pertinent question to him while May was in their bedroom, tidying up before they left. 'When are you going to make an honest woman of my sister, Henry?'

He was genuinely shocked. 'There's nothing going on between us, Pomona, I assure you.'

'Though you wish there was?' she dared to ask.

He was spared the need to answer when May appeared with a final bag.

'Take care with that – fragile! It's a present for your parents.'

The telephone rang as they were about to leave. Henry was already loading the car, so Pomona, who was bringing up the rear, called, 'I'll answer it!' When she didn't reappear for several minutes May went to find out why she was delayed.

Pomona replaced the receiver, her cheeks flushed with excitement. 'That was Mum, ringing from Spain, believe it or not! She wished us both a happy Christmas.'

'Did she sound all right?' May enquired anxiously.

'Well, yes and no ... she said to come and visit her in the spring, if we can before civil war breaks out–'

'*Civil war?* Oh dear! Is she safe where she is?'

'She says so. Perhaps if we did go, we could persuade her to return to England with us?'

Henry was honking the horn. They looked at each other. 'Don't let's talk about it now.' May closed the front door firmly behind them.

The Wrights were accustomed to having their festive dinner in the evening. After attending midnight mass on Christmas Eve and hurrying back in a flurry of snowflakes to the rectory as the bells rang out the joyous peal for Christmas Day, they needed a few hours' sleep before they trooped off to church for the morning service. The visitors were excused this.

'We open our presents round the tree in the drawing room after a light lunch – there should be a good fire going by then. Then it's all hands in the kitchen!' Mrs Wright informed May and Pomona.

May thought it would have been perfect if Bea were here, too. However, Bea and Danny were spending Christmas with his family. 'Wish me luck,' Bea said when they spoke on the telephone.

'You'll love Danny's family,' May promised, 'and they'll love you!'

Tired after the journey and busy evening, both May and Pomona slept through the family's preparations for the morning service. Henry woke them with tea and biscuits and a cheerful, 'Merry Christmas.'

'Pass me my stocking please,' Pom yawned, sitting up in bed. She nudged her sister. 'Don't you want to look at yours, too, May? Thanks, Henry, I presume this was your idea? Sit down next to me,' she invited, patting the side of the bed.

He unhooked the long woollen socks from the bedpost. 'I planned to wear these in bed,' he joked. 'It's so much colder here. I'm glad you appreciate the sacrifice. I knew you were used to

189

opening your gifts in the morning, but we always save ours for after lunch.'

'I must drink my tea first,' May sipped the hot liquid, warming both hands round the cup. 'Then I might be able to open my eyes properly and see what's what.'

'Oh!' Pomona squealed. 'A pencil with a rubber on the end. Very useful – but the Fry's chocolate cream goes better with the tea!'

Henry smiled at them. No seductive night-dresses, he thought, with tantalizing glimpses of bare flesh. Both girls were clad in flannel pyjamas, wisely provided by his mother, for this was a large, draughty house. He'd hoped for a closer relationship with May after the occasion when he'd revealed his true feelings. He wouldn't have needed much encouragement to take things further, but it hadn't been forthcoming.

May observed how relaxed he was in Pomona's company. She realized, with a start, that Pom was flirting with him. Actually, she thought, they have more in common than he and I do, being clever old sticks.

'I presume,' Pom was saying, 'you didn't win the pig in the Co-op draw? May told me about the piglet in the straw in the pen outside the shop. He would hardly have made much of a Christmas dinner.'

'I thought you were the animal lover,' May put in. 'If I'd won with my sixpenny ticket I'd have kept him as a pet.'

'Would you indeed!' Henry grinned. 'I'd have raffled him again for the church organ fund.'

'You wouldn't!' May cried.

190

'No, of course not. I don't think he was the actual prize, I guess that was a joint from the butcher's.'

'Oh, I *have* got a pig! Look, May, a sugar one with silver-ball eyes and a curly string tail. I shan't eat him either,' Pomona said. 'I shall keep him for luck. Thanks, Henry. Let me give you a kiss for Christmas!'

'No need for that ... I enjoyed finding the little novelties.' He cleared his throat. 'Well, I must join the others in church. Selina is responsible for breakfast this morning. I'll see you later.'

When he had gone, Pomona asked May: 'Did I make you feel jealous?'

'I don't know what you mean.'

'Yes, you do. But I think you need reminding now and again that you can't do much better than old Henry.'

'Sometimes you are really annoying, Pom. I am aware that he's a thoroughly decent chap, but...'

'I know. I'm sorry I teased you. Does this mean you wouldn't mind if I...?'

'Of course not, but I would hate to see him hurt. Henry has been a wonderful friend to me.'

'And now me,' Pomona stated firmly. 'Terence is a callow youth, in comparison. Anyway, he couldn't stop talking last night about that girl he works with. The only thing we had in common, now I think about it, is the pair of tights we wore, in turn, in *Cinderella*.'

'They didn't find a place in my memory box.'

'Unlike the flamenco dress. Did you bring it, to wear today?'

'Certainly not. As Henry said, it's very chilly

191

here. I feel like staying in pyjamas and dressing gown all day, and hugging the fire!'

'Boiled eggs,' Selina said, tapping the tops of the eggs with the spoon, after placing them in the pink china eggcups. 'Toast – or bread and butter? Excuse me if I sit down, my back plays up if I'm on my feet too long.'

'Not surprising, with all that extra weight,' Pomona grinned. 'Are you sure it's only one baby?'

Selina wasn't offended. 'My dear little brother remarked on my girth, too.' She appeared to have shed her shyness with her pregnancy, and patted her enlarged front complacently. 'But I'm very grateful for my dad's old nightshirts! Mum never throws anything away, fortunately.'

'Where is Terence?' Pom enquired, dipping her spoon into the egg. 'Just right, Selina, thanks ... I do like a runny yolk.'

'Oh, he was actually up early and went to church with the others.'

'When is the baby due?' May asked.

'I've a few weeks to go yet,' Selina said cheerfully. 'There are compensations: I've been told I can take the rest of the day off and put my feet up, while the rest of you peel buckets of potatoes and do endless sprouts. I just have to ensure the pudding is simmering for hours and hours.'

'Pudding patrol!' Pomona said, tongue in cheek.

Bea had spent the night in a single bed alongside little Cluny's. Brigid was aware that Danny and Bea were a couple, but, as she said to Pomona, when she ushered her into the small bedroom, 'Cluny is full of questions – she's not old enough yet to hear all the answers.'

However, at the crack of dawn, the child scrambled out of her bed, dragging her heavy pillowcase along the floor to the door.

'Where are you off to?' Bea asked sleepily, but of course she guessed. She clicked on the lamp on the table between the beds. 'Now you can see where you're going.' What a beautiful child, she thought, with dark hair like her father: a cherub in a plain white cotton nightshirt.

'To wake Nanna and Grandad, and they'll knock on the wall to Daddy – then I'll get in the middle of the bed and Daddy will get in at the bottom of the bed and Grandad will say, "Why have you got such big feet?" Daddy, not me, of course. Then I'll show them all my presents.'

'Sounds fun! I'll see you later, then,' Bea turned, plumped up her pillow. 'Happy Christmas,' she said belatedly, but Cluny was already out of the door.

Five minutes later a whisper in her ear startled her. 'Make room for me.'

'Danny?'

'Now, who else would it be. I missed you last night.'

'I missed you, too.'

'Will you marry me, Bea?'

'You know I will, but not yet. You're too young to be tied down Danny, you might change your mind.'

'I won't. I'm not Paddy. He should have married his first love.'

'Am I your first love?'

'Almost,' he admitted. 'But the only one I've slept with. How about you?'

'You know the answer to that – and I'm glad you were the first for me. Shall we open our presents now, or seize the moment?'

Danny reached out and switched off the bedside lamp.

'Did anyone see you come in here?' she asked anxiously.

'Only Paddy, and he won't say anything.' He drew her close. 'Come on, Bea, relax – even if we're caught out, it'll be worth it, I promise.'

Later in the day, with the good cooking smells wafting from the kitchen, the vegetable brigade put down their peelers, and peeped in the dining room en route to the drawing room. Selina had laid the table with the best silver and there were folded hand-embroidered napkins by each setting. But it was time to gather round the tree, dug up each year from the garden. This year it was a rather weedy specimen garlanded with old and much-loved decorations. Henry set a big log to burn and remarked: 'Worth all the blisters on my hands, sawing the wood, while my little brother was busy cracking walnuts.'

'You'd better watch what you say to me – I'm bigger than you now,' Terence said cheerfully.

'I hope you haven't eaten all the nuts, that's all.'

Osmund took the first present from the pile round the tree. 'For you, Henry – stop the banter, you two.'

There was a general burst of laughter when the

194

wrappings were removed. '*Nutcrackers* – with Mr Punch's head,' Henry said ruefully. 'Thanks, May!'

The mystery parcel, well-wrapped, was for Emma and Osmund Wright. A beautiful, shining bowl in blue and silver was revealed. 'Oh, did your Tatiana make this? Thank you so much.' May received a hug and a kiss.

There were more kisses under the mistletoe that Terence had fixed over the door to surprise the girls in turn, when they joined the family in the warmest room in the house. Henry ignored such frivolity, but wore his paper crown from a cracker; Pomona caught him out eventually with a cry of, 'Got you!' May, like Henry, tried to steer clear of the sticky white berries.

She unwrapped his gift, relieved to find a warm, fluffy scarf and not something more personal. 'Just what I need in London, to keep out the fog.'

'I thought of buying you a necklace, but I know you are not one for jewellery, apart from the amber pendant you always wear. That is obviously very special, eh?'

May said, before Pomona could reveal her secret, 'Yes, it is.'

Emma nudged her husband, 'Next present please – you're neglecting your duties!'

The room was awash with discarded bright wrapping paper by the time it was time to adjourn to the dining room for the splendid Christmas dinner.

195

Twenty-Six

January, 1936.

King George and Queen Mary also spent Christmas in East Anglia, at Sandringham, in Norfolk. From there the King made what was to be his final broadcast to the nation. In the middle of January, the newspapers reported that his Majesty was suffering from a feverish cold, which did not cause undue concern. However, his condition rapidly worsened, and a few days later a bulletin revealed that 'The King shows diminishing strength.' The silent vigils began; crowds gathered outside Buckingham Palace. At 9.25 p.m. the news came: 'The King's life is moving peacefully towards its close.' Just after midnight, a lone figure crossed the courtyard and replaced the notice on the railings...

London was now a city of mourning. Great Tom, the bell in St Paul's, boomed solemnly. City workers flocked to a memorial service at midday in the cathedral. In the Tower of London and in Hyde Park there were gun salutes, marking the seventy years of the sovereign's life. Flags were at half-mast, but were soon to be raised when heralds proclaimed the accession of King Edward the Eighth.

'They say the new King ordered the clocks to be put back at dawn,' May told Tatiana, as they sat at the long table in the studio, working together on the catalogue for the New Year exhibition, which had been postponed because of the royal funeral.

'Sandringham time, isn't that what they called it? That was the decree of his grandfather, I'm told.'

'The new King is very different from his father,' May observed.

'He is a man of the times, as King Edward was before him. George the Fifth returned to Victorian values. Royalty here is still revered, unlike in my native country. Well, we appear to have accomplished our list. Will you dispatch this, with the photographs, to the printer please?' Tatiana paused: 'Have you a suitable outfit to wear for our big occasion? Please do not be offended, but I will be happy to supply one for you, if you wish.'

'And I am happy to accept your kind offer!' May replied.

'Have you decided when to take your holiday?'

'It really depends on my sister – at the end of this term, I hope. Pomona wants us to visit my mother in Spain. I'm not sure...' May hesitated.

'You are not sure if you can afford this trip? Look, you could, if I give you a business commission, eh? I have a contact there, as you know. Another designer has asked if I would like to display some of her new designs with mine, in the studio, to our mutual benefit. You have a good eye, I would trust you to choose these and arrange their transport. Would that help?'

'Oh, Tatiana, of course it would! Thank you.' Before the holiday, she thought, there is someone else I want so much to see...

'Would you like to invite a friend to come to the preview?' Tatiana asked. 'Perhaps the kind Henry?' They had met, and he had her approval.

'Henry – I'm sure he would be delighted. Tatiana, I should perhaps make it clear; we live together, yes, but he is just a friend.'

'He would, I suspect, like to be more than that?'

'Yes. Perhaps, one day, I will have to settle for affection, rather than romance.'

'I was influenced by my godmother, Olga. She never cared to marry, but she was successful and happy with her single state. But, you, my dear May, I think would like to have a husband and children? This never appealed to me! Have you met the right man yet?'

'I met him years ago, when we were both too young.'

'Is it too late now?'

'It could be, but I am trying to get up the courage to find out.'

Visitors to the West End Gallery were greeted by a young woman wearing a simple silk shift in brilliant peacock blue, sleeveless, but fastened at the shoulders with sparkling diamante clasps. She had been attracted by the vibrant colour; it reminded of her flamenco dress, although the material of that had faded to a softer blue. Her shining dark hair hung long and loose around her shoulders. There was a soft bloom to her complexion, although the only make-up she wore was lip gloss. Earlier, when she regarded herself earnestly in the cheval mirror, in Tatiana's house, she had been startled at the resemblance to her mother,Carmen. I can't deny my heritage, she thought, and now I don't mind looking more Spanish than English.

'You are the most beautiful object here,' a voice said in her ear.

'Henry! You look very smart, too. Have a programme.'

'I can't afford to buy anything, but it is a dazzling display. You will be away for the weekend; I shall miss you. You and Tatiana will have a lot to discuss, after all the excitement is over.'

He is assuming I'll be with Tatiana for the next two days, she thought. 'Enjoy the exhibition,' she said. 'I'll be with you later.' She turned to a group who had just entered the gallery. 'Tatiana is expecting you, please join her and enjoy a glass of wine...'

Tatiana, a diminutive figure in gold lamé, with her hair in a topknot to add an illusion of height, was at the centre of an admiring circle and her voice could be heard, loud and clear. She gestured with expressive hands, the rings on her fingers flashing under the bright lights. The lustre jugs, plates and bowls were displayed on tall, white-painted stands all around the gallery.

May was learning to distinguish between the serious buyers, mostly older men, who examined the items for sale intently, and made notes in small books with silver-encased fountain pens, before moving on, and the press, in more casual attire with rakishly Windsor-knotted ties, who commented cheerfully and scribbled shorthand symbols in larger lined pads. There were society ladies, even a well-known film actor with an immaculate sweep of blue-rinsed white hair, which May suspected was an expensive wig. She smiled to herself, thinking how Pomona would have enjoyed meeting him!

She whirled round when someone unexpectedly touched her bare upper arm.

'May – I didn't mean to startle you. I knew it must be you.'

He was not instantly as recognizable as Danny had been, with his red hair. Danny was still boyish; this was a man who was inches taller than she recalled him, with broad shoulders and close-cropped black hair, but the blue eyes were unmistakable. His suit was well-worn but he obviously cared about his appearance, with his clean white shirt and polished shoes. The hand which shook hers was calloused as a result of his work.

'Paddy! I know I told you in my letter that I would be working in the gallery this evening, but I didn't expect you to come *here!*'

'I couldn't wait any longer,' he said simply. 'I rang your employer before you left – she told me she would speak to the doorman and I would be allowed in without a ticket.'

'She didn't say!' She recalled Tatiana going to answer the phone, while she was occupied with changing into her new outfit.

'I asked her to let it be a surprise. I borrowed Dad's old car.'

'Where are you staying tonight? I was catching the train first thing tomorrow and expected you to meet me then.'

'I hope you'll agree to me driving you to my home later tonight.'

'But Tatiana...?'

'She said it would be your decision; she didn't mind at all.'

A polite cough alerted May to the fact that there were guests awaiting her attention. She also became aware that Henry was standing near by. Had he heard their conversation? She beckoned him over.

'Henry, this is an old friend of mine, Paddy. He ... he is Danny's brother. Paddy, meet Henry. Please excuse me, while I talk to these gentlemen.' *Bring your bag with you,* Tatiana had said casually before the taxi arrived to transport them to the gallery. Now May understood why.

By 9 p.m. the guests had departed. The gallery staff in their white coats and gloves were carefully packing the exhibits into crates. These would be delivered to the studio the following morning. Wine glasses were rinsed, dried, and replaced in cupboards. The cleaners were waiting with their brooms.

'I would help, but it seems there is nothing for me to do.' Henry thanked Tatiana for a lovely evening, shook Paddy's hand and said it had been good to have his company. Then May walked with him to the door. Outside, it was moonlight, and the night air was chilly. She shivered. 'You need a wrap,' Henry said, concerned.

She gave him a hug. 'Thank you for coming, Henry – and for not asking questions. I don't have any answers, yet.'

'We got on well, he and I. All I want is your

happiness, May. Good luck.'

'I do love you, Henry,' she said impulsively.

'I know you do, but not in that way. You're not leaving me yet?'

'Of course not! I won't just walk out of your life, I promise.'

'See you on Monday, then. Go back inside, or you'll catch cold.'

Paddy held out her coat for her to slip her arms into the sleeves. She saw him looking at the pendant, nestling in the hollow of her throat. 'You are still wearing it, after all these years,' he said in wonderment.

'I haven't taken it off, since you gave it to me.' May buttoned her coat to the neck, hiding the necklace from his gaze, which she found disturbing.

'Go now, May – you must be very tired,' Tatiana said.

'I can sleep in the car. How long will the journey take us?' she asked Paddy.

'About three hours. The car doesn't have the speed of modern motors.'

'I hope Brigid doesn't wait up.'

'Don't worry about that,' was his enigmatic answer.

He tucked a rug round her knees in the passenger seat. It took a few minutes to warm up the engine, but when it throbbed into life, they drove through London at night, where the lights from theatres, restaurants and shop windows dazzled May's eyes. She soon closed them, and settled back to nap.

When she awoke she was suddenly aware that

they were in the country, that they had stopped outside a village inn.

'Another Swan, but in Buckinghamshire,' Paddy said. 'I need more petrol, and the garage will be closed. We'll have to stay overnight, and leave early in the morning. I can phone my mother from here.'

'I have some money, if you need it,' she said quickly.

'Thank you. I hope I have enough, but I'm not sure. I should have checked there was petrol in the can–'

'But you left in too much of a hurry.'

'Yes. I'm sorry. Well, I hope we are not too late to book in.'

'We can only offer a family room,' the elderly man behind the desk told them. 'A double at one end, and a child's bed, in the alcove. Would that be all right for you and your sister?'

Paddy didn't correct the assumption. He gave May's hand a reassuring squeeze. 'Thank you. Is there any chance of something to eat? I appreciate it is late.'

'My wife does the cooking, she's already abed. I can knock up some ham sandwiches and a pot o' tea. Will that suffice?'

May nodded, not trusting herself to speak.

They were given the keys to the room. 'Top o' the stairs. Beds are made up. Bathroom next door – no hot water until tomorrow, now.'

Paddy carried May's bag upstairs. 'I didn't bring one – I thought I would be home tonight. I'll go back down and use the phone and collect the supper, while you get ready for bed. Take the

203

double, of course, the other will be fine for me, remember I slept in the barn on the straw at West Wick.'

She smiled then. 'You've grown since then!'

When he returned she was sitting on the blanket box. 'Oh,' he said, 'I thought you'd be in bed by now.'

'I don't like crumbs in the bed – Pomona was a pickle in that respect! Also, I think I should take the little bed; your feet would stick out at the end.'

'We'll see. Have a sandwich. Hope the bread isn't too dry, but the ham looks good. I suggested mugs of tea rather than a pot.'

'Thanks. I need the tea more than the food.' She sipped at it gratefully.

'I'll be in the bathroom while you undress,' he said, as she opened her overnight bag.

When he returned, with a towel tucked around his waist, she was still struggling to release the diamante clips on her dress. 'I didn't realize they'd be difficult – Tatiana fastened them for me...'

'May I?' Paddy moved closer and examined the clasps. He removed one and then the other. The silky material slipped from her shoulders, drooping in a loose fold round her hips. 'I'm sorry, I didn't intend...' he said, as she quickly folded her arms across her bare top.

'I know you didn't,' she returned. 'Tatiana said the dress was too slinky to wear anything underneath, that I didn't need it...' She was floundering now.

'She was right: you are petite, but you have a very womanly shape,' he said, without a trace of embarrassment.

'Would you turn your back while I make myself decent, please?'

'May – it's been so long, but I knew the moment I saw you that we must go on from where we left off, though I honestly didn't plan this.'

'I believe you,' she whispered. She moved closer. The peacock-blue dress slithered down to the ground. She held on to his arm as she stepped free of the heap of material. 'Don't let's waste any more time,' she said softly, backing towards the big bed.

Twenty-Seven

She woke with a start and realized she was alone. She felt the hollow beside her in the feather mattress: it was still warm. He couldn't have been gone long. He'd tucked the covers under her chin. The curtains were not drawn. She couldn't discern the time on her watch.

A torch flickered on her face. 'I didn't turn the light on, May, I didn't want to disturb you. I borrowed your dressing-gown, I hope you don't mind.' He tugged the sleeves to cover his forearms. 'It's a chilly morning.'

She caught a glimpse of the blue dress neatly folded on the bed rail. He'd retrieved it from the floor. 'I don't mind, Paddy, but you look comical; it's not much of a cover-up! What time is it? Have I overslept?'

'No. It's not seven yet, breakfast at eight. You

don't have to get up immediately. May.' He hesitated, then: 'Last night – will you forgive me? I assure you, I didn't intend it to happen.'

She sat up, clutching the sheet to her. 'You don't need to apologize because I was the one who – who couldn't help myself. I thought you felt the same way! We both said we wanted to carry on where we left off, all those years ago.' Tears welled in her eyes and spilled down her cheeks. She dabbed them with the sheet.

'It wouldn't have happened then,' he said softly. 'We hadn't reached that point. No, I should have been the responsible one, being experienced in these things, unlike you.'

'Please don't say you made love to me reluctantly.' She was sobbing now.

He reached across and stroked her hair. 'Of course I didn't. I always hoped we'd meet again, that our reunion would be joyful, and we'd live happily ever after. I'm free to marry again, but I have an uncertain future, no home of my own, and a small daughter.'

'I'd support you with all my heart. I'm not afraid of hard work.'

'You've made sacrifices already – looked after your sister since you were a child yourself. It wouldn't be fair. You've a job now which you really enjoy, the chance to have an easier life; it wouldn't be like that with me. And what about Henry? He can offer you more than I could.'

'Henry will always be a dear friend, but...'

'Move over,' he said softly. 'We'll have to restrain ourselves for the rest of the weekend. After all...'

'You still use the same toothpaste,' she murmured as his lips sought hers. It was the last thing she said for some time.

Brigid guessed, of course, as soon as she saw them walking up the front path together, hand in hand, like young lovers. She held out her arms in welcome to May.

'It's been so long, far too long, but here you are at last!'

Cluny was tugging at her grandma's skirt. 'And here's our little Cluny, who's looking forward to meeting you – I told her all about the Punch and Judy lady! We saw old Punch strutting and cracking his stick, didn't we, Cluny? At the village fête last summer.'

Cluny's thumb went into her mouth as she regarded May gravely. She nodded her head, stubby braids bouncing on her shoulders. May smiled at her. 'I hope he didn't frighten you. Don't worry, *my* Mr Punch is retired now.'

'What's retired?' the child asked.

'It means he doesn't work any more, and nor do I. Not with the Punch and Judy show, anyhow.'

'Why don't you take May into the barn to show her what you've got there?' Brigid suggested. 'Tell Grandpa to join us in the kitchen: I've asked Brendan to put the kettle on. Paddy will take your bag upstairs,' she added to May.

May followed Cluny along the brick path to the nearby barn. She glanced back at the modest stone-built cottage, thinking it must have been a two-up, two-down originally, but a recent extension had been added to one side. It was a cold day, and she was glad she'd packed warm clothes and stout shoes to wear over the weekend, but she would have liked to go indoors to relax in the warm.

The barn was draughty, but an oil stove in a corner provided a little comfort. Stout wooden benches ran the length of the side walls, and the wood-shavings on the floor, and the tools, were signs that this was a workshop.

Paddy's grandpa was nothing like May's beloved old relative. Grandpa John was tall, broad-shouldered, with a mop of iron-grey hair, a ruddy face and blue eyes like his grandson. He could have been taken for a man in his sixties, but May was aware that he was nearer eighty. He hadn't lost his Irish accent.

'Young May Moon, I presume? I'm very pleased to meet you. Well, Cluny, you've come to check your little lad is still here, eh?'

Cluny ran straight over to a box beside the stove. 'Look, May. Come and see what Daddy brought home from the market last week! He hasn't got a name yet, because Daddy said *you* would know what to call him.' She lifted up a warm, wriggling pup from the blanket.

'Toby,' May said immediately. 'Little dog Toby.'

'Daddy says he's a Jack Russell. That's smaller than a fox terrier, and your Toby was hairy and he's smooth-coated, but will he do?'

'He will indeed,' May said huskily.

Grandpa winked at her. 'You can tell this young lady how to train him, I reckon. Pup stays out here with me and Paddy during the day, because

208

he still makes puddles in the kitchen.'

'What happened to Bertie?' May asked, as the pup was transferred to her arms. She cuddled him up. His markings were very similar to his namesake: black smudges round the eyes, which made them appear larger, and brown ear-flaps. She'd wondered if Bertie would still be around, a reminder of his mother, her old dog.

'He chased a rabbit out of the cabbage patch, he was ten years old and he–'

'Flopped down and went to sleep for ever,' Cluny said earnestly. 'Grandpa John said it was a good way to go. In action. That's what *he* hopes to do.'

'Not yet, I don't,' said Grandpa. 'Did Brigid mention a cup of tea?'

'Yes, come on. We'll take Toby, and I'll make sure he performs by the holly bush, so he doesn't puddle the kitchen floor!'

Brendan actually looked more careworn than his father, but he put aside the schoolbooks he was marking at the kitchen table, and rose to greet May. Paddy appeared then and slipped an arm casually round her shoulders, as he asked his father: 'Well, Dad, she hasn't changed much, has she?'

Brendan's eyes twinkled like his father's. 'I think you'll discover she has, my lad. You've both grown up since you last met, you know.'

'That's true,' Paddy admitted.

'Sit down and drink your tea,' Brigid said. 'Cluny, offer our guest a piece of my walnut cake.'

'If you don't like nuts, pick those out and give them to me,' Cluny said with a giggle.

'You sound just like my sister Pom at your age.'

'Pom – Grandma told me that was short for Pomona. She said most people called you Young May Moon. Why is that?'

'Stop the inquisition!' Brigid mock-scolded her granddaughter.

'Inqui – what's that?'

'Don't be so inquisitive,' Brendan put in. 'And you know the meaning of that!'

'Cluny's taken to you, that's good,' Paddy told May when he escorted her upstairs to the room she was sharing with his daughter. 'This is where your friend slept at Christmas.' He gave a wry grin. 'Danny was in my room. So you see

'Yes. Until yesterday I would have been in complete agreement with Brigid! Don't say anything yet, Paddy, please.'

'I won't. Perhaps this is a good time to tell you about my marriage, while we've a few minutes on our own. I intended to put you in the picture as we drove here, but you obviously needed a nap, after all the excitement.'

'I know you married very young, and that it didn't work out.'

'Janey was eighteen, I was twenty. She was a popular girl, loved dancing, and I caught her on the rebound from a broken engagement. The chap concerned was a merchant seaman, and she was not prepared to wait for him while he was away on a long voyage. We'd only been going out together for a matter of weeks when she told me she was pregnant. Our parents insisted that I should do the honourable thing and marry her immediately. I was making a name for myself

210

with my work, and at first all seemed well. I soon discovered she had a very quick temper, and it was then that the rows started. She didn't want to stay at home, or to be a mother. Then came the revelation: she couldn't be sure whether the baby was mine or her former lover's. I was shocked. I confided in my parents, and their advice was "wait and see".'

'Cluny is obviously your daughter!'

'Yes. But Janey didn't change her mind: she was indifferent to the baby, and to me. When Cluny was six months old, and the debts were piling up, Janey packed her bags and left. Our only communication since then has been through solicitors. My parents took us in, and I owe them so much. They love Cluny like the daughter they never had, and I couldn't take her away from them now.'

'*You* can't leave her, either, I understand that,' May stated. 'It might be best – if we don't go – any further, just now. Don't look so worried, I don't regret what happened, but you don't want to rush into another hasty marriage. I didn't tell you, either, that I am planning to visit Spain in April, and to contact my mother. I'm not sure what the outcome of that will be.' She managed to smile. 'Let's enjoy the weekend now, like the good friends I'm sure we'll always be.'

'Thank you, May.'

She moved towards the door. 'Come on then, let's join the family.' My heart is breaking, yet again, she thought, but I mustn't let him know that. The only person I can confide in is my dear friend Bea.

Twenty-Eight

April, 1936.

May planned to travel to Spain by train and boat on the Tuesday after the Easter bank holiday. Pomona had returned for the break to Henry's house, the place she too now thought of as home. She'd decided that her studies must come first and that she wouldn't be able to accompany May. She said: 'Henry will be a great help with any problems – after all, he did the same course and *he* ended up with a First.'

'You mustn't expect too much of him,' May reminded her, 'after a long day at the bank.'

'He doesn't mind, do you, Henry? Can you hear me behind that newspaper?' They were lingering at the breakfast table over a fresh pot of tea, there being no rush as it was not a working day.

'I can hear you,' Henry replied equably. He folded the paper. 'I'm more concerned about May travelling on her own. More disturbances in Spain. The situation there is nearing flash-point.'

'I'll only be there ten days. Mum has booked rooms for us in Barcelona – she said it would be easier to leave from the city if there should be reason to do so. She is already there. I had to go to Barcelona anyway, to see Tatiana's contact,' May said, more sharply than she intended. She hadn't slept well since her return from Buckinghamshire, and she thought that Henry was no doubt wondering how the visit had gone, as she hadn't said much about it to him. She and Paddy had only exchanged a letter apiece since then; his had enclosed a couple of snapshots of his family, but not himself, as he had taken the pictures. She also felt a trifle piqued, she had to admit, at Pomona's manipulation of Henry. Her sister had always been strong-willed, of course.

As if he knew what she was thinking, Henry said mildly: 'I seem to have exchanged one pair of sisters for another. I'm used to playing the part of the big brother. If that involves tutoring, well, I don't object at all.'

Later, when Henry was not around, Pomona and May exchanged a few sharp words. 'You're jealous because Henry likes having me around – I know he does! *You've* turned him down, and well, I intend to help him get over all that.'

'He's more than twelve years older than you, Pom!'

'That doesn't worry me – it's good to talk to someone on the same intellectual level. I need a steadying influence, now that you've given up your role in that respect!'

'That's true, certainly.' May was hurt at the implication that she was not as clever as her sister, or Henry. She thought, I've always been there for Pom. Maybe it's good I'm about to embark on this journey alone, to prove I can do it. I was confident in the Punch and Judy days; I looked after Pom, but now she doesn't need me any more. She's a young woman with a promising career ahead of her, and I'm only just taking the first steps in that direction. Before that I was glad just to have a job, and not much ambition. Things could easily have gone the other way with Paddy. I should have followed my heart, but what really hurts me is that he gave in so quickly.

Henry saw her off on the boat train. 'Take care of yourself, I shall miss you.' His words seemed to evaporate with the clouds of steam from the engine. He kept a firm hand on her back as she stepped up into the train corridor. The carriage was filling up fast: Henry secured a place for her and lifted her cases to the overhead rack. He held out his hand: 'Be vigilant. I'll look after Pomona, don't worry. Have a good journey.'

'I will. Don't worry, Henry.' On impulse she stretched up and kissed him, disregarding her fellow passengers, four shabbily attired young males, travelling light, who talked openly about embarking on a big adventure, eager to be involved in the distinct possibility of future conflict.

He stood on the platform as the train departed. She was not near enough the window for him to glimpse her waving goodbye. He shouldn't have let her go, he thought, but he was aware that he couldn't have stopped her.

Carmen met her elder daughter from the train almost at her journey's end. May had enjoyed her first experience on the boat, but had found the last part of the journey tedious. After travelling overnight, dozing on and off, and waking stiff-limbed and cramped, May emerged into the sunlight and saw her mother walking towards her. Carmen's hair was greying now, her figure was

214

decidedly thicker, but she was as flamboyant as ever, in a tight red frock with a flower in the lapel of her white jacket.

'Welcome to Spain, to Catalonia, to Barcelona,' Carmen called, as she clicked along the platform in her high heeled shoes. 'Hurry, I have a taxi waiting!'

Even as they hugged, May realized that Carmen was not carrying a handbag. She would obviously have to pay for the taxi, when it would have been cheaper to catch the bus, on to which most of the other train passengers were filing. May struggled with her luggage, as Carmen didn't offer to carry one of the bags, but urged her forward to the taxi rank. 'The hotel is some distance: I will point out some interesting places as we go.'

The taxi driver drove round bends in narrow, often steep roads at reckless speed, and the scenery blurred before May's eyes. The smell of petrol made her feel sick. She was only half-aware of Carmen's commentary: 'See! The Jewish mountain – Montjuic – and the castle! Alas, not a place to visit – there are many dissidents imprisoned there.'

The driver honked his horn loudly at a gathering of angrily gesticulating people, brandishing placards and spilling over into the road as men grappled one with another.

'You see, May, you should not venture out alone. It is not safe, even in the countryside; churches burn, workers strike, miners are in revolt. We have more elections. I am not political. This beautiful city is threatened ...'The taxi screeched to a halt outside a modest hotel. There was a military truck

215

parked outside. A soldier stood beside it, rifle in hand. He stared at them, but said nothing.

'He is not concerned with us,' Carmen told May. 'Pay our driver, he is anxious to depart.'

There were few tourists staying in the hotel, and they had to wait some time before they were attended to at the reception desk. Their accommodation was up two flights of stairs, there was no lift and no-one to carry the luggage. May felt exhausted by the time Carmen inserted the key in the door and announced: 'This is the bedroom; we have to share. That door is to the bathroom. We will have to go out to eat – they don't serve meals here, except for breakfast. You look tired, May. Take off your shoes and rest on the bed. There is a kettle, I will make us coffee.'

'I have some biscuits in my bag,' May said faintly. She hadn't eaten for several hours and it was surely time for lunch, she thought?

May stretched out on the coverlet, which didn't look too clean, but she was past caring. Fortunately she had fastened her hair into a knot in the nape of her neck as it was more practical for travelling, and was not wearing her best clothes.

She awoke to the strong smell of coffee, and this proved too much for her; she gulped and ran barefoot to the bathroom, where she was violently sick in the grubby hand basin. She groped for a towel, after rinsing her face in cold water, aware that Carmen had not bothered to follow her.

'Your coffee is cooling,' Carmen reproved her when she returned. She looked long and hard at her daughter. 'If I did not know you better, May, I would say you must be pregnant.'

216

May subsided into the depths of the one armchair. She'd had her suspicions, of course, but had refused to believe it. How could she have been so foolish?

Seeing the tears stream down her daughter's wan face, Carmen set down her cup, kicked off her own shoes and padded over to the chair. She sank on her knees beside May and rested her face on May's shoulder. With a sigh, she asked: 'You didn't know?'

May shook her head. 'No, but I do now.'

'Not the good Henry, surely?'

'No.'

'You are ashamed?'

'No!' May repeated.

'The man concerned – will he stand by you?'

'I don't propose to tell him. Don't ask me his name. I don't want to trap him into another marriage–'

'He has been married before?' Carmen demanded, eyes flashing.

'Yes, but he is no longer married. Please, no more questions.'

'If I find out, he will be sorry!'

'I'm sorry, Mum, if I have disappointed you–'

'You silly girl! What example have I been to you? It happened to me, you know, I was always impetuous – so was your father. We had to marry because *you* were on the way. We were not suited, as you know; it did not work. Don't look at me like that. You blame me, no doubt, but Jim was a hot-blooded young man.'

'He loved you at the time, I'm sure of that. But you were not compatible.'

'And this man – is it like that for you?' Carmen demanded.

'Oh, Mum, I love him, I probably always will, and he says he feels the same way, but – well, what happened between us – it wasn't the time or place. He would feel obliged to marry me, and I don't want that.'

'What will you do, then?'

'Mum – I was hoping to persuade you anyway – come back with me – help.'

'I will think about it. We will see how we get on, eh, during the next week or so? I have no money, I have not worked for some time. I do not attract the attention of such as Carlos. I can still dance, but I do not look the part. Maybe I can make up for being a bad mama when you were young. Now, tell me, how is my darling Pomona?'

'She sends her love. She is longing to see you before she goes back to University for the summer term.'

Twenty-Nine

Two of the odd assortment of guests at the hotel were Canadians, one of them obviously a news reporter who monopolized the telephone in the foyer. He scribbled in a notebook, tore out the page, folded this and passed it to his companion without comment. These scraps of paper were lit by a match and burned in a large ashtray on the table. The two men exchanged cheerful greetings with those sitting at the breakfast table, drinking coffee and breaking rather stale rolls of bread into pieces to spread with soft sour cheese.

'If they were caught,' Carmen whispered to May, 'they would, without doubt, be arrested. We have to pretend not to see.'

May couldn't face the strong coffee, so Carmen arranged for them to have a pot of tea. 'You should drink it plain, no milk, with a slice of lemon,' she advised her.

'Oh, I'm used to that now, as that's how Tatiana serves it.'

'Eat your roll. I shall dip mine in the tea. I don't advise the cheese – it smells old to me.'

'I'd rather finish off the biscuits,' May said, producing a couple of crumbling ones from her pocket.

'We must visit the shops after you have seen to your business, though I doubt if there is much left on the shelves. Too many strangers in our midst. Nevertheless, there are places I should show you, before...' Carmen glanced around to see if anyone was eavesdropping.

They overheard a conversation themselves. A stout pair of matrons from New York were at the next table. They were studying a tour guide. Their voices were loud, whereas most of the other hotel guests spoke in muted tones, often furtively. May suspected that there was a good reason for this. The first American said: 'We need to get out early if we are to obtain tickets for the Society of Contemporary Music Festival next week. The soloist is Louis Krasner, he is performing Alban Berg's Violin Concerto – it is the world premiere!'

'I can't wait... We also ought to visit the La Sagrada Familia church, designed by Antoni Gaudi; the guide says it is incredibly beautiful, despite being modern and not yet finished.'

'It might never be completed if...' her companion broke off, suddenly aware that they had an audience. She dabbed at her mouth with her napkin. 'Let's make the most of today.'

'Our appointment is at eleven,' May reminded Carmen. Once the arrangements are made in that respect, she thought, I believe we should return home as soon as possible.

As if she could read her mind, Carmen hissed: 'Monarchists – Republicans – the fascist Falangists – anti-clerics: Spain is truly divided. I wish to return to a country which is celebrating the crowning of a new King.'

She hasn't read the worrying rumours about Edward who, heaven forbid, may abdicate if he is not allowed to marry the woman he loves, May thought.

Henry wound up the gramophone at Pomona's request. She'd chosen a recording of 'Cheek to Cheek' from *Top Hat*, the musical film in which Fred Astaire and Ginger Rogers once again reprised their dancing partnership.

'Did you see the film?' she asked him. It was late evening, and they were sipping cups of hot cocoa, but they'd both felt like some light relief after discussing an assignment she'd just completed for university.

'No, I didn't go to the cinema much before May joined me here.'

'Oh, she and I went together when the film came to Kettle Row – long after the premiere, of course! Ginger Rogers wore a beautiful dress, decorated with ostrich feathers – I saw later, in a movie magazine, that feathers flew all over the stage when they danced together. Fred Astaire wasn't keen on her wearing it in the first place. It probably made him sneeze. Wouldn't you like to dance in a top hat and tails?'

Henry smiled. 'Can you imagine it?' he asked ruefully.

'Oh come on, you can sing anyway – probably better than Fred. Let's dance cheek to cheek!' Obediently, he stood up, and with her encouragement they began to sway round the furniture in the confined space. Pomona was almost as tall as Henry; she came up to his chin, so his cheek actually brushed against her golden mop of hair. Daringly, she clasped both her arms round his neck. He kept his left hand firmly in the small of her back.

'Heaven, I'm in heaven...' He caught his foot in the rug and they landed, giggling on the sofa.

'I suppose I'll have to kiss you, if you won't take advantage of me,' Pomona challenged him.

'I wouldn't do any such thing,' he murmured, before she kept her word, determined to make him respond. She was not disappointed.

'Oh Henry, I didn't know you had it in you,' she breathed, before he gently disengaged himself.

'I'm sorry, Pom – it's not that I didn't enjoy our embrace – it's just that...'

'You're still in love with May! You must know that nothing will come of that. She's still hanker-

221

ing after Paddy.'

'I'm aware of that, but they don't appear to have got back together, do they?'

'Look, please forget what just happened, Henry. I don't want to lose a good friend.' Pomona was determined not to reveal how hurt she felt at his rebuttal. I have my pride, she told herself.

'Of course you won't. You'll meet the right man before long, I'm sure, and you'll wonder what you ever saw in a dull chap like me. You need your beauty sleep. Time to say goodnight, I think.'

The shrilling of the phone made them both jump. Henry answered it. The voice on the other end sounded faint, there was crackling on the line, but he got the message.

'Henry, I'm coming home in two days' time – with my mother. I hope you don't mind. Please, can you meet us, and I'll explain all then? I'll ring again with the time of arrival. Love to you and Pom,' May said.

He turned to tell Pomona the news, but she was already halfway up the stairs, with her back to him. Best to break it to her in the morning, he decided.

Pom didn't cry easily, like May, but she clutched at her pillow in bed and told herself not to be a fool. Henry was still in love with May, and that was that.

The next morning May and Carmen realized that the two Canadians were missing. The Americans were vocal, as usual. 'They were arrested during the night. I think we should move on from here, too.'

'What about the concert?'

222

'No point in hanging around, but we'll contact the American embassy, and see what they advise.'

Carmen nudged her daughter. 'What did your friend say when you telephoned him last evening?'

'I – I didn't give him a chance to say much, apart from hello.'

'We must see how soon we can travel, eh?'

'I still have the shipment of the ceramics to arrange. I hope I can do that today. Did you notice that the shelves were almost empty in Maria's studio? She must be packing up in case she needs to leave in a hurry, too. I only got a glimpse of the pots she was sending to Tatiana; the crates were ready to be closed.'

They had not discussed May's condition since her revelation soon after their reunion. Now, unexpectedly, Carmen patted her shoulder. 'You must not worry so much, it will do you no good. I will care for you, as I said.'

'Thank you, Mama,' May said, unconsciously using the old, affectionate term.

Henry didn't let them down: he had already been waiting, an hour for the train to arrive. It was the first time he'd seen Carmen, but there was no mistaking the likeness between the two women. He greeted them in turn with a warm handshake; found a porter to wheel the luggage to the car.

May sat with her mother in the back seats. Carmen shivered. 'It is so much colder here,' she complained. 'I had forgotten how different the climate is from my country. Where is the sun?'

'I'm afraid you'll have to wait a month or two for that,' May reminded her. 'You will need a warm coat.'

Pomona was hovering on the doorstep to greet them. 'I've put the kettle on, and dinner is almost ready. Mum, you look just the same!'

'You know that is not true,' Carmen said crossly. 'But you,' her tone softened, 'my darling, are more beautiful than ever.'

She didn't hug *me* like that, May thought; Pomona was always her favourite. But she can't deny the fact that I am like her in looks, if not in character.

'So clever,' Carmen enthused, 'You make me very proud, Pomona. What is it you are cooking?'

'Henry's favourite, not a Spanish dish, I'm afraid, you'll have to show me how to make those. This is cottage pie – about my limit. Cooking is not my main interest.'

'You like to dance now?'

'Not flamenco. May gave that up long ago, so I never learned the steps from her. But Henry and I enjoy an occasional dance together, don't we, Henry?' Pomona added, with a sidelong glance at May. 'I'll show you your room, Mum.'

'I hope I do not put you out,' Carmen said.

'No, in fact you will be sharing the big bedroom with me. May, I moved your things into the other room, I hope you don't mind?'

I am the only one paying for my board, May thought, but of course she didn't say it. She shook her head instead.

Later she rang Tatiana to let her know she was back and that the crates of china were on their way. 'I can come back to work as soon as you would like me to,' she offered.

'You will need time to settle your mother in and to enjoy your sister's company before she returns to Cambridge. Next Monday will be soon enough. I look forward to seeing you then. I am sorry you had to cut your holiday short because of the situation over there, but thank you for seeing Maria as promised.'

After Carmen and Pomona had gone to bed May went out into the kitchen to see if Pom had done all the washing up, as she'd promised airily to do.

'You must be tired after all that travelling, May,' she had said.

As she suspected, the baking dish and saucepans had been left to soak in the sink, and rinsed crockery was piled on the draining board.

With a sigh, she bent over the sink, and began to scour the pans. Henry came up quietly behind her, put his arms round her waist to support her. 'Let me do that, you must be exhausted. Pomona expects too much of you.'

'She always has. It's my fault, I indulged her.' She turned suddenly, rubbing her wet hands on his jersey. 'I'm sorry, Henry – maybe I'd better get it over with now. I have something important to tell you – you may think badly of me when you know what it is.'

'I would never do that,' he said quietly. 'Look, leave that stuff, I'll do it later. Let's go back in the living room and talk.'

'There's no easy way to tell you, Henry, but I'm expecting a baby.'

He didn't remove his comforting arm. 'Ah,' he said.

'It was Paddy, of course – but you mustn't think badly of him. It just happened, that's all. I hope you can understand?'

'If you mean, do I mind – well, of course I do. If only it had been you and me. What does he say about this?'

'Nothing! He doesn't know, and I don't want him to. It happened to him once before, and he had to get married, but he has this dear little daughter, and he is struggling to make ends meet. *She's* the one he must look after, with the help of his parents.'

'You are thinking of coping with this on your own? May darling, you don't have to. Marry me, I have no objections to a ready-made family. I love you, you know that.'

'Henry! I couldn't expect this of you–'

'Why not? You often tell me how fond you are of me – we are the best of friends, too, and I believe that's a good basis for marriage. When's the baby due?'

'November, I think. I haven't seen the doctor yet.'

'Well, if you agree let's get married as soon as possible. Have you confided in your mother?'

'She guessed. She doesn't know who the father is.'

'And Pom?'

'Mum might tell her if I don't.'

'No-one else needs to know. Not even Bea, because of her involvement with Danny, Paddy's brother. What do you say to my proposal, May?'

'Yes, Henry, yes!'

He hugged her close to him, making soothing

noises while she sobbed, and he rocked her gently in his arms.

I feel like a baby, now, she thought. Henry will be a wonderful father.

Thirty

'My dear May, you don't look as if you have been on holiday at all!' Tatiana greeted her on her return to work. She cupped May's face with her two small hands. 'Your complexion is pale under the peaches! Dark smudges under your eyes. What is wrong? Will you tell me?'

'I was sick first thing this morning,' May said.

'You are recovered now, yes? If not, I shall insist you go home.'

'Tatiana, I might as well say, before it becomes obvious – I am pregnant. I won't blame you if you feel you must dismiss me but, well, I need to carry on working for as long as I can.'

Tatiana's eyes flashed. 'Who is responsible for this?'

'I imagine you can guess. *He* is not to know. Henry has asked me to marry him.'

'Have you agreed?'

'Yes, for the baby's sake. It will need a father.'

'What about *you?* D'you feel you need a husband?'

'He is the only one I would consider. My mother said she would look after me, but I'm afraid she never did in the past, although I have forgiven her for it.'

'Your mother – she will be looking for employment? I know she is a flamenco dancer, from Andalucia, and an idea occurred to me. Tell me what you think. I have a good friend, a fellow émigré, we were at school here together. She became a ballerina, while I, as you know, studied in my art. Evgenia has a dance studio near here, and many pupils: rich young ladies, some with talent, some not so much, but all enjoying the experience. The dances taught are various, some modern, ballroom, also rhumba, samba and tango. My friend mentioned she wished to add flamenco to her list. Can I recommend your mother to her?'

'I must ask her first, but I believe she would seize such an opportunity,' May exclaimed.

'If she is interested, bring her to see me. I think, am I right? that you do not wish for too much attention at the moment, and that if she has an occupation, you would both be happy.'

'Oh, Tatiana, that's *exactly* how I feel! Now, would you like me to start with the correspondence? I want to go on working for as long as possible.'

'Even after you marry?'

'Yes! I can't sit brooding at home all day.'

'I must dye my hair before I meet your Tatiana and her friend!' was Carmen's reaction later. 'You were my only pupil in the flamenco, May, and though you have disappointed me in not continuing to dance, I succeeded with you. Pomona, help me with my hair, eh? Yes, now!'

They disappeared up the stairs to the bathroom,

while Henry, who'd just arrived home, stood in the hall to be greeted with an unexpected hug by May. 'They'll be shut in the bathroom for hours, Henry. Mum is about to restore her raven locks! Don't you dare comment, unless you want to compliment her on the result. I'll put you in the picture before she reappears.'

'How did your day go?' he asked.

'Very well, Henry. I told Tatiana; I felt it was only fair, and she was supportive. I am fortunate to have such a good employer.'

'I heard from Selina while you were away,' he said, as they relaxed in the sitting room before dinner. 'We, you, Pom and myself, are invited to young William's baptism next Sunday. I thought you would still be away, and of course, Selina was not aware that Carmen would be here, so I said it would just be Pom and me.'

'I think you should keep it like that. I – I don't feel I could go – hold the new baby. He'll be passed around for cuddles. And Danny will likely be there with Bea. I've just realized, though, that Pom is due to return to Cambridge around then.'

'That's all arranged, too. Terence will be there for the weekend, and he suggested that he could take her back there with him, on his motorbike. I can see you are alarmed at the thought, but I assure you, he is much more mature than he was! Pom jumped at the chance of riding pillion.'

'I'm sure she did! I have to keep reminding myself she's an adult now, and I must stop treating her like a child.'

'By the way, Pom doesn't appear to know about your condition. Your mother is more discreet than you think, and I gather you've not told either of them yet about our plans to marry?'

'I'd rather not say about that, until I've seen a doctor,' said May. 'Please don't mention it to your family yet either. It's William's big day, after all.'

'I'm laying the table,' Pomona called out from the kitchen. 'Mum's coming down, but she's concealed her wet hair under a turban.'

'Definitely no comment then,' May said wryly to Henry.

Bea was disappointed not to see May at her nephew's baptism. 'You know your mother would have been welcome to come, too,' she told Pomona.

'There wouldn't have been room in the car, with my luggage. I hope Terence has empty panniers on his bike to put all my things in.' She had been secretly pleased to have Henry to herself on the journey to Kettle Row.

As godmother, Bea held William with some trepidation. She appealed to Danny: 'Wouldn't you like to take him for a bit?'

'I'd rather not. Anyway, I'm not his godfather, and *he* moved away when he saw, as I did, the baby's face go red and an ominous sound from his nether region. Don't forget I had some experience of *that* with Cluny when she was younger.'

'Where's Selina? I'm wearing my best costume; I don't want it leaked over!'

'Look on it as a practice run for when we–'

'You want a family, then?'

'Of course. Don't you?'

230

'I hadn't really thought about it,' Bea said. 'May's the same. We never drooled over babies in prams when we were girls.' She relinquished the whiffy William, with some relief, to his doting father.

Pomona and Terence slipped outside to admire the motorbike. She sat astride the saddle, 'to get the feel of it,' as she said.

'I hope you're not going to wear a skirt tomorrow,' he observed, 'or a silly hat.'

'Why do you always lecture me?' she demanded crossly. 'I shall be wearing slacks and my old school shoes – and your father's ancient tweed cap, so there!'

'I've some spare goggles and gauntlet gloves for you.' He sighed ruefully, as she dismounted without his help. 'I'm sorry, Pom, it's become a habit to snipe at each other, hasn't it? Can't we call a truce? I actually approve of your saucy hat, though I reckon it's too small to stay on your head on a windy day.'

They were facing one another in the shed in which the bike was housed, along with garden spades and forks, a bucket or two, a few empty terracotta pots and a bale of straw.

Terence took off his glasses and rubbed them with a clean handkerchief. When he looked up Pomona took in, with a start, the luminosity of his long-lashed blue eyes, which were usually hidden by his spectacles.

'Why don't we kiss and make up?' he suggested.

'Why not?' She took his glasses from his hand. 'It might be easier if you can't see it's *me*.'

When they went back indoors, to witness the

cutting of the christening cake, with William in a clean romper suit, Henry was not the only one to notice the odd piece of straw clinging to their clothes. Maybe, he mused, Terence had been the right one for Pomona all along.

Terence and Pomona left for Cambridge the following morning.

'Hug me tight round the waist,' he instructed, as she climbed on to the pillion, while he held the bike steady, and she didn't object at all.

It was a typical April day: sunshine and showers. They sped along country lanes, whizzing past livestock in farm fields: leaping lambs, and grazing sheep and cattle. Being a Monday, washing blew on lines fixed between two trees in cottage gardens and in a school playground they glimpsed youngsters dancing in a circle and chanting, 'Farmer's in his den.'

At lunchtime, before they reached the outskirts of the city, they stopped by the river for lunch. Emma had packed egg-and-cress sandwiches and two pieces of the rich fruitcake, complete with icing. They glimpsed a flotilla of moorhens on the water, who disappeared in the reeds, and were glad of their protective clothing as they were constantly flailing their hands at flies and stinging insects.

'This is fun,' Terence observed without irony. 'We ought to meet up now and again – hire a punt perhaps. What d'you think?'

'I think,' said Pomona, 'your girlfriend might not approve!'

'My girlfriend? Oh, she's hardly that. She's someone I work with. In fact, she's been overseeing me – she's already qualified. I only mentioned her at Christmas to rile you.'

'To make me jealous?' she suggested.

'You could say that. I suddenly realized you were a beautiful young woman, and I was over-awed. It wasn't that I didn't want to ask you out, it's more that you seemed superior, being at the university–'

'You could have been too,' she pointed out.

'I'm not sure I would have made the grade, like you. Anyway, I prefer to learn on the job. You need to be intelligent to work for my company, I'm told, so it's not a lesser option.'

'You made me think you didn't want me as a friend any more.'

'We were forever arguing – remember?'

'Yes, but I always secretly *liked* you,' she admitted.

'As I did you, Pom. Actually, I thought you were more interested in old Henry.'

'Oh, that was just a crush – he's far too old for me,' she said.

'Well then, it seems it's just you and me.'

'It always was.'

Evgenia said: 'I would like to offer you the position: it would mean working afternoons and evenings, but I imagine you are used to that?'

'Yes, the hours would suit me,' Carmen agreed. 'However I would expect to be provided with a taxi home at night, I don't care for the tube.'

'That could be arranged.' Evgenia looked Carmen up and down with a keen eye. 'You are a little overweight...'

'It will disappear when I am dancing every day again,' Carmen said confidently. It was a good thing, she thought, that Evgenia didn't ask my age, though I suppose we are probably both around fifty, so I'm glad I dyed my hair.

'When can you start?'

'As soon as you like,' Carmen said, as they shook hands.

That evening May was told the good news. She thought it better not to remind her mother that she had promised to take care of her during her pregnancy. She had really not believed it would happen.

'I shall be able to lie in, in the mornings,' Carmen said, with satisfaction.

When May related that to Henry, he smiled wryly and said: 'At least we will be able to get into the bathroom first thing now, eh? Also, it will give us the chance to discuss future plans in the evening.'

May wasn't so sure about that. She felt she was in denial about the baby, it didn't seem real. As for wedding plans, she wasn't ready for all that, just yet.

Thirty-One

May faced the doctor over his desk when the examination was over. The nurse who had been present gave her a reassuring smile before she left the room.

The doctor regarded May for a moment, noting her hands tightly clenched in her lap. 'I confirm that you are pregnant...' he paused, 'Miss Jolley. From your dates, and the examination, I calculate that you can expect to produce your baby in the first week of November. However, it might be wise to keep this news to yourself until the third month. There is a slight chance of miscarrying before that stage – not, I must say, that I have any reason to think this could happen in your case, but I would advise you to take things easy for the next fortnight or so. I'm afraid I cannot give you anything for the nausea, but I assure you that that, too, will pass. I will see you again in two months' time, unless anything untoward should happen.' He rose, held out his hand. 'You will, I presume, be thinking by then of booking the nursing home. I do not recommend a home birth in your ... um ... situation.'

'Thank you, Doctor,' May managed. *Nursing home*, I hadn't thought of that. November ... cold, dreary weather. *I* was fortunate to be born in the spring.

'How did you get on?' Tatiana asked anxiously when she returned to work. 'What did the doctor say?'

'That everything was all right – I think, but the doctor had very cold hands.' May shuddered at the memory. It had been rather an ordeal. She forced a smile, added brightly, 'Now, where is the list you wanted me to type?'

That evening, after dinner, she tried to delay the moment when Henry would surely put the same question. Instead, he asked: 'Would you care to come to church with me this Sunday? I'd be at the organ, of course, but you might like to sit next to the vicar's wife, she's not so much older than you, but she already has three children.'

She guessed the reason behind the invitation. 'You want us to talk to the vicar afterwards?'

'Yes. I thought we agreed that when you had things confirmed we should take that first step.'

'Henry, could we wait until I feel better? The doctor tells me I will, in a little while.'

'You haven't changed your mind? Don't keep it from me, if you have. I want you to stay here so I can care for you. It's obvious Carmen has discarded her good intentions.'

'She's enjoying her dancing again. I don't mind, because she's happy. She mentioned a new friend, Ramon, who teaches Latin-American steps, who has a spare room in his flat, within walking distance of the studio. She might well take him up on his offer.'

'I hope it's ... well, a *genuine* offer.'

'Henry, my mother has always done what she wanted to do. I was hurt by her desertion of us when I a child, but I now accept her as she is. She's a survivor, after all.'

'So long as *you* don't leave me,' he said softly.

'I can promise that. I will accompany you to church, I haven't heard you play since the Singing Kettle days.'

The doctor was right, May felt better by the time she was three months pregnant. She was also relieved, thinking the danger of losing the baby was much less. She let out the waistband of her office skirts, and looked at herself side on in the long mirror in the bedroom. She had lost weight as a result of the sickness, and there wasn't much in the way of a baby bump for anyone to see, or so she convinced herself.

The postman arrived one morning just as she and Henry were leaving for work. He greeted them cheerily: 'Just two for Miss Jolley today, no bills!' May tucked the envelopes in her bag; there was no time to stop and read these now.

She didn't remember the letters until lunchtime. She and Tatiana had been busy tidying and rearranging the ceramics before a prospective buyer arrived at eleven. The client, an old friend of Tatiana's, insisted on taking her friend out to a smart new restaurant.

'I'll hold the fort; don't hurry back,' May told Tatiana.

'Break for lunch as usual, ignore the telephone,' Tatiana advised.

The first letter May opened was from Pomona, telling her she had joined the rowing club.

'Big, strong girl' they requested, so I applied!! Terence says he'll hide in the bushes on the river bank to admire all those rippling muscles and hefty thighs in shorts, not blue stockings!

May smoothed out the enclosed newspaper cutting and read the headline:

STUDENT'S DREAM OF SWIMMING THE CHANNEL

'Fame at last, Pomona! Even if you haven't got

there yet,' she said aloud. 'Well, you made the local paper, anyway.' She was pleased at the mention of Terence; the two of them obviously shared the same sense of humour, she thought.

She recognized the writing on the second envelope too, and her heart missed a beat. The letter was from Paddy. There was a drawing in crayon. It was recognizable as Toby, due to the dark circles round the eyes, and the perked ears. On impulse, she kissed the picture. Paddy wrote:

Had been hoping to hear from you. It is Cluny's birthday next week and we two are coming up to London on Saturday to visit the Natural History Museum in Cromwell Road. Is there any chance you could join us. We could lunch out (my treat). I would suggest meeting at eleven a.m. Regards to your mother and to Henry – we got on very well, having your friendship in common.
Warmest regards, Paddy

Friendship, warmest regards; he's letting me know where he stands, she thought. She would discuss it with Henry.

'Maybe you would care to come too?' she suggested to him.

He hesitated. 'Are you sure that's a good idea?'

'Your moral support, that's important, Henry. He won't ask too many questions, I feel, if you are with me.'

'He might suspect you are pregnant.'

'If I say *we* are engaged...'

He hoped she wouldn't observe the anguish in his eyes. 'Then I think it is time we went shop-

238

ping for a ring, don't you?' he said.

'Nothing too expensive,' May insisted. 'Not modern, I don't mind a second-hand ring – Victorian, perhaps?'

The jeweller produced a tray of modest rings. Henry gave a small sigh. He'd been thinking of an engagement ring, but he wanted May to be happy with her choice. She picked out a slender gold band with a garnet stone in a claw setting, tried it for size. 'There! that's the one! May I keep it on?'

'Of course, you may.' Henry agreed, although he wished she'd allowed him to slip it on her finger.

Back home, he said: 'We should tell the rest of the family now that we are engaged, don't you think?'

'I agree. But leave the other news, please, a little longer,' she said. 'Well, I'd better unwrap the fish and chips – that was a good idea of yours, as it's a bit late to start cooking now. It seems strange without Mum here, but...' Carmen had moved into Ramon's spare room the previous day.

'We are better on our own,' he finished for her.

'At least we know where she is and what she's up to. The situation in Spain is grave now.'

Henry smiled. He wasn't so sure about that, but wouldn't say anything.

In the kitchen, May put their supper plates into the oven to make sure the food would be hot. She closed the oven door, remarking, 'It won't take long.' As she straightened up, he came up behind her and gently fingered her hair aside, before he kissed the nape of her neck. 'I love you so much,

May,' he murmured.

'That was nice.' May was unsure how to react.

'I'll shift your things later back into your old room,' he offered.

'Thank you, Henry, that's good of you. Will you lay the table now please, and don't forget the vinegar and the tomato sauce.'

May felt the need of an early night. When she went upstairs she found that Henry had not only transferred her belongings to the big bedroom, but that he had changed the bed linen and turned back the corner of the sheet for her to climb straight in. He had obviously retreated to his own room while she was in the bathroom. She undressed quickly and sank thankfully into bed, glad of the clean, cotton sheets.

A tap of the door. Henry opened it and called 'Goodnight.' He, too, was ready for bed, in his pyjamas, decently covered with his old dressing-gown.

'Come in, Henry,' she invited. 'I want to tell you how pleased I am with my lovely ring. Look, I still have it on! I won't let you down and change my mind on Saturday. How could I, after what you said when you kissed me tonight?'

'I meant it.' He came over to the bed. 'Can we talk?'

She yawned. 'I thought we had. I promised you–'

'I won't hold you to it. The ring ... well, we're not really engaged; we're both pretending to ourselves that it makes a difference. It's time to be open with each other, for you to tell Pomona and Bea, for me to inform my family of your predicament, because they think of you as one of us, and will support you, as I still intend to do. You must talk to Paddy, and you can't do that with me around, so I won't be coming with you to the museum. His family, when they know, will, I'm sure, be there for you too, whatever the outcome between you and their son.'

'They were so kind to Pom and me, all those years ago – they sort of adopted us into their family, just as yours did, later.'

'You and the O'Flahertys have a common background. At heart you'll always be the Punch and Judy lady, May. It's a part of you in which I can never share. Before all this happened, I was considering following in my father's footsteps, as you once did with Jim. I wish I had met him. Can you see yourself as a clergy wife?'

'I don't know,' she admitted.

'May, be honest with yourself. When you met Paddy again, you knew, didn't you, that you still had strong feelings for him? What happened then was inevitable. May I look at the ring? You didn't really give me a chance to do so, earlier.'

She stretched her hands out to him. Carefully, he slid the ring off her finger. 'It's very pretty, but it's a friendship ring, not an engagement ring. Wear it on your other hand ... and think of me.'

'That's a promise I can keep,' she said softly.

Thirty-Two

May, 1936

Saturday dawned, damp and cold. The garden was rimed with frost. May decided to wear her fawn mackintosh, unbelted, over her skirt and blouse. She tied a kerchief over her hair, turned her collar up, and carried her umbrella. She thought: I look drab, and I'm almost twenty-seven. I'm far removed from Young May Moon and even from the attractive girl in the peacock-blue dress. Was that really only three months ago?

'You can always bring them back here you know,' Henry said. 'I can make myself scarce. Are you sure you don't want me to run you into London in the car?'

'Thanks, but I'm used to the train now.'

'I hope all goes well.'

'I think it will: I shall follow your advice.'

Paddy was waiting outside the museum, with his hands in his pockets and rain dripping off his hair on to his collar. The wind whipped a discarded scrap of torn paper along the pavement, which clung to his trouser leg. He bent to brush it off and when he straightened up, she was standing there, shaking her umbrella before closing it. He didn't appear to recognize her immediately.

'Sorry if I'm late,' she said breathlessly.

'You aren't – I was early. Shall we go inside? It's perishing out here, no-one would think it was May.'

Does he mean, he didn't realize it was *me* – May? she wondered, asking belatedly: 'Where's Cluny?'

'She came out yesterday in some blisters, which Mum says is chickenpox. She insisted I should meet you as arranged, and I've promised Cluny we'll go round the museum and buy some post-cards, so she can see what she's missed.'

May wasn't sure whether she was relieved or not that Cluny had been unable to come, but it would be easier to talk later, she thought.

He took her arm, guided her up the steps. He said in her ear, 'I had a shock when I looked up and saw you. Why on earth didn't you tell me, May?' The flapping mackintosh had revealed her secret.

'We can't talk about it now, not here.' I should have been aware he would guess I was pregnant, she thought; after all, it's happened to him before.

The gigantic mammoth skeleton was amazing. 'I think Cluny might well have been overawed by it,' Paddy observed. 'She became interested in dinosaurs when she looked at a couple of my old books. Dad told her a lot about them; he's immersed in ancient history.'

They went from gallery to gallery, where the displays amazed them both. 'The dodo! What a pity it is extinct.' May stumbled, and his arm went firmly round her shoulders, supporting her. 'You've had enough, I can tell. Let's buy the cards, then find somewhere to eat.'

'I want to choose a birthday gift for Cluny, too,' she said, 'but I have to sit down first, I ... feel faint. I'm sorry.'

'It's me who should apologize. I had no idea, and I should have had. It's all my fault, and I feel awful about it.'

'*Don't*. It was – just as much me as you.'

After she had chosen a mug with an illustration of the museum building, for Cluny, a chair was provided for May to rest upon, while Paddy selected a batch of cards for his daughter. 'The mammoth doesn't look so formidable cut down to size.'

She looked around her and upwards at the vaulted ceiling. 'What a wonderful place this is. You must bring Cluny here later; she'll love it.'

'If you say you'll come too. I'm glad you took to each other.'

'Little Dog Toby helped, in that respect!'

Later, they sat in a crowded café at a small table for two in a corner. They ordered soup and rolls. 'Not quite what I had in mind,' Paddy said, 'but it was far enough for you to walk. I didn't come by car. Cluny was looking forward to travelling on the train, and I'd booked our seats.

'Everything other than the soup seems to smell of onion and be swimming in grease. This, at least is hot and the rolls are fresh. Eat up, then we'll choose our dessert. What would you like to drink?'

'Tea, I think. Not yet though – I don't fancy coffee.'

'May, why didn't you tell me?'

'I – I thought you'd feel you had to marry me.

I believed you regretted what happened, because we hadn't had time to get to know each other properly again. I though that you didn't want to rush into another relationship because of Cluny.'

'I'm ashamed to admit I got cold feet,' he told her humbly. 'I've regretted letting you go ever since, hence the invitation today. I thought you'd come because of Cluny, not me. I can remember you ignoring me when we first met, because you considered I was brash. Mum said we were made for each other, and that this time I mustn't let you go.'

'Dear Brigid.' Her voice was husky. She cleared her throat. 'But you didn't expect this, did you? Nothing has changed, has it, with your situation? I know you can't afford to set up home on your own, especially with Cluny to consider. You mustn't unsettle her.'

'I suppose I was hoping for a proper courtship and, in time, earning enough to become independent. The depression seems at last to be lifting, but what with the unrest here, civil wars in countries like Spain, and the threat of Nazi Germany, another world war seems inevitable. Will small businesses like mine be viable then?'

'I wish we could go back to West Wick. It was an unexpectedly good summer, after the sadness of losing my father. It was when I grew up, I suppose.'

'And fell in love with me, as I did with you.'

She took a spoonful of vanilla ice cream. He'd already finished his spotted dick pudding and custard. 'This is nice.' She came to a sudden decision. 'I don't think either of us wants a hasty marriage, Paddy. Courtship sounds good to me. I can stay on at work, and live at Henry's until I have to give up, when the baby is due. I will save all I can from my wages, and you can concentrate on building up your business. We'll keep in close touch, and I shall need you by my side in November. *Then*, we can be married. What d'you think?'

'If you think it will work ... then I agree.' His relief at her decision was palpable. 'May, I have to catch the train back at five o'clock. There's not much point going to a park in the rain. How about seeing a film?' He grinned and she was reminded of the young Paddy. 'We can have a crafty cuddle in the dark,' he added.

'As long as you don't squeeze me too tight.' She looked ruefully at her slight bulge.

Henry didn't question her on her return home. He waited until she was ready to talk.

'We're going to be married, Henry, but not yet. I hope I can stay on here with you, work with Tatiana, and get to know my mother better.

'He is pleased about the baby, I think, although he didn't actually say, but he wants us to be together, when the time is right.'

'It must have been a shock to him,' Henry said charitably. 'Of course you can stay on here, I've become accustomed to the company. No strings attached, I assure you. I rang my mother, by the way.'

'I hope she wasn't too shocked!'

'My dear, she wants to help all she can. They all send their love and best wishes. Perhaps, tomorrow, you will feel like contacting Bea?'

'It's a relief to have this out in the open. I hope Paddy's family will feel the same.'

'I'm sure they will. Oh, Carmen rang. She said she wanted to talk to you. I told her where you were.'

'I hope nothing's wrong. She was pleased about her move.'

Ramon, that dapper dancer with snake hips and good looks, was fourteen years younger than Carmen, but he knew how to flatter a mature woman. Carmen had been bowled over instantly by his charm. She had certainly not taken in the fact that, while he flattered the female pupils, he was more interested in their male partners.

The room she now occupied was up a flight of stairs; it was small, under the eaves and rather airless. He advised her that she should not open the window because of the noise from the traffic outside. There was a list of rules taped to the wall.

1. USE OF THE KITCHEN PERMITTED
   ONLY BY ARRANGEMENT,
   ONE HOUR a.m. and ONE HOUR p.m.
2. OBSERVE ROTA FOR BATHS.
3. CLOTHES AND LINEN TO LAUNDRY.
4. OTHER ROOMS STRICTLY PRIVATE.
5. DAILY SWEEPING OF STAIRS
   REQUIRED.

To one who had never concerned herself with housework, let alone sweeping stairs, this was outrageous. She soon became aware of why the rest of the flat was out of bounds; because Ramon invited his friends home after he had finished his stint at the dance studio.

Carmen decided to return to Henry's house, where she could bath as often as she liked and cook what she fancied in the kitchen. Henry or May were always on hand to deal with the washing up.

'Henry,' May said apologetically, 'Mum wants to come back.'

'Perhaps it's a good thing. We could be, with our unusual set-up, the subject of unwelcome gossip. Carmen would soon put a stop to that, I think! I imagine you said she can return here?'

'I wouldn't presume to do that without asking you first. I did say that now she's working she would be able to contribute to the household expenses. I feel we should do the same when Pom is here.'

'That's a different matter,' he said immediately. 'She needs a home base, and I am happy for this to be it. When would Carmen hope to move back?'

'She'll give a week's notice, she says. I have to ring her back.'

He smiled. 'Shall we draw up our own set of rules, eh?'

'Oh Henry, you're far too tolerant for that!'

There was a shoal of letters the following week for May, all pledging their support. May felt so much happier now that her two families, as she thought of the O'Flahertys and the Wrights, were behind her.

It would soon be her birthday, and she was invited to spend it with Paddy and his family. 'Cluny will be over the chickenpox by then,' Brigid wrote. 'We can't wait to see you again!'

Thirty-Three

'Not much use bolting the stable door,' Brigid re-marked, as she showed May into Paddy's room. 'You two need some quiet time to find out more about each other, that's what Brendan said. Anyway, we already think of you as our daughter-in-law, and Cluny is just as excited as we are about the baby... We'll sing Happy Birthday to You, dear Young May Moon tomorrow. Cluny and I have baked you a cake! Welcome to the family.'

'Oh, I'd love to hear you singing again, I have such happy memories of that,' May said.

She noted with relief that the two single beds were set apart by a chest of drawers. Of course, this was the room Paddy shared with his brother when he came home.

Brigid patted her arm: 'Paddy doesn't want to rush things either. But you could always push the beds together. You must be tired after the journey – take the bed by the window, pull the curtains across and have a rest before dinner at half past six. You'll be undisturbed until then. Paddy promised to take Cluny out with the dog.'

May removed her shoes, blouse and skirt and lay under the coverlet on top of the bed. She thought, I'll wear something more comfortable this evening, that skirt is becoming too tight. Tatiana's artists' smocks were specially made for her by a local seamstress, and she'd kindly ordered a couple of these roomy frocks for May. The material was serviceable cotton, one in pale blue, one in green, with two buttons at the neck and loose three-quarter-length sleeves. May had embroidered a daisy-chain along the yoke seams, white looped petals with yellow French knot centres. This livened up what was essentially a workaday garment.

There was a jug of flowers on her side of the chest, which included large white daisies. Brigid, pausing by the door, said: 'Cluny picked those for you.'

May didn't expect to go to sleep, but she did. She awoke to a strange sensation, a fluttering in her abdomen. Then she realized that the baby was making its first discernible movements. She placed her hands on the spot where the upheaval had occurred. There it was again ... she was trembling with excitement. She looked up and saw Paddy sitting on the other bed, regarding her with a pensive look.

'You looked so peaceful, I didn't want to wake you up, but Mum said to tell you the meal will be on the table in ten minutes.' He rose. 'I'll see you downstairs, eh?'

May sat up. 'Paddy – wait a moment, I've something exciting to tell you. The baby just kicked for the first time! Oh, there it goes again!'

'Can I feel it, too?' he asked diffidently. He moved towards her.

She nodded. 'Hurry, before it stops!' His warm

hand covered hers and through the rayon petti-
coat she was wearing, they shared the special
moment. Paddy gave her a quick kiss on the top
of her head. 'Thank you for sharing that with
me,' he said.

'I know it was a shock when you found out
about the baby, but you're happy about it now,
aren't you?'

'I can honestly say that I am. Well, get dressed,
let your hair down, and I'll tell Mum she can dish
up!'

It was a birthday that May would never forget. It
began after breakfast on Sunday morning, when
she opened her presents from the family. Grandpa
had carved her a perfect apple from walnut,
complete with stalk and curled leaf, which sat by
her plate; Brigid and Brendan gave her a record,
and she was thrilled to see it was labelled: *Young
May Moon, a popular tune.* 'We'll wind up the
gramophone later,' they promised.

Cluny said: 'I picked you the flowers and iced
the cake.' Then Paddy felt in his pocket and
produced a little polished heart-shaped box that
he had made in the workshop. He'd lined it with
a scrap of red velvet over a raised pad. 'It's for a
ring, but I want you to choose *that.*' May glanced
at the friendship ring on her right hand, given her
by Henry, which Paddy hadn't commented on.
There would be more presents to open when she
arrived home; it wouldn't have been tactful to
bring them with her. The O'Flahertys' modest
gifts were all she wished for today.

Cluny had chosen the birthday tea menu, which

included wobbling orange and green jellies, pine-apple chunks, tinned salmon sandwiches, short-bread, cheesy scones and a chocolate cake with icing smothered in hundreds-and-thousands, plus a fingerprint or two bestowed by an enthusiastic small chef.

After a slice of the cake Cluny was whisked away to wash her face and hands by her grandma. Brendan cleared the table, Grandpa offered to help wash up, Toby cleared up the crumbs under the table, while May and Paddy were told to retire to the sitting room to await the entertainment.

The two of them hadn't talked last night, as May had been already asleep when Paddy came upstairs. He'd turned the light off, but lay awake in his bed for some time, thinking over the day's events, especially the moment when he felt the baby kicking. I mustn't let her down, he told himself. I wish we'd got married right away, but I must respect her wishes.

They sat on the settee, and Paddy drew her close, so that her head rested on his shoulder. 'I love you,' he murmured.

'I know you do. I love you, too. D'you realize I'm twenty-seven years old today?'

'You don't look much older than you did at sixteen. You'll always be Young May Moon. I like your party dress! Your favourite green, I see. I'm glad you didn't bob your hair.' He twirled a lock of it round his finger.

'The thing about black hair is it seems to go grey earlier. Mum has to dye her hair, but perhaps I shouldn't divulge that fact!'

'We'll likely go grey together – me having dark

hair too.'

'I wish we hadn't been parted all those years, but I know you wouldn't be without Cluny.'

'I'm looking forward to us presenting her with a baby brother or sister.'

'So am I. Paddy, Brigid is the mother figure in her life, but I believe Cluny and I can be the best of friends.'

'Of course you can. Listen – did you hear that? I wondered what other surprises they were cooking up!'

'It sounds like Brigid's harp!' May exclaimed.

'Time to turn the lights low, I reckon, and switch on the standard lamp,' he said, rising to do just that.

Into the room they came, Brigid and Brendan in their kilts, Cluny in the one worn by her uncle Danny when he was a boy, hoiked up under her armpits and dangling to her ankles. Dog Toby followed behind, wagging his tail, pouncing on the trailing material. Grandpa carried the harp and placed it by a chair for Brigid, then he joined May and Paddy on the settee. 'Room for a little 'un,' he boomed, easing in his considerable bulk. 'Sit on my lap or you'll get squashed,' Paddy whispered to May. His arms gently encircled her middle. With perfect timing, the baby began its gymnastics.

'First,' Brendan announced, 'The Singing O'Flahertys will lead the company with their rendition of *Happy Birthday* to Young May Moon!'

They sang all the old songs, with the addition of one or two more modern lyrics. May requested *Tea For Two*, and the middle-aged couple before them seemed transformed into the glamorous pair they had been on stage more than ten years ago.

Then Brendan played his fiddle and young Cluny improvised a dance; more a slipper-shuffle: when she twirled, her kilt dropped round her ankles. May smothered a giggle as she and Paddy recalled her stepping out of the peacock-blue dress, and what had happened next.

Cluny wasn't embarrassed; she pulled the kilt up, clutched it with both hands, then danced on, to warm applause.

Paddy's whistling ended in laughter too, when Toby raised his head to howl loudly, drowning him out. 'I didn't realize it was that bad,' he said ruefully.

The entertainers paused for breath, when May requested that her birthday record should be played. 'I won't alarm you all by attempting the jig,' she sighed, with a smile.

Finally, Cluny performed her party trick; she fetched her hairbrush and brushed her grand-mother's hair vigorously in the dark. Sparks flew, always brighter when red hair is involved.

'Almost as good as fireworks,' Grandpa said cheerfully. They all clapped the display.

May managed to keep awake while she waited for Paddy to come quietly into the bedroom. She closed her eyes as he undressed and switched off the light. Then she said tentatively, 'Paddy...'

'Yes, what is it?' He stumbled over his shoes on his way round to her bed. 'Are you all right? The excitement hasn't been too much for you?'

'No, of course not. It was a lovely evening, just like the End of the Pier Show at West Wick. When you sang *Just a Song at Twilight,* I thought of dear Jenny and Percy, who loved each other all those years, and I wished *we* hadn't let so much time go by.'

'I haven't sung for years, you know. Danny inherited that talent – it's good he's still using it. Well, goodnight. We have to make an early start in the morning.'

'Paddy, I need a cuddle – just that. What about you?' she said softly.

'It's a bit late to shift the beds together now, eh?' His warm breath fanned her cheek, he was getting nearer.

'I'll make room for you with me,' she said, and she did.

Thirty-Four

July, 1936

Carmen was ready for the dance studio doors to open and the young ladies, as Evgenia called them, to step eagerly on to the sprung floor and greet each other with air-kisses and gossip, before the music began and she called them to order.

For the first time since she had last worked, in Spain, Carmen had managed to squeeze into her flamenco dress. The sight of her so dressed, with a flower in her hair, elicited gasps of admiration.

She had their undivided attention. The young man who wound the gramophone and carefully positioned the needle on the records, looked on wistfully. He hoped eventually to partner one of the lofty girls, but alas, he had not finished growing yet, and was too short to be considered. Meanwhile, he memorized the sequence of steps.

Carmen was inspired this evening: the young ladies were in awe of her expertise. The interruption, when Evgenia appeared followed by a swarthy-looking man in an ill-fitting suit, made her stop in her tracks, hands on hips, eyes flashing.

'I apologize, Carmen for disturbing your performance, but, as you will see, I have this gentleman with me, who says he is your husband, from Spain.'

'My husband?' Carmen spat out the words. 'No! I am widowed, as I told you. I know him well, he was once my partner in my act. His name is Carlos Rivera.'

'The class must continue – another record please, boy. You should talk in private with this ... person, I think, and send him on his way, if he is unwelcome... You may talk in my office. I will watch the action here for you,' Evgenia said.

The man said nothing, but waited for Carmen to lead him outside. Carmen sat behind Evgenia's desk, facing Carlos. 'Why are you here?' she demanded, eyeing his dishevelled appearance. He had been so dapper in the days, when... She shook her head at the thought.

'I heard you were in Barcelona, through a mutual contact. I was involved with the Republicans, fighting the Nationalists, but when we heard that Franco was about to return from exile and the Nationalists were promised support from Germany and Italy, many of my comrades were rounded up and imprisoned. I escaped and made my way to where I believed you to be. I thought you were my only hope, and would help me because of Isabella.'

'Where is she? I heard nothing from her foster parents after I went to Barcelona to meet May. We had to leave there very shortly after–'

'I know. The manager at the hotel gave me your daughter's address in England. It is a long story, but here I am, humbly asking your help. All I have with me is my guitar. I sold all my possessions to enable me to travel.'

'Isabella? You did not answer my question. Is she safe?'

'Why should you worry, when you abandoned our child, just as you did your other daughters? I put myself at risk to bring her with me, to show her that one parent cared for her! She is safe. She waits outside in the taxi, for you to tell us where we can go.'

'Taxi? I suppose you expect *me* to pay for that?'

'I am penniless, as I said. I – we – throw ourselves on your mercy.'

Carmen stood up. 'Wait here. I must tell my employer that I have to leave early. She will not like it, but I must do so. I will take you to my home, but this will be a temporary arrangement. You are, I think, a refugee, Carlos?'

In the taxi Carmen sat beside the silent child. Isabella, clutching her small bag of belongings,

257

was seven years old. There had been no contact with her mother since she was a baby – when she was considered an encumbrance for her parents, in their performing days. The only family she knew was the elderly couple who had brought her up, despite the lack of regular payment These people, who claimed to be her parents were strangers to her.

Henry opened the door to them. Carmen had not changed her dress, just snatched up her handbag after a brief explanation to Evgenia. His eyes widened at the sight of her companions, a scruffy foreigner carrying a guitar case, and the little dark-haired child with an unmistakable likeness to May, who now joined him. She'd recently arrived home from work and was upstairs, when Carmen banged on the front door.

'I told him, my dear Henry,' Carmen said, without explaining who the strangers were, 'You would give him and the child refuge here–'

'*Carlos?*' May interrupted, as she came into the room. 'Is it you? And *who* is this?'

'She is your half-sister: Isabella. She does not know us, we ... gave her away, at a few weeks old. She does not speak to us.'

'Perhaps she only speaks Spanish. Didn't you think of that?'

May, now five months pregnant, bent with difficulty to address the forlorn child. She offered her hand. 'Come with me, Isabella. I hope you can understand me; my Spanish is rusty.' She gestured up the stairs at the bathroom. 'When you have washed, we'll have dinner. You'll have to stay tonight for the child's sake. Mum, you must deal with Carlos. You and Isabella can share my bedroom tonight, and he will have to use your room. Henry, I must apologize on their behalf for this intrusion.'

'We will discuss this in detail in the morning,' Henry said. 'Don't forget that Pomona will be arriving here for the vacation tomorrow. Meanwhile, I will make sure there is sufficient food for all.'

The child stood passively as May washed her face and hands for her and dried them with a soft, clean towel. She spoke at last. *'Muchas gracias,'* she said, adding in halting English: 'Bella, they call me Bella.'

May drew her close. 'That means beautiful. I am May, your sister, and I am glad to meet you.'

'Yo amo mi abuelita ...' Tears spilled from Bella's eyes.

'You love your little grandmother? I understand. You miss your family.'

May tried to suppress the anger she felt for Carmen – how could she give up her third daughter, just as she had May and Pomona? Why had she never mentioned Bella to them? But we had Jim and Min, she thought, who loved us and brought us up, and this small girl only had someone she called Grandma. Still, it sounds as if her foster parents loved her.

Henry, kind as always, told Carlos, 'I will try to get something sorted out with the authorities, who should know of your arrival in this country. Bella can remain here with her mother and her sisters. There should be no problem, because of the blood-ties between Carmen and May.'

'I have had an idea,' Carmen announced the following morning. 'I might be able to procure Carlos some work with me, playing the guitar for my dancing class. Pomona will be here to look after the child during the long holiday.' She did not thank Henry for his generosity, or offer to care personally for her child.

'She has her studies,' May put in. 'I shall shortly be working part-time for Tatiana, mostly mornings. I can help with Bella.' They were sitting at the table after breakfast, and the child reached for May's hand under the overhang of the tablecloth. May squeezed the small hand reassuringly.

As Henry left the house for the bank, May having been given the day off by her considerate employer, he remarked to her: 'Well, it's quite a houseful for a confirmed bachelor, isn't it?'

'Dear Henry, you are the *perfect* host!' She doubted that the new arrivals would be considerate guests.

If only I could be the perfect husband, he thought.

Pom and Bella took to each other immediately.

'Fancy!' Pomona exclaimed, 'A sister arrives out of the blue, and May looks very pleased with herself. How about producing a boy for a change, May?'

'I can't promise, Pom, but I think of the baby as Jim, after Dad. Paddy doesn't mind, but Cluny rather likes the idea of a sister.'

'I guess Mum is as maternal as ever,' Pomona said. 'I shall do my bit by encouraging Bella to speak English before she goes to school in September.'

'Mum will, no doubt, be planning to teach her the flamenco as her contribution,' May said wryly.

Later, while they watched Bella bouncing a ball the back garden, they caught up on family news. 'Seen much of Terence?' May asked.

'When I can escape the cloisters.' Pomona grinned. 'He watched our team rowing, and when we had a boat out on the river ourselves he said I could take over the oars as I was better at that than he is. We still argue, you know.'

'I guess you always will. You obviously both enjoy it.'

'We've both left Henry out in the cold. But then, it wasn't me whom he desired.'

'Not very delicate to put it like that, Pom. Paddy and I, well...'

'You couldn't help yourselves, that's obvious!'

'Pom, you'll understand one of these days, when you meet that special chap.'

'D'you know, I already have. We just needed to grow up, that's all. We've agreed not to, you know, be *rash*, before we can even think of marriage. Two more years before I graduate, and the same for him, with his apprenticeship.'

'Is that how you think of Paddy and me – that we acted rashly?'

'You have no regrets, that's what matters. It was meant to be.'

Carlos had moved to a hostel but, unlike most of the other inhabitants, he had some work. Only part-time, but it was a definite advantage. He supplanted the boy who wound the gramophone in Carmen's classes, but Stanley continued with his task for the other groups. Carlos actually offered to teach him to play the guitar when he learned of Stanley's wish to be involved with the flamenco.

Relations with Carmen were cordial now that Evgenia had expressed her approval of his expertise.

One day, Carlos believed, he and Carmen would again top the bill, but somewhere more illustrious than the end of the pier at West Wick. Their young daughter had no place in such dreams.

The new King had planned a holiday at the end of July in the Riviera, in a secluded property with a private beach, but the eruption of civil war in Spain saw many refugees flooding over the border into France. The French government advised against the royal visit.

On the morning of 26 July, as commandant of the Royal Canadian Mounted Police, Edward went ahead with the Anglo-French ceremony at the Vimy Ridge to unveil the memorial to the 60,000 Canadians who had perished during the Great War. He was greeted by many of the survivors, who had fought for the motherland. He was popular with the Canadians because of a visit to North America when he was a young and dashing Prince of Wales.

This same day, Germany and Italy joined Franco's struggle to fight with the Nationalists in Spain.

Thirty-Five

August, 1936

The King's involvement with Mrs Simpson, an American divorcee, was common knowledge, but since Edward's accession to the throne the newspaper headlines had changed: the King's official duties were chronicled, but his private life was now strictly out of bounds. However, the rumours continued. There was important news though regarding rearmament worldwide, and there was a drop in unemployment, as factories became busy once more, and new enterprises flourished. The recession was over at last, but the ugly spectre of World War Two was becoming all too real. Fascism, Communism; it seemed the Spanish Civil War had been the catalyst.

May had some exciting, unexpected news to share with Henry. She was worried that he'd seemed withdrawn in her company lately. She was aware that he didn't approve of Carmen's attitude towards her youngest daughter, or of her mother's continued presence in his house. Pomona took the hint and after May left work to prepare for the birth of the baby, she decided to spend a couple of weeks of the summer break at Kettle Row, with the Wrights, who promptly invited Bella to accompany her. May wished she could go too, when she learned that Bea, Danny and Terence would also be enjoying a breath of country air with a visit to the rectory.

May decided to talk to Henry after their evening meal, while Carmen was at work. She sank down thankfully beside him on the settee, for now she was heavily pregnant. 'I heard from Paddy today.'

He folded his paper and looked up. 'All's well, I hope?'

'More than that! He has been offered a good job with a big marine aviation works! They have a new government contract to build many more bi- and seaplanes, which have wooden floats as well as propellers! Carpenters are still in great demand. It's not like being in charge of his own business, he says, but the money is better!'

'Is this in Southampton?'

'Yes; there is accommodation available a few miles away, which won't be a problem as Brendan has said Paddy can borrow his old car until he can afford his own motor, and – he wants *me* to join him there – to be married *now*, rather than later.'

'That's very good news, but what about his child?'

'Cluny is happy to stay on with her grandparents, but we would, of course, have her to stay with us on a regular basis. Oh, Henry, I'm sorry to spring this on you so suddenly, but I'm aware that you have delayed plans of your own because of me and, now, my family. I'm so glad you are happy for me.'

'I didn't expect this,' he said quietly. 'However, I have felt all along that your place was with

Paddy. Naturally, I will miss you, May. I can tell you now that I was offered training for the priesthood in September. As this would mean giving up the house and going to a northern college, I didn't think it would be possible; I'd committed myself to caring for you until after November. Then there was the fact that Pomona thinks of this as her home, and Isabella is due to start school here next month. Let alone the problem of Carmen.'

'I wish you had said! I'm so sorry to have been such a burden!'

'You've never been that, May, believe me. It's just that things seem to have escalated beyond my control.'

'It's not too late, is it, to accept the college offer?'

'I have until the end of next week to make up my mind.'

'Then do it! Go! With my blessing. Does the bank know?'

'They actually offered to support me – they said they appreciated my loyalty and hard work over the last decade.'

'Well, what are you waiting for? I'll send a telegram to Paddy, talk to Mum, and *then* work out how to deal with the rest of it!'

When Pomona heard about the changes ahead, she spoke first to Terence, then confided in Emma and Osmund, while Bella was out of earshot.

Emma said immediately, 'You must think of this as your home from home now, Pomona, just as Bea's Danny does. You and Terence will eventually settle down together, then we'll have another daughter, eh?'

'I don't know what to say...' Pomona cleared her throat. 'But – what about Bella?'

'We'll take her on, won't we, Ossie?' Emma said to her husband. 'When she asked if she could call me Nana, I knew she wanted to stay. She's a little country girl, after all, used to living with older people, but here, there's a good mix, with Selina's lot. Bella's very attached to you, too, Pomona. She can go to school here in September.'

'That's *wonderful!* I hope Carmen will agree.'

'I'll write to her myself, and I'm sure she will!' Emma said.

'And I'll phone her soon,' Pomona decided.

May's telegram to Paddy, bore just three words: YES YES YES. When she returned from the Worple Road post office, early the following morning, she busied herself while waiting for her mother to come downstairs at 11 a.m. with her imperious demand of: 'Where is the coffee?' At least, she thought wryly, Henry and I had breakfast in peace together.

Carmen had bathed, but appeared wearing her robe, with her black hair bundled on top of her head. However, she'd applied the usual scarlet lipstick. The sight made May wince, for the imprint those lips left on the cups was difficult to shift. As Carmen opened her mouth to repeat the irritating words, May indicated the steaming cup of coffee on the table and the plate of assorted biscuits. She sat down beside her mother and sipped her own lemon tea. This was a taste she'd acquired at Tatiana's.

Carmen looked at her daughter. 'Well, aren't you trying to tell me something? I have something to say to you, too. You, first.'

'Mum, you have to make other living arrangements. Henry is giving up the house, and I am joining Paddy. We will be married now, before the baby arrives.'

Carmen set down her cup in the saucer with a clatter. 'You cast your mother out? Let me tell you, I am going, anyway. Since I became so successful teaching flamenco, and Carlos is returned as my partner with his music, my fame has spread. A father of one of the young ladies has booked us to perform at his daughter's coming of age party. Evgenia agrees to let us go, as this has led to more such invitations. We will be able to afford to stay in hotels, as in the past, and soon, I think, we will be in cabaret; there are many clubs in London, and word spreads of our talent.'

'You are back together then, you and Carlos, as a couple, as well as dance partners?' May could hardly believe her ears.

'He knows his place. Not yet in my bed. I have him under the finger–'

'Under the thumb!' May couldn't resist the correction.

'So you see, you tell me to go, but, no matter. I am a survivor.'

You are also my mother, May thought. Pomona and I have dealt with this problem most of our lives. We don't need you now, but, 'What about Bella?' she asked.

'Pomona telephoned me late last night, after you were in bed. The child wishes to stay with your friends at Kettle Row. She is not attached to me. Yes, I admit it is my fault, Carlos is guilty, too, but I cannot play the role of mother. I was unready for that when I married your father, and now I accept that I am too busy to deal with a child.'

'You will, I hope, keep in touch with all of us,' May said.

'You must not expect too much—'

'We don't. But you are still our mother.'

'You will shortly find out for yourself what that means. However, you are Jim's daughter and you follow his ideals.' Carmen rose. 'I shall begin my packing.'

'Mum, d'you remember the present you gave me, when you left West Wick?'

'You still have it? My first flamenco dress?'

'Yes. I wore it several times. Would you mind if I passed it on now to Bella?'

'I would like that very much. It may not seem so, but I love you all, my daughters,' Carmen said.

It was time to say goodbye to Tatiana. May was taken into the studio to see her friend's latest work, and was presented with a cup, plate and bowl for the 'baby's bottom drawer'.

'These are lovely!' May exclaimed. 'I didn't expect you to paint Mr Punch. He looks benevolent, which is good.'

'I don't want to frighten your baby, just make him smile.'

'Oh, you think it's a boy, too! Actually we don't mind if the baby is a girl.'

268

'I will miss you, my dear May. I haven't found the right young lady to replace you, yet. You will write to me, I hope?'

'Of course I will.'

'Now, I have another small gift for you. Please do not refuse.' She handed May a sealed envelope. 'Wait until you are home, to open.'

'Will you stand there, in your doorway, while I take your photograph. It's an old camera, but it still works.'

When developed, the snap was naturally in black and white, but when May looked at it, as she did often, she could picture it in colour, matching Tatiana's lively personality. She would miss her friend, too.

One last shopping trip down the Worple Road; the car was loaded with provisions, and Henry was the only one to wave them off and wish them all the luck in the world. That merited another snapshot. With Henry about to leave the place himself, May thought, there will be no reason to return.

A few days later, Paddy and May were married in a register office in Southampton. It was a quiet wedding, with no family able to be present, and the witnesses were unknown to them: strangers passing by in the street. The bride and groom wore their best clothes, and each had a button-hole flower. No music, no hymns, just the solemn vows and a kindly registrar, who shook their hands warmly and wished them luck.

They had opened Tatiana's envelope and discovered ten five-pound notes. This would enable them to have a brief honeymoon, a night in a hotel. Their new home was an upstairs apartment in a redbrick block of flats.

That evening they stood looking out over the harbour, at the lights blazing on the great liners. The steam tug *Calshot* was busy, carrying passengers to one of the liners. 'Maybe movie stars,' Paddy murmured. He hugged her close to his side, it was a cool evening. 'You are *my* star. I'm the happiest man in the world tonight.'

Thirty-Six

November, 1936

May was out of puff when she arrived at the door of the apartment. One of those days, she thought, as she put down her shopping, eased off her shoes and reached for her slippers. Damp and murky, no doubt foggy over the water. She'd caught the bus into the city because the estate had only a couple of shops, a newsagent and a general stores. She'd lugged home two heavy bags of provisions – for it was possible the baby might arrive soon, and she wanted to stock the larder. Paddy had insisted he would do the shopping at the weekend, and she knew he would be cross that she hadn't stayed at home, with her feet up.

Still restless, she went into the spare bedroom and checked the baby toiletries packed into the chipwood basket she'd been given by the local

270

shop. It still had a faint smell of apples, although she'd covered it with blue sateen after padding over the wood. She murmured aloud: 'Vinolia soap and powder, roll of cotton wool, zinc and castor-oil ointment, card of nappy pins, bath sponge, muslin nappies to line the terry ones, baby hairbrush, and gripewater.' The crib, which Paddy had brought with him when he collected her from Raynes Park, was the one he and his brother had used as babies and which in turn had been handed down to Cluny. May, being superstitious, hadn't made it up yet, but there was a neat pile of blankets and baby clothes on the spare bed. Satisfied, she closed the door and went into the kitchen to start cooking Paddy's evening meal.

She experienced that little niggle low in her abdomen again. The baby had been quiet for the past few days, which the midwife said meant it was almost time for the birth. 'The fluttering,' she advised, 'is perfectly normal. Carry on as usual. You'll know when to stop.'

May peeled potatoes, lit the gas and set them to boil. She shredded cabbage, scored the fat on plump lamb chump chops and heated them gently in the frying pan. Paddy didn't like them cooked in lard; he said they didn't need it.

I need to sit down, May told herself. She'd suffered from backache this last month. Paddy worked a long shift on Fridays; he wouldn't be home until around seven. She was making a favourite supper, because it was also pay-day. She turned the gas low. No need to hurry the cooking.

She shouldn't have sat in the easy chair, because once she relaxed she drifted off to sleep. She woke to darkness, because she hadn't turned the light on in the living room. The cabbage had boiled dry, she realized instantly. A horrible smell. Even as she heaved herself out of the chair she was aware of a strong contraction, which made her gasp and clutch her middle. When the pang subsided she went unsteadily to the switch and the room was flooded with light. The fire was burning low, but her first priority was to rescue Paddy's dinner.

The plump chops had shrivelled to half their size, the fat from them spat in the pan. She rescued the potatoes and turned off the gas rings. The cabbage was scraped into the bin, and the pan put to soak. May mopped her forehead with the tea towel; she was sweating profusely, but at the same time she felt very cold.

Another contraction; she held on tight to the kitchen table. There was the sound of Paddy turning the key in the lock, and the next moment he was beside her, supporting her and helping her towards the bedroom. 'Stay there! I'll have to go downstairs to ring the hospital from the hall telephone.' He fetched a spare blanket from the airing cupboard and covered her with it on the bed, as she lay on top of the eiderdown, too exhausted to crawl under it.

'Your dinner ...' she managed.

'Don't worry about that. I can heat it up later. Your bag is packed isn't it? I expect they'll want you in hospital right away.'

'But you don't have a first baby that quickly. The midwife said–'

'Shush, darling. Save your breath. Try to relax

272

between the pains. I'll be as quick as I can.'

It was a short drive to the hospital, but not a comfortable ride for May, cramped in the passenger seat, hanging grimly on to her bag in her lap.

'You must be hungry.' She was concerned that he hadn't eaten.

'Please don't worry about me.'

They were met at the hospital entrance by a porter with a trolley accompanied by a nurse. May was pushed away down a long corridor to the maternity ward, while Paddy answered the queries at the reception desk.

'Yes, you can stay with your wife until the birth is imminent,' he was told, 'then fathers are banished to the waiting room until it's all over. The nurses can't be doing with strong men passing out on the delivery room floor. Good luck,' the receptionist added with a smile.

May was in the bed nearest the ward door; there were rows of beds and all were occupied. She was aware of a constant groaning and bells ringing, as patients reached for the pull cord above their heads. Nurses swished by, and there was a strong smell of antiseptic, which was a reminder of where she was. Paddy was at her bedside, rubbing her back, as instructed by the midwife, who told him that May was almost at the third stage, when she would be removed to the delivery room next door.

May was trying to tell him something. He listened intently. 'Paddy – when they – brought me here – I thought – I was in the trap – going to West Wick...'

273

'Shush,' he said. 'It won't be long now.' He prayed he was right.

The rubber mask went over her nose and mouth. 'Breathe deeply,' a man's voice said. The doctor had been called. Despite all her efforts, the baby was not yet born.

May seemed to float off into space. Through the haze she heard the echo of old Mr Punch: *'That's the way to do it!'* as James Patrick O'Flaherty, Young Jim, came, with a loud cry, into the world.

Paddy, wearing a white gown over his clothes, held the baby in his arms. There were tear stains on his face, for he had wept as he paced up and down in the waiting room. He'd waited a long time because there had been an emergency after the birth; May had lost a lot of blood and needed a transfusion. She was the medical team's main concern: the baby was wrapped in a blanket and left to cry lustily, which was a good sign. Now, both he and his mother had been washed, but they remained in a side room, until May was stable enough to be moved back into the ward.

May had not yet regained enough strength to sit up, but she was smiling and talking. 'What do you think of your son, Paddy?' she asked.

'He's a champion. Did they tell you he weighs almost nine pounds?'

'Yes. He's dark-haired, like both of us, but maybe he'll have curly hair like you.'

'Are you all right?' he asked anxiously.

'Are you all right?' she countered. 'You need to go home, eat your dinner, and then go to bed. I'll see you tomorrow afternoon, and you can ring the hospital tomorrow morning. I need a good night's sleep too.' She yawned. 'Phone home, and tell Cluny she has a little brother, and that we love her very much.'

'I will. What about the others – Carmen, Pomona, Bella, Tatiana – Henry?'

'Send telegrams in the morning.'

'What shall I say?'

'Young Jim arrived safely. All's well, love from...' her voice faded away. Her eyes closed. She was asleep.

'Young May Moon and Paddy,' he whispered.

May arrived home with her baby on 8 December, a fortnight after the birth. Two days later, on Thursday the tenth, the newspaper headlines were stark and sombre. The King was to make a statement which would be read in the Commons and the Lords that afternoon. General business was first discussed, and then Mr Baldwin, the Prime Minister, presented a document to the Speaker, declaring it to be a message from His Majesty.

The Speaker read the handwritten document aloud to the hushed Commons. The King had abdicated, and his brother, the unassuming, hard-working Duke of York, would succeed to the throne.

Prince Edward, as he was now to be known again, made a farewell broadcast to the nation on 11 December, he spoke warmly of his brother and the fact that the new King George was a happily married man, with a family. He ended his speech with 'God Save the King!'

That same night the Prince left Windsor Castle and went into exile.

Young Jim spent his first Christmas with his parents in Buckinghamshire, with his greatgrandpa, and his grandparents, Brendan and Brigid. Cluny was entranced by her baby brother, and rushed to comfort him whenever he cried for attention. Dog Toby took to sitting by the pram in the garden, or lying across May's feet, while she fed the baby. There were other visitors over the Christmas weekend: Pomona and Terence arrived on their motor cycle, and Bea and Danny, who'd been at Kettle Row, came by excursion train. They were about to begin rehearsing for a new production in January. There was another celebration meal, with a capon and a Christmas pudding saved for the occasion.

It was a time of laughter and love, May thought, and she found herself the centre of attraction, with Young Jim in her arms. The anxiety over the abdication had evaporated, and the new King and Queen were already assured of a firm place in the affections of the people, not only in the United Kingdom, but throughout the Empire.

Then it was back to work for most of the company, while May and the baby established a new routine at home in Southampton.

May told Jim little stories when she was bathing him, or settling him down to sleep in his crib. He appeared to be listening, with a solemn gaze; but sometimes he would gurgle, and she'd mop his dribbles with a muslin piece and ask: 'What's the joke, Jim?' When she mixed his baby gruel and he opened his mouth like a baby bird, she scraped the bowl with the spoon and told him that Mr Punch was pleased he'd left a clean plate. She played ridiculous games, which made Paddy laugh when he caught her unawares, as she powdered the baby's bottom while he wriggled on his tummy, on her lap, with a cry of: 'Flour the pastry – roll it over!' She sang, too: *Bye Baby Bunting* and *Lu-la bye byes*, when she was trying to get him to sleep.

Paddy was worried that she might feel lonely while he was a work, but she assured him: 'How can I be lonely, when I have Young Jim?'

Thirty-Seven

Coronation Year, 1937

The invitation arrived out of the blue. May recognized the thick manila envelope, having typed many addresses on these when she worked for the estate agents. She studied it for a few moments before opening it. Paddy was taking his turn with giving Young Jim his breakfast, before leaving for work. 'Who is that from?' he enquired, adjusting Jim's bib to catch the spills.

'Um – from my old office, the new secretary hasn't cleaned the typewriter keys, all the "e's" are clogged up. I'll read it to you:

277

Dear Miss Jolley, or rather, Mrs O'Flaherty,
We were all surprised to hear your good news. Con-
gratulations on the birth of your son and heir! We
raised a glass to you in the Kettle Drum. I meant to
write before, but now seems a good time, because I am
enclosing an invitation sent to your old address (the
farm), which was forwarded to the Kettle Row house
where you lived with your aunt, and thence to us, as
the agents for the property. I'm sure you will find it of
interest.
Yours sincerely, Lionel Davies.

'Well, aren't you going to read that out, too?'
Paddy asked her.

'It's from the West Wick council offices. A
special celebration is planned for the coronation
in May! They want to revive the End of the Pier
Show and the old-time beach entertainments on
that day – which will be a public holiday! I am
asked if Pomona and I will set up Jas Jolley's
Punch and Judy booth on the front, or, if inclem-
ent weather, in the school hall! They want to
know, too, as soon as possible, if I am in touch
with – wait for it – the O'Flaherty family, and
Carlos and Carmen, the flamenco dancers! Apparently, we were all named on the request list
which appeared in the local paper.

'Oh, Paddy, I must reply today. This letter is
dated March, and it's April now – it has been to
several addresses before arriving here, what shall
I say?'

'Say we'll come! Young Jim and all!'

'Just a thought. Your family still sing, and Mum
and Carlos are dancing partners once more, but

Mr Punch hasn't been out of the trunk in ten years, there's only the wooden Toby you made that time, and can I remember the script?'

'Dear May, the other day I overheard the version of it that you made up for Jim, and he was impressed. So – what are you worried about?'

She hugged him tight. 'After those reassuring words – only that you'll be late for work, if you don't hurry!'

Coronation Day, 12 May. Most parts of the country woke to cloudy skies, but this was nothing unusual on such occasions. The pomp and pageantry of the London scene were to be recorded by the British Broadcasting Corporation's fledging television service, which had been launched the previous year, in 1936, but only a minority would view the footage; the majority would gather round their wireless sets for the live broadcast and or the King's speech scheduled for that evening.

Tatiana travelled to West Wick by taxi, with Carmen and Carlos. She was so delighted to have been asked to join the family members that she insisted on booking a suite of rooms for them all, in the big hotel that was recommended by her travelling companions.

'I never imagined when I visited Mum here all those years ago that I would ever stay here,' May said, as they settled into their room, prior to the 'light lunch' at midday, which they'd ordered earlier. 'I do believe the receptionist is the superior one who was behind the desk then.' She bounced on the bed to test the springs, laughing like the Young May Moon, while Paddy inspected

279

the cot and then put Jim in there for safety, while they sorted out their luggage.

A tap on the door: Tatiana and co had arrived. 'I hope you are going to wear your peacock dress?' she asked May.

'Not for the Punch and Judy Show, but tonight I'll be sparkling in the stalls at the end of the pier show! Which room is yours?'

'I'm next door to you, and Carmen and Carlos, who signed in as Mr and Mrs by the way, are in the room beyond. Your parents, Paddy, are on your other side, and Pomona and Bella are sharing a room further along with your friend Bea. Her brother and Pomona's boyfriend will be on the second floor.'

'A wise move!' Paddy managed to keep a straight face.

'That was naughty of you!' May teased him after Tatiana left. 'I hope Jim doesn't make a mistake on my lovely dress, that's all.'

'I'll hold him, or one of the girls will, I imagine, if I decide to be on stage with the family. Just take a good supply of muslin wipes. Did Dad tell you he hoped you'd do your jig?'

'I'm still thinking about that. I'll see how this afternoon goes.' She thought, I hope Cluny doesn't divulge our secret. I taught her the jig while she was with us over the Easter holiday in March. Of course, I didn't know, then, about the exciting time ahead!

It was deemed too chilly to be on the beach. A notice directed the crowds to the school hall. This was a new addition to the school since Pomona and Danny had been pupils there. The booth was erected on the small stage and rows of chairs were already in place. The hall was full of excited children and parents by 2 p.m. Earlier, in the playground, the family had watched as the school children danced round the maypole: bunting fluttered in the breeze while small girls attempted to hold down their skirts, and curls unwound as hair was blown about, too.

Pomona observed that the odorous block of latrines was no longer in evidence – indoor sanitation had arrived in West Wick! She pointed out to Terence the tree in the field beyond where, on a hot day, she'd slaked her thirst with tepid water from a bucket placed in its shade. 'I wonder what happened to the old tin cup?'

Before the performance began, the children were called by name to receive a coronation spoon, with a royal crest on the handle, from the headmaster. Brigid, who was holding the sleeping baby while his mother was on stage, overheard a mother say: 'Just right for the jam dish.' There were also free tickets for some of the rides at the fair, due to arrive on the green on Saturday.

'My brother's not well, so he's not here,' a small girl told a teacher, who replied: 'I'm sorry, but the tickets are only for those present now.'

'Seems rather harsh,' Brendan whispered to his wife. 'We gave mugs to every child, present or not, yesterday.'

'Shame you had to miss today, at your school.'

'They understood; I came with their blessing,' he said. 'I'll be there for the party on Saturday.'

Pomona was not bottling today, as she had

done when she was eight years old, but she helped May put the puppets in place inside the booth, then emerged to make the introduction.

'Boys and girls of all ages, I am proud to present Professor Jas Jolley's Punch and Judy Show!' Then she descended the stage steps and took her place in the front row, with Terence, Bea, Danny, Bella and Cluny. The little girls were now good friends. Paddy stayed out of sight in the wings, fingers crossed. May was on her own now, but she needed to know he was near by. Tatiana sat with Brigid and Brendan, but Carmen and Carlos decided to rest back at the hotel before the big show, that night.

The curtains swished open and Mr Punch appeared with his familiar cry of:

Boys and girls, Pray how do you do?
If you are all happy, then I'm happy too.

May relaxed and began to enjoy herself. The audience was responsive, and the words came out loud and clear. She remembered all the changes, and it was if she were transported back to the days when she was, as Paddy always said, the Punch and Judy Lady.

When the curtains closed and the little play had ended she hoped that her father would have been proud of her. She was about to leave the stage when Paddy rushed forward and told her to take another bow. The clapping seemed to go on for ages.

'You're still a star!' Paddy murmured, as he escorted her back to her seat. 'Pom and I will pack it all away: I guess the applause has woken Young Jim, and he will be calling for his mum!'

'Life is easier now he is learning to drink from a cup, and has a bottle at nights,' May said.

'You've got your figure back,' he said appreciatively, which earned him a playful cuff on the head.

Back at the hotel, they listened to the King's Coronation speech at 6.30 p.m. on the wireless, in the sitting room. All had gone according to plan, with the sun shining briefly in London. As the King finished speaking, there was a general chorus from all the guests of: 'God Save The King!'

Cluny and Bella were excited about going out in the evening. 'It'll be midnight before we get to bed!' Bella whispered to her friend. She was envious that Cluny would be appearing briefly with her grandparents and her uncle Danny, and wearing her new kilt, bought for the occasion.

'You, Bella,' Carmen said unexpectedly, 'shall learn the flamenco. Surely one of my daughters shall follow in my footsteps?'

They had front-row seats, and Paddy sat next to the aisle, where Young Jim was tucked up in his pram, which was of the folding variety so easy to transport in the dicky-seat of their present motor car, which they'd bought when they returned the one on loan from Brendan. 'I'll take him out for a bit and wheel him around on the pier if he cries,' Paddy promised May.

'I don't want him to catch cold,' she worried.

'He seems to be quite content, and the lights

will soon go down. There's always the emergency bottle of milk, eh?'

Some of the earlier acts were new to them. The snake woman contorted her limbs in seemingly impossible poses; the magician produced endless bunches of paper flowers and two white doves flew round the stage when he raised his top hat. A comedian with a false red nose told some rather dubious jokes, and was jerked off stage into the wings. The O'Flahertys appeared as the final act before the interval.

They came on in their green kilts, with harp and fiddle, and Cluny raised a cheer when she was led on by Danny. They performed the old repertoire, *Tea for Two* and *Danny Boy*. Then Brendan came front stage and called: 'Are you there, Young May Moon? Please come up and join the party.'

'Go on!' Paddy urged her.

'Did you know this would happen?' she demanded.

'I can keep a secret–'

'Well, so can I.'

She wasn't dressed for the jig, in her peacock blue dress, but, 'just in case', she was wearing her dancing shoes. 'Follow me,' she encouraged Cluny. Together, they danced, arms at sides, with raised knee, pointed toes, hopping, then three little steps back. Cluny was sometimes a step behind, but her enthusiasm was obvious. Feet were tapping in the audience at the lively fiddle music. The applause was deafening, and woke Young Jim. Paddy rocked the pram.

The curtains closed, and the performers joined the family party.

Carlos and Carmen were the main act in the second half. Carmen appeared years younger, partly due to skilful make-up and newly dyed hair. She embodied the free spirit – the *duende* – of flamenco, in her frilled, tiered skirt and high-heeled red shoes in which she strutted to the staccato beat. Carlos, in matador breeches, Cuban-heeled shoes with polished buckles, strummed his guitar and sang from the heart.

However, as the programme noted, the end of the pier show was for one night only, and would not be repeated.

May and Paddy were in their room. It was indeed midnight, as the children had predicted. They were already asleep. Young Jim had been whisked away by his grandparents, his cot wheeled into their room.

'You two have never had a proper honeymoon,' Brigid said to May, making her blush.

There were lovely flowers on the dressing-table, for Tatiana had arranged for bouquets to be delivered on stage to her friends. It was typical of her generosity.

Paddy enjoyed a bath, despite the late hour, but May decided to go to bed. She'd just wait, she thought dreamily, for Paddy to return in the white towelling robe provided by the hotel, then she'd ask him to undo the diamante clasps which held her dress up. She knew exactly what would happen then.

The publishers hope that this book has given you enjoyable reading. Large Print Books are especially designed to be as easy to see and hold as possible. If you wish a complete list of our books please ask at your local library or write directly to:

Magna Large Print Books
Magna House, Long Preston,
Skipton, North Yorkshire.
BD23 4ND

This Large Print Book for the partially sighted, who cannot read normal print, is published under the auspices of

THE ULVERSCROFT FOUNDATION

THE ULVERSCROFT FOUNDATION

... we hope that you have enjoyed this Large Print Book. Please think for a moment about those people who have worse eyesight problems than you ... and are unable to even read or enjoy Large Print, without great difficulty.

You can help them by sending a donation, large or small to:

The Ulverscroft Foundation, 1, The Green, Bradgate Road, Anstey, Leicestershire, LE7 7FU, England.
or request a copy of our brochure for more details.

The Foundation will use all your help to assist those people who are handicapped by various sight problems and need special attention.

Thank you very much for your help.